# Claws and Fangs

## By Lauren

# Claws and Fangs

## by Laurann Dohner

### Scarred and Kilt

Matty has a new neighbor, and she strongly suspects the kilt-wearing hottie is a vampire — he only goes out at night, has weird visitors and the blood bank is making regular deliveries. But he doesn't seem to hurt anyone, so "live and let live" is Matty's motto. Until she sees a guy armed with crosses and wooden stakes breaking into the neighbor's house. Matty charges to the rescue — and ends up in Mr. Hottie's bed…and on his desk…and…

### Lacey and Lethal

Lacey hunts vampires — vile monsters who leave death and shattered lives in their wake. They murdered her sister and she wants revenge. Until she captures a big, sexy blue-eyed vamp, and the strong attraction she feels contradicts everything she's become. But she can't resist getting closer.

Lethal can't believe the little lass got the better of him. He's been drugged and chained, but he's more insulted than concerned. She swears he's her enemy, but he's determined to be her lover.

# Mine to Chase

Jasmine met the guy of her dreams, who unfortunately wasn't interested. She's spent a year filled with lustful fantasies and soul-deep yearning for a man who doesn't want her. Now she's locked away in a dark hole, kidnapped by a madman, her life almost over.

She was supposed to be his a year ago, but Chase had walked away to protect her from his world. He's a mixed-breed — vampire and werewolf — and his list of enemies is endless. His current mission is to hunt down and kill a rogue vamp who's preying on humans, but what Chase finds changes everything. Jasmine's one of the victims. Instinct demands he protect her, possess her. He won't be denied again. This time, she's his — for keeps.

Claws and Fangs

Scarred and Kilt Copyright © January 2017

Lacey and Lethal Copyright © January 2017

Mine to Chase Copyright © January 2017

Editor: Kelli Collins

Cover Art: Dar Albert

ISBN: 978-1-944526-77-1

# Scarred and Kilt

# Chapter One

*He's back.*

Matty leaned closer to the window, glanced at the clock on her nightstand table and realized he'd barely beaten the rising sun. Her focus returned to the house across the street as the man climbed out of the back of the limousine, his near-white braid trailing down his back to his waist, seeming to glow from the streetlamp.

He turned and bent down, talking to someone inside the black vehicle. She could hear his deep chuckle through her open window. His muscular arm braced on the roof of the car, thick biceps displayed in the black tank top he'd chosen that stretched across a broad chest.

"Have a good one," he told his ride home, the brogue as clear as the deep baritone of his voice.

It gave her the good kind of chills every time she heard it. He pushed the car door closed and glanced at the sky, before striding briskly toward his home. She loved the way he moved, with those broad shoulders and that manly grace.

Matty grinned while she studied the blue plaid kilt he wore. She never thought she'd find a guy wearing a skirt hot but that was before she'd glimpsed "Kilt". She'd dubbed him that since she didn't know his real name. She'd raided his mailbox a few times out of pure curiosity, but the only name on the junk mail had belonged to the old homeowner.

His legs, revealed under the material, were as muscular as the rest of him. He wore solid blue socks with black leather boots. It was an interesting look, but attractive. She'd glanced at photos of other men in kilts on the Internet. A lot of the men sported high-tops or tennis shoes. Kilt dressed more old fashioned in his footwear.

He'd moved in three months before and it had become a habit of hers to watch him whenever possible. He had become the most fascinating person on the block. She hated it when he unlocked his door to disappear inside. He kept all his curtains closed so she couldn't catch glimpses of him.

Lights turned on and off as he moved through the house. She knew where he'd go; it was always the same routine. The first two floors of the house went dark. She looked up and, sure enough, lights shone through the vent from the attic, barely noticeable unless someone was looking for it. He slept there during the day.

*I have it bad for a guy who I'm pretty sure is a vampire.*

The thought made her back away from the window. She normally wouldn't believe in such things but it made sense. She'd never seen him during the daytime. He never answered his door while the sun shone, only seemed awake at night, and he always made it home before dawn. It would account for his occasional weird evening visitors too. Most of them dressed strangely from various time periods.

He could have a rare allergy, one of those people sickened by the sun, but she'd noticed the white van making deliveries every Monday and Friday. She'd called in a favor with her friend at the police department to run the plates—and it had been registered to a blood bank.

It all fit, and the facts seemed clear.

She remained seated in her chair, waiting for the sun to rise, and knew she'd go to bed soon. Matty had her own reasons for keeping the hours she did. She'd let her guard down once during the night and now the darkness frightened her.

Dawn broke and the sky pinkened with streaks as she watched. She stood, stretched her arms high and twisted her hips a little to alleviate the stiffness from sitting too long.

A black van pulled up to the curb across the street and she frowned. It wasn't one she'd seen before. Where they parked, it could mean they planned to visit her house or Kilt's, but neither was feasible. No one ever came to see *her*, and anyone who knew *him* wouldn't arrive after the sun rose. It was also too early for it to be someone trying to sell something.

She stepped back into the shadows, watching as a man climbed from the driver's side. He opened the sliding back door behind the driver's seat and leaned in. Matty grabbed her binoculars and could make out the interior of his van.

The guy had crosses, two long wooden stakes, and what appeared to be a squirt gun of the gallon-sized variety that kids loved to play with during the summer.

*Oh shit.*

Kilt seemed to have been discovered by someone who obviously intended to do him harm. She watched as the stranger wedged the stakes and crosses between his pants and belt, then hoisted up the plastic weapon she suspected held holy water. The van door slammed closed and the man studied Kilt's house. He crept toward the side gate.

Matty bit her lip. She shouldn't interfere…but she liked to watch her neighbor. He hadn't ever bothered her, no one on the block had disappeared, and he wouldn't have blood delivered if he were a killer. He'd be getting it for free by attacking people.

"Damn," she muttered, rushing to her nightstand.

She grabbed the Taser gun, not wanting to kill anyone. Then reconsidered and took the handgun too. It could be deadly to face off against someone who might have one, only holding something that didn't fire bullets herself. It was better to be safe than sorry.

The small screwdriver she kept to change the batteries on her remote came with her, then she jogged out of her room and down the stairs. It only took seconds to tap in her code to shut down the alarm and open the front door.

Hesitation struck. Some of her early rising neighbors might look out a window and spot her. Memories surfaced of when she'd allowed that to happen in the past. They weren't good ones. Her gaze fixed on the van though, and she exited the house, closing the door behind her. Vanity wasn't worth Kilt dying. She had to do something.

The grass chilled her bare feet as she jogged across her lawn, then the paved street, only stopping when she reached Kilt's front porch. One darted glance around revealed how empty of life the other houses seemed to be. No one stared or came out to see what she was doing. She bent, staring at his door handle.

The locks were flimsy and she doubted he even had an alarm system. Any security company would have strongly suggested he upgrade them. She grimaced. It was stupid not to use technology to help keep himself safe, but maybe he didn't want responders coming to his home if his security system was ever triggered. There wasn't even a deadbolt. She used the screwdriver to stab into the crack between the door and jamb. It took a little wiggling but she managed to pop it open. She pushed on the door, stepping inside.

*Yeah, I'm definitely going to have a talk with my neighbor about his cheap taste in hardware. I might as well, since I've pretty much appointed myself the neighborhood watch.* She glanced around, closed the door behind her and sprinted up the stairs. The intruder was probably still trying to work his way into the house. They were all similar models on this block, so she felt she knew Kilt's house almost as well as her own. The intruder would have to either figure out how to remove the family room's slider from its track or break a window, if he couldn't find one unlocked. She doubted he'd be brave enough to smash glass, for fear of drawing attention to his trespassing from nearby homeowners.

She avoided the bedrooms, sure Kilt wouldn't be there, and strode to the end of the hallway. She hesitated when her fingers touched the handle to the attic door. Every vampire movie she'd ever seen flashed through her head, and she drew back. No way would she invade his sleeping space. Her neighbor could attack her.

She spun instead, stepped into the laundry area and waited.

11

The bedrooms all had thick curtains, the doors open, but hardly any light filtered into the second floor. Her ears strained and she heard someone coming up the stairs a few minutes later. The stranger had a heavy tread, breathed loudly as if he'd done something to get a workout, and her hand gripped the gun she'd shoved inside her robe pocket. Her fingers curved around metal. The weight comforted her as she slid her other hand into the matching pocket, grabbing the stun gun. *Prepared for anything. That's me.*

A light clicked on near the stairs, illuminating the hallway. She hesitated before inching forward. She peeked around the doorway to watch the stranger disappear into the first room closest to the stairwell, and she tiptoed down the hallway. She pressed against the wall next to the bedroom he searched, and waited.

The closet jerked open inside the bedroom, the guy obviously looking for Kilt, and he softly cursed. Matty's hand tightened on the button of the stun gun, her other hand ready to jerk out the handgun if needed. The shadow moved on the floor as the man stalked closer. Her heart pounded but she had surprise on her side.

She lunged as the shadow grew larger.

The guy startled when he faced Matty. His brown eyes widened as he stared at her face. She shoved the stun gun at him. The metal bars touched the guy just as she pushed the button.

The repetitive clicking noise seemed to create a beat for the stranger to dance to as his body began to shake and twitch, and she watched him pale. His arm shot out while he jerked around. He struck her face, but it didn't hurt. She pulled away quickly but kept her arm outstretched. She didn't ease up on shocking him until the guy collapsed on the floor, unconscious.

A few long seconds ticked by as she watched him to make certain he wasn't faking it. She stepped over his body. Her gaze swept the room and landed on the drape ties hanging uselessly from the wall. She retrieved them, returned to the intruder, and used her foot to roll him over.

His limp body flopped onto his belly. She crouched, braced her knee on his ass, and quickly tied his wrists behind his back. She returned to the wall to remove a second set of drape ties. It didn't take long to yank up each of his ankles, and she hogtied him tightly before removing all his weapons.

She tossed the crosses, his plastic water weapon, and both stakes toward the window. It wasn't easy, but she pushed him onto his side. Sliding her hands over his body, she found a knife hidden inside an ankle strap. He also kept a folding knife stashed in the front pocket of his shirt. She tossed those into the pile too. Matty let him drop onto his stomach and rose to her feet.

A quick study of her handiwork assured her the guy wouldn't be going anywhere without someone untying him. Now she had to decide what to do with him. It would be bad to call the police. She'd broken into the home herself. They would also search every inch of the house and find the sleeping vampire. She couldn't allow them to find Kilt.

"Damn," she whispered.

The only option would be to leave the guy there and hope he didn't wake and somehow get free. It was also possible he'd start yelling for help and a neighbor might hear him. The cops would come, and again, Kilt would be found. The whole point of saving him from dying would be for nothing.

Her last option would be to wait with the jerk on the floor until her braided neighbor woke. She could stun the jerk if he began to yell, keeping him quiet. Then again, Kilt might not be thrilled to find two unwelcome visitors inside his home. It was possible he might feel the need to kill her for the trouble she'd gone to.

It was a difficult decision. She backed away and glanced around the room again. The desk beckoned, and she approached it. Maybe it would give her a clue as to just how dangerous or harmless Kilt actually was.

He didn't have anything personal inside the drawers, no bills stated his name, and no letterhead on his print paper. She turned on his computer but it was password protected. Her disappointment rose. She wanted to find out *something* about her mysterious, hunky neighbor, knowing she'd never get another opportunity to be inside his home, but this idea had been a bust.

Matty decided to return home, put on actual clothes, and lock up her house. She'd sit with the stranger for a while and keep him quiet. It was possible when he woke that she could scare him, possibly convince him it was *her* home instead of Kilt's. Once she opened the curtains and stood in the sun, he'd realize she wasn't a vampire. A threat of having him arrested might send him fleeing. As long as she was back home safe before the sun set, her neighbor wouldn't be any kind of danger to her.

She turned to leave—but something blocked the bedroom door.

Her mouth fell open as Kilt stepped into the room wearing just the blue plaid kilt, a big, dangerous-looking sword gripped in his hand. His blue eyes were striking as they shifted away from the intruder and met her stare. A frown curved his firm lips but he didn't speak. His unbraided hair had obviously just been washed, the damp strands flowing down his muscular chest to his waist. Drops of water dotted his tan skin as if he'd just jumped from the shower.

Mute, Matty gawked at the bronzed god who silently watched her. His sword lowered when she met his gaze again. His intense eyes fascinated her. *It's probably not a good idea to stare into them in case movies are right and he can control my mind.* She still didn't glance away. He wouldn't be calmly standing there watching her if he wanted to do harm. He'd have attacked already.

He tilted his head slightly, his gaze roamed down her body, and he took a step closer. "Who are you and what are you doing inside my home?"

She cleared her throat. "Um, I live across the street. I saw that dirtball park in front of your house and realized he meant to break in. I'm kind of the neighborhood watch." Her ratty robe embarrassed her. He probably thought she was insane. "I'm not with him."

"Did you call the police?"

She hesitated in answering. It was possible he wanted to know if help was coming before he used that sword. It would be difficult for him to explain a bloody mess and two dead bodies to armed officers. Then she remembered that she wasn't defenseless. The weapons she'd brought were reassuring weights against her legs in her robe pockets. "No."

"You tied him well. Thank you."

She loved his husky voice and the accent was flat-out hot. So was he, with his handsome good looks. The danger factor actually made him sexier. A real vampire stood feet away—and seemed grateful to her.

*A real vampire*. She resisted the urge to faint. She'd been half joking, but the laugh was on her.

"I'd like to repay you. Name what you want."

She hadn't dated in the five years since her attack, and it definitely made her lonely. It had also made her socially challenged. She was aware of that, even if the one thing that came to mind wouldn't have been wrong to ask of him.

She shook her head, refusing to ask him to show her what he wore under that kilt, despite the curiosity she'd had since she'd laid eyes on him. *Totally inappropriate and don't go there.*

"I should be going home now. I'll leave you to deal with your intruder."

# Chapter Two

Blaron regarded the woman, inhaling the scents inside the room. The hunter on the floor wore cheap, offensive cologne and stank of sweat and fear. It nearly masked the sweeter, tempting feminine fragrances of his neighbor. He hadn't seen her before but he believed her reason for being there. His gaze traveled down her well-worn robe, her shapely legs peeking from beneath the thigh-length material, and her bare feet. She wouldn't have gone far dressed that way.

Her face intrigued him. A scar ran down the side of her jaw, another at her temple, and at her cheek near her ear. They didn't distract from her delicate, attractive features. Her big blue eyes stared at him with a mixture of awe and wariness. He didn't pick up fear coming from her but her heart raced. He could hear the fast beat, tormenting him just a little. He wasn't hungry but she tempted him all the same.

He'd been showering, oblivious to the happenings inside his home until he'd turned the water off. The noise of someone moving around the floor below him had been alarming. The hunter surprised him—Blaron had been careful to hide his identity—but the female stunned him. He knew humans fought crime by watching their neighbors' homes, but he'd never thought a woman would take on a criminal in her bathrobe. Most would dial for the police.

She had mentioned being the neighborhood watch. That meant she must have some sort of surveillance to have seen the hunter. It worried him that his senses had failed to notice her scrutiny.

She took a hesitant step toward him, her intent to flee, but he didn't budge from blocking the doorway. He wasn't allowing her to leave until he assessed the threat she posed to his future safety. It was odd that she hadn't called for assistance.

His study switched to the hunter on the floor.

The male lay on his side by the bed, awake now, his arms and feet bound at the center of his back and his terrified gaze on Blaron. He noticed the pile of weapons, and his lips pressed firmly together. The male had intended to kill him.

He glared at his enemy. "Who are you?"

"I have friends," the guy whined. "They will come, evil demon." The guy twisted his head to shoot a murderous glare at the woman. "They'll kill your minion too."

Confusion made Blaron frown. "My what?"

The hunter jerked his head at the woman. "*Her*. Your lover who guards you while you're in your death sleep. Release me, son of Satan! It's my duty to send you back to hell!"

He hid a wince, glanced at the woman, and knew he couldn't just allow her to stroll out of his home. She'd seen and heard too much. "Good luck with that, hunter. You're the one who has been caught."

"My friends will come, and they'll kill you and that hideous bitch who feeds you! I can see why she'd sink so low as to protect a monster. *She's* one too."

Blaron instantly noticed how the woman's features paled. She lowered her head to allow some of her curly blonde hair to drop forward to hide the worst of her scars, and her shoulders sagged a little.

Anger hit him instantly that the insulting words had made her courageous spirit withdraw. Only a strong female would attack a larger male and come to a neighbor's defense, both of which she'd done for a stranger. He admired her for that. She was probably sensitive about her flaws, and he moved before he allowed his temper to cool. His bare foot nailed the rude bastard in the side.

The hunter gasped from the pain. The sharp kick knocked him against the bed and he blacked out.

The female raised her head, realized what Blaron had done—and she stared at him with a mixture of amusement and, finally, fear.

"I detest rudeness from a guest, especially an uninvited one." He paused. "My apologies, lass."

She held his gaze confidently and licked her lips. The sight of her pink tongue darting out did something to his body that stunned him. His cock twitched, filled with blood, and he lowered his sword in front of him to rest the tip on the floor. The flat metal hid his response by keeping his kilt from lifting in the front.

"Five years ago, I awoke to a burglar who decided to try to rape me at knifepoint. I fought, he sliced my face a few times and stabbed me." She

19

paused, emotional turmoil making her voice tremble. "I kept fighting. He ended up dying while I survived." Her eyes glinted with pride. "I'm not so pretty anymore but I'm still breathing. I count that as a win."

"I'm sorry for what was done to you. Why did you try to save me?"

"It sucks being awoken to some jerk intent on causing harm. I've had that done to me. You haven't eaten anyone on the block, I assume you're bag-fed since you get those nifty deliveries, and we sleep during the same hours." She hesitated. "I have a live-and-let-live policy. I don't care what you are as long as you're not hurting anyone."

Shock tore through him once again. She knew what he was, or at least suspected. He could see it in her wary regard. He wondered if she figured it out after disarming the hunter of the weapons used to kill a vampire according to myth, or if she'd guessed long before.

"You added a bathroom in your attic?"

Her question came out of nowhere. "That's what you wish to know?"

"You sleep up there. I don't leave my house, so I watch the neighborhood a lot. You come home and go up there before the sun rises. I didn't see any contractors do work on your home."

She did intrigue him. "The last owner had a bedroom and bathroom created up there. It's why I bought the house. I added a steel door at the top to protect me." There was no harm in answering her question.

"Oh. So this jerk wouldn't have been able to reach you?"

He glanced down at the hunter. "It's possible he might have set my home on fire once he realized it's where I spend my days. Most of us stay underground for extra protection against the sun. I don't. I would have been trapped. Burned by fire or by daylight if I jumped out a window to escape the flames."

"None of these homes have basements."

"True enough."

"You probably should have bought a home with one, then dug out an escape tunnel in case of fire. I would if I were you." She gave him a tight smile. "Do jerks like him come after you often?"

"No. This is the first time in some years since I was found."

"You grew lax. I mean, *I* figured it out, and obviously this guy did too. You don't want to die."

He reevaluated what she said. She knew about the blood deliveries to his home and had taken note of the fact that he hadn't fed on anyone on the block. *Yet she still came to my aid and is giving me advice on how to stay safe.*

It made his cock stir more, the blood he'd drunk before his shower flowing there, and he wondered how vampire-friendly she would be if she guessed how attracted he was to her.

"Even if you aren't technically alive, the motto still applies." She took another hesitant step closer. "Could you please move? I'm up past my bedtime, and I assume you are too. I'll leave you to deal with him. As far as I'm concerned, I never saw him, this didn't happen, and you're just a regular guy. I'm not going to tell anyone about you."

"Is that why you didn't call the police?"

"I figured they'd find you if they searched the house. I planned to babysit him today until just before the sun went down, then leave him for you to deal with. I won't have a moral dilemma over this guy's fate. I see my mirror every time I'm in the bathroom. I wish someone had taken out the jerk who attacked me before he broke into my home. You'd be doing the world a favor. What if he tries to stake someone else, or even makes a mistake by going after someone who just likes to act as if they're a vampire? There's a kid a block over who dresses like one. She's totally into Goth but I've seen her during the day. I should leave now."

"Nay," he murmured. "You can't go yet, lass."

She backed up, alarm registering on her face as she crossed her arms over her chest. "Don't make me regret what I did. I've heard no good deed goes unpunished, but it would suck if that's true." She grimaced. "Forget the suck part. Bad pun I didn't intend to make, considering the circumstances."

Blaron really liked her. He managed to stifle a grin. "We're not safe. My home has been invaded and his friends may be watching it. They tend to travel in groups. You're a target if you leave. They believe you're in cahoots with me."

He didn't believe it. Group hunters traveled in packs but they also attacked in them. They'd have arrived already if the hunter had friends watching his back. Blaron wasn't willing to allow the woman to leave yet though. She intrigued him. Spending a little more time around her proved too tempting to resist.

He'd release her when he was ready to. She'd pose no real threat to him once he abandoned his home. He'd have to move; he'd no longer be safe where he lived after one hunter had found him. And no one would believe her if she decided to rant about vampires once he was gone. No one ever did.

"I'll not hurt you." He wanted to assure her, feeling the brute if he frightened the wee bonny lass after she'd shown such bravery. "I wouldn't be able to live with knowing you were harmed because of me. I also wish to know why you came to my aid. It was very courageous of you to help, knowing you'd be facing me."

"I actually thought you'd be sleeping."

"I don't fall to my death sleep when the sun rises, as they portray in movies and books. I'm able to move around, but I do need to avoid the sun."

Interest sparked in her pretty eyes. "Really? So the whole dead body thing while you sleep is false? That's interesting."

"Truly." He glanced at the water gun. "Holy water is just wet, the spike would've hurt something fierce, but I doubt that scrawny wretch would've gotten close enough to do me any damage. I tend to be a light sleeper."

"I bet." She shifted her stance. "So what happens now?"

"I need to call some friends. They'll come get us. I need to go somewhere safe."

Her gaze flickered to the thick drapes covering the windows, sun lighting the edges. "The sun is up."

"That's unfortunate but I'm old enough to withstand a little of it before I suffer any real damage."

He didn't miss the curiosity in her gaze. He guessed she wanted to ask him his age but refrained. It was a question all vampires suffered.

"I have a gun in my pocket. I'll be perfectly safe returning home. I just live across the street and I have no qualms about shooting idiots. It's even registered so I wouldn't get into trouble if a neighbor sees me shoot someone. The cops would come, I'd say I thought I saw an intruder sneaking around my house, and my butt is covered."

He grinned, unable to resist. She was brave and cute. "Thank you for not pointing a weapon at me."

"I doubt bullets would hurt you. Besides, I came over here to save you. Not take you out. Live-and-let-live motto, remember?" She glanced at the hunter and anger sounded in her voice. "I just get pissed when someone like that goes after another person to do harm. Been there, survived that."

Bullets would hurt all right, but he wasn't about to admit that. She wouldn't be able to kill him but if she shot him enough times, she'd sure slow him down enough for her to flee outside. He wouldn't dare pursue her into the sunshine across the street. He kept that information to himself.

"I'll make that call." He backed up for the phone on the bedside table, lifted it, and his body tensed in case she attempted to dart past him. He glanced away to dial but she remained still. The phone rang a few times and someone at the club answered.

"I've been compromised," he stated softly. "A hunter is tied up and I need an evacuation for three immediately."

24

"Yes, sir," the male growled. "We're coming."

He hung up and adjusted again to keep his kilt from lifting, his weapon once more pointed down in front of him so as not to alarm the lass.

"They are on their way."

"For three?"

"You should come with me. My people will scout the neighborhood to make sure he's alone and you can be returned later, when it's safe."

"Who are your people?"

He hesitated. "Friends."

"Not vampires?"

"No." He made sure to keep his sword in place even as his body started to cool. He noticed a discoloration forming on her cheek, having missed it before, and realized she'd been harmed. "He hit you?"

She reached up and rubbed the spot, her fingertips brushing tenderly over the area. "It's okay. He flopped around a bit when I tagged him with the stun gun and he got in a lucky slap before he fell down."

Blaron moved before he considered she might feel threatened as he advanced. Her arm dropped and she instantly backed up. He paused but continued to get closer.

"Easy. I'm just going to take a look."

She bumped into his desk, not having anywhere else to go, and he paused just a foot in front of her. He noted her much shorter height, realize she really was a wee bit of a lass, and he reached up to gently trace her skin with his fingertips. She was soft, warm, and peered up at him with a mixture of fear and curiosity. His body responded to her appealing scent and her lovely eyes.

"I'll not harm you." He dropped his voice to a husky tone.

His gaze lowered from her eyes to the mark on her pale skin. It was slightly warmer and he inhaled, picking up a very slight hint of blood scent coming from her. He wanted to groan as his body tensed and his fangs began to ache under the gums where they were hidden, matching the awareness of his equally affected cock.

"He cut the inside of your mouth."

Her eyebrows shot up with surprise. "How did you know that?"

His fangs grew longer and he muted the groan he nearly uttered. "I can fix it for you." He traced his tongue over one fang, careful to keep them hidden from her, and lowered his head. "Will you trust me?"

"I don't know."

She was too damn cute. "Close your eyes, tilt your head back and open your mouth."

"No way. I had a boy tell me that once and he tried to kiss me."

"That's what I plan to do. I can heal you with my tongue."

She strained against the desk. "I think that's a bad idea, and I don't even know you."

"You came to my aid. I owe you, lass. Allow me to heal what that wretch did. It won't hurt. I promise I won't be biting you."

# Chapter Three

Kilt was absolutely the sexiest guy, in Matty's opinion. His eyes stared deeply into hers and she had the urge to allow him to do anything he wanted. She wondered if he had an ability to control someone's mind but she didn't feel any different. The inside of her mouth *did* hurt, and the coppery taste of blood wasn't her favorite. The fact that he promised not to bite or hurt her made her less afraid.

A gorgeous, half-naked man wanted to kiss her to fix her boo-boo.

*He's a vampire. Don't forget that*, she warned.

*Too bad I wasn't hurt in a more interesting place*.

That thought made her want to wince. The mental image of the tall, muscular vampire dropping to his knees to place his lips on other parts of her body assured her that she'd spent way too many years dateless without sex.

Matty decided to do something rash. She'd learned how short life could be after she'd nearly lost hers. Regrets were a bitch. She wanted him to kiss her, wanted to feel alive for once, and Kilt was too much of a temptation to resist. *You only live once, and what do you have to lose? Your life isn't exactly exciting.*

"Okay, but only because you haven't eaten any of our neighbors and you haven't even tried to disarm me. I'm willing to trust you."

He smiled. Then his lips pressed together and he lowered his head until their faces were a mere inch apart. His eyes were beautiful and something she could stare into for hours without getting bored. She remembered he'd wanted her to close her eyes, which would totally screwed up that "look into my eyes" movie stuff if he were trying to control her mind.

She closed them, tilted her head back and slightly parted her lips. Her body tensed, waiting to see if she'd just made a horrible mistake or if he was as honest as he seemed. He got credit for not denying what he was. He could have flat-out lied, denying being a vampire.

He wasn't a butterfly kisser, a man who just tenderly brushed his lips over hers. The vampire was more direct. He dominated with force when he took possession of her mouth by firmly covering hers lips with his. His tongue invaded, delved inside and explored. He tasted sweet, and he knew what he was doing.

Her hands splayed on his bare chest for something to cling to, another surprise, because for a dead guy, he was literally hot. Firm muscles were just under his skin and his arm wrapped around her waist to tug her tightly against his solid body.

Matty felt something hard press between their bodies but it was shoved to the side, and she realized it must be his sword, or perhaps the weapons in her pockets. Then she barely noticed the sound of the sword bumping the wood of the desk and the soft thump when it hit the carpet.

His arm around her waist adjusted her a little until her butt eased onto the top of the desk and his hips pressed against her thighs. She spread them slightly, lost in the passion that surged between them, and didn't care that it should have alarmed her to respond so strongly to a stranger when he deepened the kiss.

28

His hips nudged against her legs tighter, spreading them wider, until her robe parted enough for the soft material of his kilt to brush her inner thighs. That wasn't the only thing she felt, as another hard object pressed against her mound. It wasn't his sword this time—and she knew he was as aroused by their kiss as she was.

His free hand curved around her rib cage and he cupped her breast through the material of her robe. She moaned against his tongue and her hands trailed up his chest, loving the feel of him, and she wrapped her arms around his neck.

Her fingers slid into his platinum tresses until they found his scalp, pulling him even closer. He had silky, wonderful curls that felt right laced around her fingers. His touch on her breast was firm as he squeezed. She moaned louder as a throbbing ache between her thighs made her spread them farther apart, hoping he'd step closer.

She felt his fangs extend while they kissed but it didn't alarm her. It was probably normal, considering he was a vampire. She ran her tongue over the point of one and he growled deep in response, his hips grinding against her pussy. Desire turned into a burning need to have him inside her. Matty couldn't remember wanting a man more.

He moved his hips in a way that mimicked fucking her, the hard press of his cock rubbing against her clit, and even through layers of clothing it was enough to make her hotter, needier and insane with wanting him. She didn't care that he was a vampire or she wasn't one to end up sitting at the edge of a desk wrapped around a stranger. All that mattered was that he didn't stop.

Kilt released her breast, bowed his back to put room between their stomachs, and his hand slid between them. She felt a tug at her waist when he yanked on her robe belt. It came free, and he yanked open her robe. She wrapped her legs around the backs of his thighs, trying to pull him closer, but he stopped rocking his hips against her.

He found the bottom of her nightshirt, jerked it up, and his big hand withdrew. She tried to break the kiss to protest the fact that he wasn't rubbing up against her clit anymore, a little stunned at how fast things were progressing between them, but his mouth followed hers when she attempted to pull away. She wasn't trying hard, since she had a death grip on the back of his head to keep him tight against her mouth. Her heels brushed along his warm legs that were exposed below his kilt.

Something crashed to the floor near the desk when he knocked things out of the way by clearing the top of it with a sweep of his hand, and then her back pressed against the hard surface. He came down on top of her, bending over to keep her flat. She bent her knees up and wrapped them around his hips.

His hand returned to her, wiggling between their bodies, and she felt a tug at her hips. She didn't care, since there was only his kiss and the need to be taken by him.

Material bunched between her stomach and his, and his strong, sure fingers stroked her clit. His touch drew a moan from her and she gasped into his mouth. They were skin to skin, her panties gone, and the feeling had to be the best thing she'd ever experienced. Her body burned and she used her grip around his hips with her legs to try to make him enter her.

Matty knew she was close to climax. The guy rubbed circles over the swollen bundle of nerves and her body tensed. He leaned closer, his hand withdrew from between them, and the big crown of his shaft pressed against the slick opening of her pussy. His mouth tore from hers right as he began to enter her with his cock. He was incredibly hard, it felt amazing, and she cried out as her head flew back.

She was coming before he'd even worked his thick shaft all the way inside her.

His mouth brushed a kiss on her neck and a jolt of pain sent her over the edge into a blinding climax as pain turned into sheer pleasure. White-hot waves of ecstasy slammed into her as he began to pound in and out of her body, her vaginal muscles flexing tightly around his shaft that penetrated her deeper.

She cried out again, a small part of her mind realizing he'd bitten into her, fed on her blood, but it felt too good as another climax gripped her body. Her fingernails clutched his head tighter against the cradle of her neck and the big, powerful man nearly crushed her. He groaned against her throat and his body trembled with enough force that the desk under them rattled. His fangs withdrew, his hot tongue swiped the bite, and he cursed softly as he continued to spill his release into her welcoming body. Warmth spread inside her pussy, nearly triggering a third climax.

Matty was in a daze, panting, her body going lax as she fought the urge to drift to sleep. Her eyes opened when he raised up slightly, his handsome face all she could see, and his incredibly gaze held hers. Passion and satisfaction were two emotions she could read easily as he peered at her, because she probably had the same ones on display.

"Ah lass," he murmured. "I didn't mean to bite but I couldn't help it. That was remarkable."

She licked her lips, tried to think, but the room began to spin as she suffered a moment of lightheadedness. The gaze holding hers seemed to darken in color and flash regret.

"I'll take care of you. You're such a wee one and I took too much. It was the passion. You'll be fine. Sleep. I will protect you with my life."

For some insane reason, she trusted him. He'd just taken her blood, had sex with her, and yet she closed her eyes. A sense of peace filled her before she blacked out.


Blaron shifted his gaze to her neck. He bent, licking at the drops of blood that remained on her healing skin. He hadn't meant to bite into her but he couldn't have stopped for anything. The passion that had flared between them had been a force not even a vampire as old as he could resist.

His spine stiffened when he realized there were two added scents inside the room now, and two sets of lungs that hadn't been sucking in air before. He jerked his head around to glare at the two men who stood just inside the bedroom. Both wore leather from neck to foot, had arrived far too quickly in his opinion, and neither met his angry glare.

"Sorry," one of them muttered. "We didn't realize you were having a private moment. We just rushed in, worried about you."

"Drag the hunter out and give me a minute."

"Yes, sir," they said in unison, moving to grab the human from the floor and hauling him off by his tethered limbs.

Blaron cursed as he straightened the lass's robe. He bent, grabbed his sword, and slid it into the scabbard he'd had sewn onto the side of all his kilts. He damned the males for their quick response and himself for losing his mind over a sweet-smelling female who fascinated him.

His hands sliding under the lass, he cradled her gently in his arms and walked out of the room with her snug against his bare chest. He glanced around his house for the last time. He couldn't come back. It would be too dangerous. Regret flashed. He'd lost many homes in his long lifetime in order to survive. At least this one he hadn't grown too attached to yet.

Both brothers waited near the front door. One of them stepped forward, his arms lifting. "I'll take her from you, sir."

The other one offered a hooded cape. "This should shield you from the worst of it. We parked the van in the driveway. We have a team on motorcycles scouting the area. It will be the last thing the hunters ever do if they try to follow."

"I have her. No one touches her but me."

"But the sun wi—"

"Just toss the damn thing over my head and wrap it around me." Anger stirred. "She's mine, and not to be touched by another."

Both males backed up instantly, alarmed. The one with the cloak hesitated and approached.

33

"Apologies. I didn't know you'd taken a companion."

Blaron stared down at the scarred yet beautiful face of the woman sleeping peacefully in his arms. The idea of keeping her wasn't a bad one. He'd heard stories of vampires finding their other halves. Supposedly, there would be an instant strong attraction and an acceptance of each other. Matty had come to his rescue, admitted to believing he was a vampire. She should have wanted the hunter to take out the predator in her neighborhood. Instead she'd defended him. It made her unique—and he definitely desired her. The concept of keeping her actually made him smile. Life would be exciting with her at his side.

He made a decision.

"Nor had I, until I met her. She's the one."

Shock still reverberated through him as he stated those words aloud. Every vampire wanted to find the perfect companion but he'd never expected to find his. It had seemed more of a romantic myth, but nothing else could explain the way they'd both lost their minds the moment their lips had touched. Instant chemistry was rare when it hit that strong. He wasn't a fool. He wasn't about to let her go. She might fight him a bit at first, but that would be fun for them both. He wasn't above using seduction on the sexy little lass.

One of the brothers cleared his throat, staring at him with caution. "Did I say something amusing, sir?"

"No. I was just lost in my thoughts. Send in a cleanup crew to remove all trace I was ever here and inhale her scent to track where she came from. She lives across the street but I'm not certain which house belongs to her.

Pack her up, and make it look good when you do what needs done. She won't be returning either. Let's go."

One brother moved behind him, using the cape to cover his head and shoulders. Blaron bent forward, tucking Matty tighter against his chest. The other brother pulled the material over his arms to protect him from burning when he stepped outside.

"Is she turning? Should I cover her as well?"

"No. She's still human," he informed them.

"Are you ready, sir?"

"Let's go."

He rushed out the door the moment it was opened for him and the brothers stayed at his side, prepared to protect him and Matty. The cargo van's side door had been left open, another brother waiting outside to guard it. He climbed inside, careful not to bump Matty's still form in his arms. He settled in the back as the door slid closed, sealing them in darkness.

The club wasn't far away. He smiled, adjusting her into a more comfortable position on his lap, resting her head against his shoulder.

# Chapter Four

Matty was slow to wake, a haze of sleep and erotic dreams tempting her to keep her eyes closed. She might have drifted back off but a big, warm hand on her bare hip slid upward to her lower stomach.

"Wake for me, lass," a husky masculine voice with a sexy accent rasped near her ear. "You need to eat. I've been worried about you."

Alarm jolted her to full wakefulness as her eyes flew open to stare into the handsome face of her neighbor. Kilt was in bed with her, it was dark inside whatever room they were in, and only a few small lamps gave off enough light for her to see by.

"Easy, lass. You're safe. We're underground inside a club a friend and I own. My home has been compromised and we'll stay here until we find somewhere else to go."

She was pinned by his hand on her stomach, one of his bare, muscular thighs lay over the top of her naked ones, and a sheet was tangled between them. "What am I doing here? Where are my clothes?" She yanked the sheet up higher on her chest. Her breasts had barely been covered.

"It wasn't safe for you to go home. Remember the hunter?"

"Of course I do. You bit me." She remembered that too.

"Aye. I did. I'm sorry about that but I was lost to the passion. You're fine. I'd never harm you but I admit I took a little much. It made you weak and sleepy. Are you ready to eat? I have a fine meal awaiting you."

More of her senses were waking, now that she was getting past the alarm of being naked in an unfamiliar place with a near stranger. The room was chilly, she smelled food, and it was unusually quiet.

And before that, a vampire had amazing sex with her and had bitten her neck.

She blushed and tried to wiggle away from him. He hesitated then moved his leg to release hers while his hand unpinned her. She lunged away, rolling, but kept the sheet fisted in her hands.

The bed was a large four-poster and she gasped when she nearly rolled off the edge. It was higher from the floor than any bed she'd ever been on. She stared down at the concrete floor, knowing it would have hurt if she'd taken a dive, and he hooked his arm around her waist to drag her butt a few inches back from the edge.

"Careful, lass."

"Where did you say we are?"

The bed moved as he sat up and she turned to glance down his body. The sheet had been pulled nearly off him when she'd tried to flee. Only part of it covered his hip but there was no missing the condition of his body, since the material tented over his lap. Her gaze flew to his face.

"Underground. There's a club above us but we're safe. No one knows where we are or that this basement even exists. Would you enjoy a bath before your meal? The club serves both my kind and yours. I've been assured the food is top notch."

"You don't know?"

"I don't eat food, but we serve it for humans in the club. Blood is also served to our vampire clientele. We mostly cater to them."

She gaped at him a little. "It's a vampire club? Seriously? Isn't that a bit obvious if you're trying to hide your existence?"

"Aye, but we fit better in the setting of a Gothic club. It's too cliché to be believable."

"You mean you encourage people who dress up like Vampires to come here, along with real ones?"

He nodded. "Aye. They love to dance, dress up, and we are able to mingle with them without raising suspicion. Most of the actual vampires are the normal-looking people who visit the club."

"What's it called?"

"Mooning."

She'd never heard of it before but she hadn't been social since her attack. "Do you drink from the guests?"

He hesitated. "Not often. Don't feel fear. No one will touch you." He smiled. "What's your name?"

Her cheeks burned. She'd had sex with him, shared a bed afterward even if she hadn't been aware of it, and they hadn't even exchanged names. "Matty. And yours?"

"Blaron."

She stared at Kilt. He was so handsome and his loose, long hair against his tan skin drew her attention. The desire to touch him made her hands clutch the sheet tighter. "I should go home."

"Why don't you eat first? I'll draw you a bath."

"You have a bathtub in a basement?"

"It's outfitted down here with a few apartments. This one is mine."

"But you lived in a house."

"I got tired of living under the club. It's quiet during the day but at night, that isn't the case. I didn't want to feel as if I were working every night by hearing the thumping music from above. See why I'd choose to live somewhere else in a quiet neighborhood?"

"I guess." It sounded reasonable to her.

He rolled the other way, leaving the cover of the sheet, and she couldn't help but stare at his perfect, beefy ass. It was paler than the rest of him—he had obvious tan lines—and that confused her as he slid off the bed. He bent, reached for something on the floor, and when he straightened, he pulled up a red kilt. He secured it at his waist and turned to face her.

"I'll retrieve you a robe from the bath." He walked into the darkness, out of the reach of the nearest dim lamp, until bright light came on across the room from the open bathroom door. She glimpsed a large tub before he returned holding a blood-red robe.

"It's a bit gaudy. I apologize. A nice pale blue would be more fitting for your creamy complexion but beggars can't be choosers. We're at the mercy of my friend's sense of humor for a few days. I moved my things out and he stocked my place for guests."

"Vampire ones?"

"Of course. Some of them get a bit drunk at the club and he was shoving them down here during the day from time to time."

"Um…"

He stopped at the edge of the bed just feet from her, dropped the robe, and arched a blond eyebrow. "Is there something you wish to ask me?"

"You have tan lines."

"It was from before. You stay the way you were when you were changed. I was a farmer once, and spent a lot of time in the sun."

"You mean before you became a vampire?" It still felt odd even saying that word aloud.

"I went to war with my friend who now owns this club with me. One night, a saucy wench came to comfort some of the injured lads in camp. She chose me, and I believed I'd gone to heaven when she lured me out into the darkness." He paused. "I was flattered she seemed to want me out of all the others she could've picked. I was a lad, she was fetching, and I thought she wanted to share her charms. It turns out she was looking for some sturdy warriors to travel with and protect her. She turned me and my friend."

Matty let that information settle. "Where is she now?"

He hesitated. "She died a long time ago. She had a preference for feeding from large humans, such as me. One night, she didn't distract one enough before she sank her fangs into him."

"I'm sorry." She wasn't sure what else to say. "Did you love her?"

He shook his head. "I detested her. It wasn't my choice to be turned. She wasn't likeable, but she taught us how to survive. I was grateful for that, especially after learning my battle mates were all killed weeks after we left them. My friend and I owed her, and we did our best to keep her safe. She never allowed us to go hunting with her though. She chose to feed off a male who fought back. She was skilled with a sword."

She wasn't sure what to say. They stared at each other. He took a step back.

"Dress in the robe, eat, and take a bath. Don't leave the room. I need to make some arrangements and will return soon." He stared at her. "No one will harm you here but I can't promise that if you were to reach the club above us. There are unfamiliar vampires up there who don't know you are with me. It wouldn't be safe."

"Okay." She wanted to go home but eating and take a bath first sounded good. He couldn't exactly take her to her house until the sun went down, and she couldn't have slept all day. She wished there was a clock but a quick sweep of the room with her gaze didn't show one. "You'll be right back?"

"Twenty minutes at most. Just stay inside the room and no one will bother you. I will lock the door, and I'm the only one with a key."

"Can I ask you something?"

"Anything, Matty."

He said it in a husky, sexy way with that accent of his that she loved to hear. "Why do you always come home in a limo right before dawn? What

41

do you do every night after I assume you work here? Doesn't this club close around two?"

He hesitated.

She had a sinking feeling from the little information she'd learned that she knew what he did at night. "You hunt for food?"

"I hunt, but not for food. I'm a bagger now. My search for blood from hosts was over as soon as we were able to bribe blood banks into selling to us. Not all vampires share that approach, but we don't like harming humans. My friends and I actually go after vampires who kill humans once the club closes."

His answer confused her. He seemed to understand.

"Clubs and bars do close around two in the morning. That means victims aplenty for vampires looking for drunk humans who are easy to prey on. They risk exposing us when they murder humans to take their blood. It's too dangerous these days to leave behind bloodless bodies, and it's no longer a necessity to survive. I don't drive, and that's why I have someone chauffeur me around."

"Will you be working tonight? Can you drop me off at my house?"

He hesitated. "I'm taking the evening off. We'll talk when I return. Eat, lass. Enjoy a warm bath." He glanced around the room. "It may look a bit rough with the concrete but the amenities in the bathroom are very modern."

He spun on his bare feet and walked to the door. His sword rested against the wall. He grabbed it up as he jerked open the door and disappeared into the darkness. No lights lit the hallway. She shivered at the thought of trying to sneak out...

She was in the basement of some vampire club.

The smell of food drove her to inch closer to the side of the bed, release the sheet, and slide off the edge. The cold floor made her shiver as she tied the thick, fancy robe around her waist. He'd left a covered plate with wrapped silverware on a desk in the corner. A drink waited there as well. She lifted the lid, staring at steak and eggs with hash browns. Her stomach rumbled. She was hungry.

* * * * *

"What are you doing?"

Blaron frowned at his friend. "Informing you that I'm taking the night off. And can you have someone find me a good home? I'm not holing up with you for long, Lethal."

"You'd be safer. I told you living amongst humans wasn't the smartest thing to do. A hunter spotted you. Just move in here again."

"No."

"You're so stubborn."

"So are you. I need to go." He turned away but Lethal's voice halted him.

"I'm stunned you brought a human here. You really shouldn't have. I realize your home was invaded but you should have sent her to a hotel or something if you believed her safety was compromised. I take it that you aren't lovers yet, since you asked for the key to my place to shower?"

43

He spun around to face his friend. "We're lovers but our relationship is very new. I came on too strong so I'm giving her some breathing room. She's very special to me."

Lethal tilted his head and a grin tugged at the corners of his mouth. "I see. You've bitten and fed from her? What happened to your sworn oath of not taking blood even from willing women?"

Anger tensed Blaron's body. "She's the *one* for me."

Shock gripped the other vampire's features. "Are you certain? You said your relationship was new."

"I'm certain. We just hit it off perfectly. It's almost instinctual for me to keep Matty at my side."

"How did you find her?"

"She found *me*. She's a neighbor who saw a hunter sneaking into my home and came to save me. We just met this morning."

"That little lass you carried in came to your rescue?" He chuckled. "What did she do? Scream to warn you?"

"She had hogtied the hunter by the time I reached them. She's quick and smart."

"And you have bedded her already? That was fast."

"It happened before we came here. As I said, she's my one."

"Have you told her that you plan to keep her?"

"I'm getting there."

"Good luck. I take it she knows what we are?"

"She guessed before she ever met me. She's a brave lass."

"How did she guess?"

"It's a long story."

"Shorten it for me."

"It seems she was watching my home for a bit, since hers was across the street. I got the impression she doesn't go out much. It's given her plenty of time to study me."

His friend leaned forward, resting his elbows on the desk he sat behind. "You're telling me she figured out you're a vampire and still came to your defense when a hunter found your lair?"

"Yes. She's a special lass."

"That seems an understatement. Most of them would either want to kill you or attempt to blackmail you into turning them into one of us, ever since all those stupid movies came out. Good luck telling her that you've chosen her to spend your life with. She won't be happy."

"Maybe she will be."

Lethal chuckled. "Always the optimist. Of course, perhaps she's a vampire movie fan. Let me know how it goes when the reality of it sets in for her—or maybe I'll hear the screaming from my office. We'll go hunting without you tonight. You stay to inform your lass of her future." He opened a drawer and withdrew handcuffs lined with fur. "Here's to love. You may need these to convince her to stay."

Blaron stood. "I won't be needing those."

"Take them. It's best to be prepared." All humor faded from his features. "She's a danger to us if you don't convince her to stay with you. You brought her here and I don't wish to close the club down."

"She has no idea where we are."

"She's guarded to make sure she doesn't snoop around or try to leave?"

"No. She won't flee."

Lethal stood, glaring. "She is the enemy if she does. She could put us at risk of being attacked by her kind if they were to believe her. One post on an Internet social site and we'd have hunters from all over the world descending on us. I don't want to move. We've built a life here, Blaron. Are we clear?"

"Perfectly." Blaron gripped the handle of his sword. "Don't threaten her, Lethal. She's mine, and we'll fight if you try to harm a hair on her precious head."

Lethal's stance relaxed. "I didn't say I'd cause her harm. I would, however, make certain she couldn't tell anyone about us. Make sure we have no reason to come to blows. Friends are hard to keep as the years wear on. I don't want to lose you because I stir your anger by locking her up or trying to erase her memories."

They regarded each other and Blaron released his sword. He grabbed the handcuffs off the desk. "I'll be in my room."

"You should lock her in when you leave her alone. For her safety and ours."

"Don't tell me what to do."

"Fine." Lethal sighed. "Just be careful. I would hate for a little human to kill you if she's so inclined. You'd probably hand her your own sword to stab you with."

"Matty and I have a connection. I'm certain she'll want to stay with me once she understands that."

"I hope so, for our sakes. You put us both at risk by bringing her here."

"She's no threat. I'll romance her into agreeing to be my companion."

Lethal grinned. "Do you remember how? Would you like some pointers?"

"You're as old as I am, you bastard." Blaron grinned, remembering they were as close as brothers. Lethal wouldn't harm Matty. He relaxed. "I sure wouldn't ask advice from *you* if I needed it."

"I've taken far more lovers over the years than you have."

"I did fine with her earlier this morning."

"I'm glad to hear it. Have fun but not too much!" Lethal's amused tone irritated him.

Blaron departed quickly. "Asshole."

"It takes one to know one."

# Chapter Five

Matty rose from the warm bath, her hair washed, and tucked a towel around her body. The door in the other room opened. She froze, afraid it might not be Kilt, but instead some other vampire. The door closed and she heard a growl.

"Matty? Are you in there?"

"I'll be right out."

She knew that Scottish brogue. He'd returned. She dried off quickly, wished for clothing, but only had the robe to put back on. The blood-red color of it made her feel like a walking advertisement for a vampire meal on legs. *Bad pun. Don't go there*. She hesitated at the door but turned the handle, opening it up.

It surprised her to see that Kilt had showered and changed. His hair was still damp and the sight of him in loose black pants was enough to make her gawk. He looked like some kind of blond pirate out of a film with his long hair, the breeches, and a sword hung low from a belt secured at his waist. He stared at her with his sexy eyes when she finally stopped noticing his shirtless, muscled chest. The guy had the best body she'd ever seen.

"You ate." He looked pleased as he smiled. "I take it the food was enjoyable? The plate is clean."

"They serve good food. You were right."

He shrugged, drawing attention to those broad shoulders. "I had heard but I don't eat food anymore."

"Ever?"

"I used to but it's been a long time."

"But you *can* eat it though?"

He hesitated. "I don't need it, and I lost the urge to eat with others a good hundred years ago. Blood is what I need."

She unconsciously reached up and touched her neck. There wasn't a mark where he'd bitten her, she'd check in the mirror, but the memory remained. Kilt followed her hand with his gaze and licked his lips. The air between them seemed to warm up in the chilly room as both of them were reminded of what they'd done together on his desk.

Matty dropped her hand quickly. "Have you eaten?"

He hesitated. "Are you offering to feed me?"

She took a step back and bumped the doorjamb of the bathroom, missing the opening, and halted. "No."

He reached for his waist, unfastened the belt, and turned his back on her to place his sword on the table by the bed. She watched him, leery of what would happen next. The guy weighed at least a hundred pounds more than her and was bodybuilder big. Their gazes met again when he faced her.

"I fed and showered to give you time to yourself. We need to talk."

"Yes, we do. I need to go home. I'm sure that I'm safe. That jerk was after you, not me."

"You haven't asked what I did to him."

She hesitated. "I don't want to know."

"Fair enough." He took a hesitant step toward her. "I'm an honorable man. I want you to know that. You'll learn, but we don't know each other yet." He stopped feet from her, watching her closely. "I'd never cause you harm, and I'd give my life to protect yours. Those are things you can always count on from me. I'm honest and I will pledge total loyalty to you. I'm a bag feeder, so there won't be any other women in my arms."

Mute, Matty listened. It sounded as if he were trying to make something more out of the crazy one-morning stand they'd had. Her heartbeat increased. The idea of dating him wasn't totally a bad one. She'd never forget him, and could admit he'd already become a part of her life while she'd watched him from her bedroom window. He said he wouldn't be returning to his house. That meant she wouldn't see him again as soon as they said goodbye—unless he was asking her out.

"In the old days, a vampire couple would've fed off humans. The best way to ensure a human could survive without knowing what we were was feeding off them during sex." His cheeks blushed slightly. "Those days are over, and I'd kill anyone who touched you, even for feeding purposes."

"Um…" No other words formed.

"I'm saying this wrong. I'm not good with words but the passion between us can't be denied. I'm attracted to you, the sex was incredible, and sleeping with you wrapped inside my arms, against my body, was heaven on Earth. I've never known such rightness as touching you."

For a guy not good with words, he said the right ones to melt her heart. She still couldn't talk though. And he shocked her further by dropping to his knees before her and staring up at her face with sincerity.

"You bring me to my knees. I pledge my life to yours, Matty. I'll do whatever it takes to convince you to be my companion."

She swallowed hard. "What is that? Your girlfriend?"

He hesitated and offered a hand, holding it out to her. She placed her trembling one in his. He brought it to his lips to place a kiss on the back of her hand, turned it in his, kissed her palm. His gaze never left hers.

"It's a lover, a friend, and you'd use the term wife. It's a lifetime commitment...and we don't age. I'm going to be honest with you. It's forever—and that could be a long time. I've met a vampire over a thousand years old."

Her knees locked together to keep her on her feet and the wall at her back kept her standing. "You want to turn me? Make me a vampire?"

He nodded, still holding her hand. "I don't want to lose you to old age or illness. Humans are frail. You'd be much stronger as a vampire."

She yanked her hand out of his and hugged her waist. "No."

Pain etched his features. "Why not? Isn't that something tempting? You'll never age and I'll always protect you. I'm a skilled warrior. Only the sun could kill you, or a beheading. No one would ever get close enough to stake you to the ground or touch that pretty head of yours."

"I...this is insane. You don't even know me. We had sex once, and while I'd only kind of thought you *might* be a vampire, you're *real*. I'm still reeling from the fact they exist! And why would you offer that to me? I don't understand."

"Kisses don't lie, nor do our bodies. You're a perfect fit for me."

51

"It was sex one time. That's crazy to think just because it was good that we should get married. We're strangers!"

"What we shared was special, Matty."

He had a sexy voice, and she had to agree on the special part. The sex they'd had on his desk had blown her mind. What if every time he touched her it was that intense? She ran her gaze over his body and the urge to touch him again surfaced.

"We'll have a long time to get to know each other." He smiled, drawing her attention back to his face and his eyes. "I look forward to it." He paused. "And if you believe that was just 'good' sex, I obviously need to take my time the next round." His gaze lowered to the tie of her belt. "Open it up. I'm on my knees already...just hook a leg over my shoulder." He brushed his hair back, winked, and licked his lips. "I'll show you greatness."

Her jaw dropped open. "You..."

"Plan to do a little worshipping of your bonny body." He reached for her.

Matty launched herself against the wall, avoided his hands, and ran for the door. The guy planned to seduce her, bite into her again, and make her a bloodsucking creature of the night. That wasn't on her "to do" list. He might be hot, have a rocking body, be totally hung, but no guy was worth giving up chocolate forever. Besides that, they were strangers.

She'd nearly reached the door when his arm snagged her from behind, around her waist. Kilt hugged her to his body, wrapped his other arm over her chest, and lifted her right off her feet. She twisted her head to stare at him with fear as he frowned at her, inches from her face.

"Don't be afraid."

"Put me down!"

"I won't hurt you. Are you afraid it's going to be painful? It won't be."

"I don't even know you, and I'm not ready to get married. Or whatever you call it." She struggled but his strong arms refused to release her. She did, however, feel his body respond when something hard pressed against her ass. She froze and gawked at him.

"Sorry." He shrugged, turned them both to face the bed, and sighed. "I can't help it. I want you despite this not being the best time to be sporting a pole."

"A pole?"

He cleared his throat. "My dick is hard anytime I touch you. Is that clearer?"

He gently dropped her on the bed and Matty rolled, sat up, and her gaze lowered to the breeches. He either wasn't wearing underwear or they were thin, because his "pole" was pointing straight out, the material of his pants stretched taut. She raised her eyes to stare at him.

"We're not having sex—and don't bite me."

"How about we make love but I don't bite? I'm prepared this time for how strongly I will react to you." He grinned. "I need to convince you it's better than good between us." He stared at her lap. "Open the robe and I'll take you to heaven."

"Um, no. Fangs and that area aren't meeting. No way. I don't have any piercings down there and never plan to get any."

He chuckled. "Do you know what fangs are good for when I'm licking you?" He parted his lips, revealing they were fully extended. "They fit perfectly on the sides of that pretty little pearl to give my tongue full access. I won't have to use my hands to keep you spread enough to get to it well. They will be otherwise occupied."

The vivid picture he painted made her breath freeze inside her lungs and her body responded. She inched back, scooting away from him. "I think I should go home."

"Damn. I was afraid of this." He frowned. "You're scared. I won't force you to turn but you've got to at least give us a chance before you say no."

"You want to date me?" She paused, considering that. They could get to know each other. It wasn't as if she had a social life. The idea wasn't scary. Of course, they wouldn't be going out to dinner, since he admitted not eating food. Maybe they could see movies together. "We could try that."

He turned and reached for the sword he'd removed earlier. Fear gripped her. Would he kill her for refusing to become a vampire?

He discarded it and fiddled with the belt he'd removed, and her fear eased. There was a small pouch attached to the belt. He finally turned, holding up fur-lined handcuffs.

The relief was short-lived when he lunged at her.


Blaron hated to do it but he needed to convince Matty they belonged together. She cried out when he grabbed her. He was careful not to hurt her, but she put up a hell of a fight when he stripped her of her robe. He

54

was careful not to bruise her creamy skin as he gripped her wrists, tugged her up the bed as her feet kicked at him, and secured her wrists through the bars of the headboard.

"Asshole!" She tried to kick him in the face.

He dodged her foot, barely, and grunted when it impacted his shoulder instead. The lass had fire, and he loved her a little more for it. His Matty was a fighter. He wouldn't bite her; he would refrain from tasting her blood. She struggled when he released her, her hips rising from the bed, her feet flat on the mattress, and his cock hurt from the sight as she twisted and wiggled.

He backed away and reached for the waist of his borrowed breeches. He hated the feel of them, the constricting material rubbing the crown of his straining cock. He sighed with relief as he tugged them down. He sat, yanking the damn things off his legs and tossed them to the floor. He was a kilt man. He moved onto his hands and knees at the foot of the bed, watching her wear herself out, and grinned at the curses she muttered. His lass had the mouth of a sailor when her temper was riled. He found it adorable.

She'd learn he'd never take her by force. He'd never be a brute to her, but the cuffs were for her own good. Lethal would try to harm her if she attempted to run away, and her old life was gone. Blaron had set the hunter free after messing with his mind. Of course, memories could return if something triggered them. If so, the hunter might remember Matty, target her. She'd be in danger. He couldn't allow that.

No, Matty belonged with him. He just had to convince her of that. Even if meant restraining her to his bed to show her he'd never harm her. Seduction was the best way. He'd love her, show her tenderness and passion.

"Easy, Matty my love," he rasped. "I bring you pleasure, not pain."

"You're scaring me."

He flinched inwardly at her words. "'Tis a wasted emotion you don't need. I'll never harm you. Never."

He tried to reach for her again but she kicked her legs at him. He pulled back, waiting for her to stop. She had fire. He'd give her that. Maybe it would be better to back off for a few minutes. He sat back on his heels at the bottom of the bed and waited.

# Chapter Six

"Now, Matty," he sighed. "Calm down."

She glared at him. "Let me go. This is your idea of convincing me you're honorable? Stripping me and handcuffing me to a bed?"

"It's not perfect but it will do."

"Jerk. Asshole. Creep!"

He grinned. "I've already heard you use more colorful terms."

"You're amused?" She'd fought the restraints until she grew tired. "This isn't funny."

"It's not." His gaze lowered down her body. "Open those pretty thighs for me and I'll improve your mood. I won't bite you this time and I won't turn you during the heat of passion. You have my word as a gentleman."

She snorted, not willing to believe him. "You're a vampire."

"I'm one who wants to pleasure you."

"You want my blood. You admitted to using sex to get women to allow you to feed off them."

He looked hurt at her words. That surprised her. Some of her anger dissipated. What if he really did have feelings for her? She felt them toward *him*. It was insane. They'd just met that morning, but in her defense, she'd been watching him for months. She'd been fascinated from the moment she'd glimpsed her new neighbor.

They stared at each other until he sighed.

"You're more than that to me."

She wanted to believe him but what if he was lying? She knew next to nothing about real vampires. It was possible they went around lying to women to get them into bed for their blood. He could discard her the second he got what he wanted. "Let me go, Blaron."

"Give us a chance first. I will convince you or give your life back."

*Why does it feel as though I'm making a deal with the devil? A hot, sexy one, who keeps staring at my thighs as if I'm a big kid's meal he's starving for.* She hated how her nipples hardened, knowing it didn't have a thing to do with the room temperature but more for what would happen if she gave him access to her pussy.

"You're saying if we have sex again, you'll let me go if it doesn't convince me to marry you?" Maybe he said that to every woman, planning on letting her go regardless. "You know that's screwed up, right?"

He smiled again. "I do love that term. Screwed. Up. Down. Hard. Fast. Slow." His eyes seemed to glow. "Any way that will please you and make you scream out my name while I'm inside that tight, wonderful sheath of yours."

Her body wanted him, tingled from his words, and it made her a little sad. It would hurt if he were lying. She'd spent years alone, and he just seemed too good to be true.

What if he really *did* want to spend his life with her? What if he wasn't lying or just telling her what he figured she might want to hear? Worst case, he'd make love to her. She'd have the memories to live with.

She'd keep her pride, though, if she didn't cave to him too easily by seeming overly eager.

"Fine. Do your worst but I'm going home afterward." She took a deep breath. "No biting."

"No biting. I love a challenge, lass."

He reached for her and she spread her thighs at his urging. She dropped her head on the pillow and closed her eyes. No matter how good he might be at oral sex, she had to protect her heart for falling for him even more. She probably had nothing to worry about. Men had gone down on her before but it hadn't been great. They sure hadn't made her scream their names.

She relaxed when the bed moved and he spread her thighs even farther apart. She glanced down, saw him sprawled out on his belly, his face inches from her pussy. He raised his arms, bracing them over her legs to hold them down. His gaze met hers and he gave her a cocky grin that showed his fangs.

"They won't cut you, and I'll show you just how much you're going to love them."

Fear and excitement fought for dominance. She'd kill him when he let her go if he bit her tender skin.

He breathed on her clit, making her more aware of the vulnerable position she was in, and she pulled on the handcuffs that refused to release her wrists. The sensation of being tied and pinned to the bed had a certain amount of sexual appeal.

He lowered his head and growled softly, a masculine sound that turned her on more. There was something almost sinful and super sexy about knowing how dangerous he could be. He nuzzled his mouth against her folds; she tensed when she felt his fangs brush her clit. They pressed tight against her skin on either side. It seemed to push the bundle of nerves closer to the tongue that teased her with a slow trace of the tip. Matty squeezed her eyes closed and her fingers wrapped around the chains of the handcuffs.

He tortured her with flicks of his tongue over her clit until it throbbed. When he applied pressure, pushed the flat of his tongue against it to rub, she tried to buck her hips but the weight of his arms kept her down. She jerked though when he reached up, and both of his hands found her straining nipples. He pinched them between his thumbs and forefingers, rolling the taut beads, and her body tensed.

Moans broke from her lips. His forearms pinned her but his fingers playing with her breasts drove her crazy. "Faster. Please?" She hated begging but she wanted to come so bad it hurt.

He refused to quicken the pace. Instead he kept up the slow gliding of his tongue until she cried out, the orgasm ripping through her body. His tongue paused until she stopped trembling and the pleasure eased. His hands stopped pinching her nipples and instead massaged her breasts, kneading them gently.

She gasped when he began again, his tongue fixating on her clit.

"I can't," she panted. "Too sensitive."

He ignored her, and she cried out when he began sucking instead. Strong tugs of his mouth with the occasional swipe of his tongue made her writhe and moan. She came again, his name bursting from her lips.

"Blaron!"

He mouth pulled away. "Will you marry me?"

"No."

"I'm not done."

"You can't mean to keep doing that until I say yes?" She had a sinking feeling he did. And damn him, he was good at it. She wouldn't survive hours of him licking her.

"Aye, lass. I do."

"Bastard!"

He chuckled. "But I'm all yours."

She gasped when he nuzzled his mouth against her pussy again, his fangs fitting around her clit, and his tongue licked her slowly. Her toes curled, feeling the sides of his ribs, and she hoped she at least tickled him. Her breathing grew faster as she panted and he refused to let up until she came again. She screamed his name that time. Her body bucked from the intensity of her orgasm. He pulled away.

"Matty?" His voice was a little rough sounding. "What say you?"

"Fuck you."

He growled. "That's next."

She gasped when he sat back on his haunches. He gripped her thighs, crawled in closer until they were spread over his own, his cock pressed against the opening of her pussy. She stared at him, a little afraid of the dark, dangerous look on his handsome face.

"I won't hurt you but I have to have you. Say yes."

She nodded, wanting him. She hurt inside, needing to be filled. The orgasms had been great but they'd felt a little empty.

He entered her slowly, her body stretching around his thick cock, and both of them moaned.

His hands slid down her thighs, cupped her ass, and adjusted her a little higher on his lap. He rocked them both, fucking her deep and fast. His thumb moved to press over her clit, and Matty went wild. The sensation of him inside her while he was touching her clit, his powerful body taking hers, was too much ecstasy to handle. She screamed out as she came and opened her eyes in time to watch Blaron throw back his head, his body tensed. He shouted out her name as he came inside her. He shivered, his muscular, sweaty body the sexiest sight ever, and his chin lowered as their gazes met.

"What say you, Matty?"

She couldn't form words. She was too blown away by what he'd just done to her and too out of breath. His eyebrow arched as he smiled.

"Again? Okay, Matty. I can go all night and day for you." He adjusted his hold on her, running his fingers over her lower stomach. "We'll both learn new limits of how much we can survive."

He began to move inside her, still hard, this time in slow, long thrusts, nearly withdrawing from her pussy, only to drive back in deep. He paused there, staring into her eyes, and withdrew. Her fingers clamped around the chains and her back arched. Blaron smiled.

"I've had hundreds of years to learn how to please a woman, but none mattered as much as you. Think of doing this every night."

She moaned in response when he brushed a thumb over her swollen clit. Her vaginal muscles clenched and Blaron groaned.

"Matty, my love, say yes to me. Agree to be mine."

She nodded, wanting to come again. His hand released her ass and he bent over her, bracing his arm on the bed next to her rib cage. His mouth took hers in a kiss that was so tender, so passionate, that she wished she could cling to him. Her wrists strained against the handcuffs and she whimpered in protest.

More of his weight came down on her, and his fingers brushed hers before she felt a hard jerk on the chain. Her arms lowered after he snapped the restraints, and her fingers delved into his hair, holding his mouth closer while she kissed him back. His hips rocked them into another shared orgasm and he broke the kiss when they both cried out.

"Love me, Matty. Allow me to love you, lass."

She opened her eyes to stare into his. "This is totally not fair."

He smiled. "Love isn't fair, but it sure feels amazing, doesn't it? We're right for each other. I'll keep convincing you."

"I'm never going to win an argument with you, am I?"

He chuckled. "I'll let you win sometimes. I like the idea of you restraining me to a bed and convincing me you're right."

The idea of him tied down at her mercy excited her.

He smiled. "I hear your heart racing. Like that, do you? I'd allow you to do anything to me you want. I'd welcome it. We'll be happy together."

Her life flashed inside her mind. She'd become a recluse, no life outside of her home, and she'd been lonely. Blaron was offering her a life with *him*.

She trailed her hands down to his cheeks, staring into his eyes, and knew she didn't want to lose him. It might be scary to face an unknown future but at least it *was* one. He gave her such a look of longing and hope that she truly believed he wanted to be with her.

"Will you have to hurt me?"

"I'll love you always, and make you happy. There'll never be pain in my arms."

"I mean turning me into what you are."

He grinned. "No. I will let you drink from me while I drink from you. It's not the way you've seen in movies. We'll sleep after, both of us tired, and when you wake you'll feel the same. You'll just need to drink blood from a bag."

She grimaced.

He chuckled. "For you, I'll drink from the bags and you can drink from me. Way more pleasurable, and it's what a good man does for his woman."

"It sounds gross."

"You know how it feels when I lick your little pussy? The fangs feel almost as good when you sink them into my skin and drink from me. It's sexual, and I'll fuck you while you do it. I promise you're going to love it. I just may have to turn the club over to my friend Lethal, since we won't want to climb out of bed for a few hundred years."

She took a deep breath. "I wish you'd give me a little more time. This is a huge decision."

Blaron saw the fear in her eyes and nodded, even though he wanted to sink his fangs into her and give her his bleeding wrist. "I understand."

"You'll give me time?"

"I'll show you what you're getting into first. How about that for a compromise?"

She seemed to debate it. "Okay. I'm not sure exactly what that means."

"We're going to get dressed and go upstairs to the club. I'll show you my world and even feed in front of you, so you aren't afraid of bagged blood." He just hoped it didn't turn her away from him.

"Thank you."

"I'm worried you'll run from me, Matty. It would break my heart. Don't do that." He didn't mention that Lethal wasn't going to be happy with him, but it was half his club. His friend could stuff it. It was more important that his woman was comfortable with accepting what he was offering her. He wanted her completely at peace with the decision.

"Let's shower and I'll go get you clothing." He'd sent a team to her house. They'd have brought her personal belongings to be stored in the club by now. He'd just have to break it to her that he'd moved her out of her home already. She'd probably be angry but so be it. He wasn't allowing her to return to danger.

# Chapter Seven

Matty felt nervous as she dressed. She'd been to dance clubs before but it had been a while. Of course, back then she hadn't been scarred. People tended to gawk at her and openly stare. It always left her feeling angry or sad, depending on their reaction. She tended to avoid putting herself on display for those encounters.

"Are you still angry with me?"

She turned, holding Blaron's gaze. He'd dressed in the bathroom while she'd done so in the bedroom. She liked him wearing the blue long-sleeved shirt with a blue and black kilt. He'd exchanged his sword for a small sheath that looked as if it held some kind of hunting knife. It was attached to a belt with a pouch that covered the front of his groin area. Black boots and matching socks adorned his feet. He'd braided his hair again, looking super sexy and exotic. He stared back at her and she remembered that he'd asked her a question.

"No. I'm starting to understand that you're just a take-charge type of man. I shouldn't have been surprised that you sent strangers into my house to pack my clothes. At least they put them in those nice hanger boxes so nothing in my closet got wrinkled."

"Werewolves are very efficient. They've had a lot of practice, unfortunately. Any time humans begin to suspect we are different, we need to move."

"Werewolves." She swallowed hard, running her hands down her skirt in a nervous gesture. "I'm almost afraid to meet them. You said a lot of them work for you here at the club?"

He nodded. "You'll be safe, Matty. None of them will harm you. They aren't ravenous beasts as portrayed in your horror movies. They actually watch them and laugh, so I've heard. 'Tis very amusing for them to see how humans view them."

"That's a bit comforting to know they have a sense of humor."

"You'll meet Chase. He's in charge of them, and a friend."

She felt compelled to warn Blaron, since he'd never been out in public with her before, and he was being nice enough to lessen her fear of the werewolves. "Um, don't get mad when we go into the club."

"What do you mean? Are you planning something? Don't try to run from me, Matty. Please. You said you'd give us a chance."

"It's not that." She walked up to him and appreciated how he peered at her face without staring at the scars. "Some people are rude enough to ask what happened to me."

He reached up and tenderly traced the largest scar. "You're beautiful."

She searched his gaze, believing he really meant the compliment. "I didn't leave my house much and only went shopping when I had to, always in the middle of the night to avoid people."

"There will be no more hiding as my woman. Wear your scars with pride, Matty. They are a part of you, and no one would dare offend you." His expression hardened. "Not twice."

She laughed. He was a big man, intimidating, and she could see how he'd discourage anyone from saying a word to her that might hurt her feelings. "You'd beat them up for me?"

"I would." He lowered his hand and wrapped his arm around her waist, pulling her closer. "I'd do anything for you."

She was falling in love with him even more. "Thank you."

"It's my honor to defend you. Even from blind, petty fools with no brains."

She laughed again. He had a way of making her happy and amused. "My hero."

"I aspire to be that, now and forever."

"I appreciate it."

He leaned in and she held her breath, heart pounding as he brushed his mouth over hers. She closed her eyes and opened her hands on his chest. He pulled away too fast, making her long for a deeper kiss than the teasing one he'd given.

"We should go upstairs. I'll introduce you to everyone and then take you to the feeding room."

"That sounds ominous."

He chuckled. "Never. One of the biggest difficulties I faced after being turned was knowing I'd need blood to survive. It's a different time now. I shall make it easy for you. We acquire our blood by buying it from humans. The werewolves run a truck that collects it a few times a week and we store it in the feeding room. We provide a little money for those who donate; they give us what we need."

"You said I could drink it directly from you, though, right?"

"Aye. It will be highly enjoyable for us both. Plastic will never need touch your bonny lips."

"But I have to give up food?"

"You could eat it, but that means you'll still have to deal with body functions."

She arched her eyebrows, not certain what that meant. She could guess but it would be better if he spelled it out.

"Your digestive system works differently for food and other drink than it does for blood. The bathroom, Matty. Once you stop eating food, the toilet only collects dust. Is that a delicate way to put it? My body absorbs blood without causing waste."

"I understand." She didn't have to give up chocolate after all. It would just come at a small price. One that she was already used to as a human. "Let's go and see what you want to show me."

He took her hand, placing it in the crook of his arm. "My pleasure."

She took a deep breath, allowing him to lead her out of the bedroom and into a living space. There was no kitchen in his apartment. She guessed he didn't exactly need one since he didn't cook. They exited through a solid door into a well-lit hallway. The basement seemed pretty large. Another sturdy door blocked the end of the hallway, behind which they came to stairs.

"Why so many doors?"

"Protection in case the basement is ever breached by hunters."

"Is there an escape route?"

"Of course. There's an old sewer system we could flee through and stay underground until the sun set. Lethal is all about survival."

"Why did you move out of here again?"

"No matter how much soundproofing we tried, the music is still audible to our kind. I grew tired hearing it every evening while the club was open."

"Ah." That made sense to her.


Blaron led her through the club's kitchen, smiling at the werewolves who worked for them. They gave Matty pleasant glances and a few waves.

One of the cooks stepped into their path, looking at Matty. "It's nice to meet you. My name is Velma. Just let me know if there are any specialty foods you enjoy, and I'll be happy to provide them."

"Thank you. That's so nice." Matty flashed him an uncertain look.

"Velma is a werewolf."

Matty's eyes widened, then fixed on Velma. "Wow. You look so normal. I never would have guessed. I mean, I'm sorry. That was so rude of me."

"Don't worry about it. I'm not offended. We hide in plain sight. We're just glad one of the masters found a companion."

"Masters?"

"That would be me and Lethal," Blaron stated. "It's a polite way to refer to us older-than-dirt vampires."

Velma laughed. "Both of them gave us jobs where we could be ourselves. We're grateful. It's difficult to work for humans. We have to watch our every move and word in case we reveal too much. The club also doesn't require drug testing. That's a great thing."

Matty's eyebrows arched. "Um, is that a problem?"

"They aren't human," Blaron explained. "A simple blood test can be dangerous if the results come back as odd. At the very least, misunderstandings happen, like assuming they purposely messed up the test to hide something."

"As if we might take drugs, when in fact only a moron would," Velma added. "They don't have the same effect on us as they do on humans. Give a werewolf cocaine and he'd puke his guts up for days. It's like food poisoning to our kind."

"Oh."

Blaron cleared his throat. "We must be going. Thank you, Velma."

She stepped out of the way. "Have fun."

He led Matty out of the kitchen and behind the bar. Chase waited there, playing bartender. He introduced them. Chase bowed, shook her hand, and winked.

"It's nice to meet you, Matty. Nice job this morning. The Barlo brothers filled me in. You tied up a vampire hunter. That was very courageous of you."

"Don't flirt with her." Blaron narrowed his eyes, glaring at his friend. "She's mine."

Chase chuckled and stepped back. "She's a beauty. You'd better keep her close, lest someone try to steal her away." He grinned at Matty. "You're with a man who wears a skirt. Not everyone could pull that off."

Blaron relaxed, realizing Chase was just being friendly. "'Tis a manly kilt. You're just jealous that you have knobby knees and feel the need to cover yours."

"Aye," Chase mimicked him. "'Tis manly since you terrify anyone you glower at."

He tugged Matty out from behind the bar. Some of the regulars had arrived already but it wasn't crowded yet. Some couples were dancing but most were sitting at tables, grouped in numbers of two to four, chatting. He immediately held the gazes of some of the vampires who picked up Matty's scent, silently warning them to think twice about approaching her. She wasn't an unattached human they could attempt to seduce and take a sip of blood from in the heat of the moment.

"Would you like to dance with me?" He wanted to hold her.

"It's eighties music. I grew up listening to my mom play this stuff. Do you know how to dance to New Wave?"

He turned his head, caught the attention of the DJ, and made a hand signal. The music abruptly ended, a slow song coming on next. He gripped Matty's hand, faced her, and then placed her other hand on his shoulder. Smiling, he put his arm around her, turning them in a circle.

"Ever waltzed before?"

She appeared stunned. "No."

"I'll teach you. Just follow my lead. This is a simple one."

"There's more than one type?"

"There are many."

"I didn't know that." She smiled though, relaxing in his hold and swaying with him.

He noticed a few of the vampires rising from their tables, taking partners, and coming out to join them on the dance floor. He looked down. Matty had also realized they were no longer alone. She stumbled when the couples began to waltz around them. He pulled her a little closer.

"What's the matter, lass?"

"I was sure we'd be the only ones out here with this elevator music playing."

She amused him. "It's called orchestra music, and vampires love to dance. It brings back a lot of good memories for the older ones, and the younger ones love the romantic idea of it." He leaned down, lowering his voice. "Ever heard of vampire balls?"

Her mouth parted in an "O" shape.

He chuckled. "We do love a good ball. We hold one here every New Year's Eve. I can't wait to bring you. I'll teach you the most popular dances and buy you a beautiful gown."

Her features softened as she peered up at him. "You're a romantic at heart, aren't you?"

"Just a bit." He spun her, loving the feel of her in his arms. "You bring it out in me, Matty."

# Chapter Eight

Matty was in love with Blaron. It was that simple. She'd had a fantastic time in the club dancing with him. It hadn't been anything like she'd expected. He'd taught her a few old fashioned dances and introduced her to some of his vampire friends. They'd been polite and likeable. He finally led her out of the club when more people arrived and the music turned to something more contemporary.

The kitchen staff was busy preparing food orders when they passed through to reach the hidden basement door. It was located next to a walk-in freezer, behind a false brick wall front. The first door at the bottom of the stairs, one they'd passed earlier, led to the feeding room. It looked more like a cozy studio apartment, with a tiny kitchen and open living room space with two couches and a coffee table.

"Surprised?"

She nodded.

He released her hand and pointed to a barstool at the counter that divided the kitchen from the couches. "Take a seat. We store the blood in the fridge here. Are you ready for this?"

"I think so." She climbed up onto the padded barstool, getting comfortable.

He paused by the refrigerator and tilted his head. "I want you to know all of me, Matty. Feeding is a requirement for me to survive. I do this every other day. I can go longer but I don't recommend it. I get a bit testy and my fangs won't easily retract when I'm feeling hunger. It's like suffering from your grumbling digestive system on an empty stomach."

She appreciated that he was being so open about things. "Go ahead. I'm ready." She braced for whatever would come next.

He turned and yanked open the fridge. Inside were bags of blood, several dozens of them. He took one out and closed the door, walking a few steps to the bar on the other side of her.

"Why are there so many of them?"

"We sell it to vampire customers at the bar, as well as what we drink. It's all stored here. My fangs act like tiny straws. Are you ready to see me feed?"

She hesitantly reached out. He held still as she pressed her fingertip to the side of the bag. "It's so cold." Her gaze held his as she lowered her hand.

"It tastes better warm. I won't lie. But the colder the better when drinking from a bag. The chill deadens the taste buds, you could say."

"I'm ready to watch this. Go ahead." She was curious.

He opened his mouth, allowing her to watch his fangs slide down. They appeared pretty sharp and long. His movements were slow as he lifted the bag with one hand over his head, using his other hand to support the bottom of it better. He winked, then bit into the bag as he lowered it to his mouth.

The blood just slowly drained out of the bag. None of it ran over his lips or onto his clothes. Less than a minute passed before he folded the empty plastic, withdrawing his fangs from it. He licked both bloodstained tips clean, then closed his mouth, staring at her. More seconds passed.

"Well?"

"That was okay. I mean, you're so neat about it."

That earned her a smile. "Good. I'm glad I didn't frighten you."

"So that's it?"

"That's it." He leaned over, opened a cupboard on the other side of the bar, and tossed the bag away. "This is what I'd do, then I'd allow you to feed from me if you agree to be mine forever, Matty. To be a vampire doesn't mean you have to harm anyone, or that you'll become a monster. We buy the blood from humans. No one is harmed or forced. You'll stop aging. The only drawback is avoiding the sun. You can still see it though. UV rays don't come through televisions. I have a video of sunrises I watch when I miss the beauty of it. It's almost like being there, only without the burning." He chuckled. "Be mine, Matty. Let me love you."

"You tempt me to say yes," she confessed.

He came around the bar and held out his hand. "Let's return to our room." Desire showed in his eyes and sounded in his husky tone. "I could convince you, lass. Let me take you to our bed."

She slid off the seat and clasped his hand. "The more time I spend with you, the less I want to be without you."

"That's how I feel as well."

They returned to his apartment and he locked the door. She led the way to the bedroom and began to get undressed. She wanted Blaron. He stripped out of his boots, the socks, and then his clothes. His body took her breath away.

"How do you stay in such amazing shape?"

He glanced down his body, then wiggled his eyebrows. "I spar with my sword."

"Is that a euphemism for sex?"

"No. I actually practice my sword skills with Lethal often. He wields a blade well and keeps working me into a sweat." He lunged at her, grabbed her, and swung her up into his arms.

It wasn't frightening. She laughed, loving how strong he was and how easily he lifted her. He tossed them both on the bed, turning in the air so she landed on top of him. She turned, splaying her hands on his chest, and stretched out over him. She loved how he felt under her, their skin touching.

"I'm a very hands-on lad," he rasped. He showed her by cupping her ass with both of his hands, massaging her. He rolled them over, pinning her under him. "You're so incredibly sexy, Matty. Do you know what you do to me?"

She wrapped her arms around his neck, playing with his hair. "I can feel. You're getting hard." She spread her legs apart to make room for his hips in the cradle of her thighs.

"Aye. You've got me wrapped around you, lass."

"I think I'm the one wrapped around *you*." She bent her knees more, hooking her calves over the back of his ass.

"It doesn't matter. We have each other, and I'm not letting you go. Say yes to me, Matty. Be my vampire wife."

She licked her lips, loving the way he watched her tongue slide over them, and the low groan he made. His cock stiffened even more, pressed against her, trapped between their bodies.

"You said something about convincing me?" She smiled, teasing him. "Show me."

He lowered his head, kissing her with enough passion to steal her ability to breathe right. He adjusted his body a little, slid his hand between them, and began to play with her clit with his fingers. She moaned against his tongue, arching her body into his.

He played with her until she was almost ready to come, then eased off her clit to reach for his shaft. He entered her slow and broke the kiss. They both made pleasured sounds as he sank into her, joining their bodies.

"Stay with me forever, Matty. Say yes."

It wasn't a hard decision to make. She never wanted to go back to her old life. Not when she could spend the rest with the sexy man who wore a kilt. "Yes."

He kissed her again, the passion between them igniting, and he slowly began to fuck her deeper. Matty moaned when he pulled his mouth away. Their gazes met.

"Drink from me, love." He brought his wrist to his mouth, bit down, and pressed it against her parted lips.

She thought she'd gag, but he began to fuck her hard and fast as his fangs sank into her neck. Pleasure and pain blurred as she drank. The taste of blood barely registered. It was just Blaron, the bliss his body gave hers, and the taste of him. She grew lightheaded as she came. The climax made her pull her mouth away from his wrist when she cried out his name.

Blaron's fangs left her skin and he licked her wound. He turned his head, met her gaze, and smiled while he licked his wrist closed.

"That's it, my love. Sleep. I'll clean us and we'll cuddle until we wake. I'm with you."

Matty closed her eyes, too tired to even speak.

# Epilogue

Matty woke when two strong arms lifted her. She was confused until she met Blaron's gorgeous eyes. The blue of them seemed more brilliant, more breathtaking, and he'd put her on his lap, straddling him, as he sat naked against the headboard on their bed. Memory returned and she stared at him as her hands gripped his bare shoulders.

"I survived? Am I dead?" She flushed at her words. "I mean, am I the living dead now?"

He grinned. "You are alive, but you're a vampire."

She hesitated, trying to see if she felt any different. She didn't. Disappointment hit. "I don't think it worked. I'm still just me."

"Are you sure?"

"Yes."

"Mmmm." He grinned. "This is going to feel really good. Just go with your instincts."

"What are you talking about?"

He released her hip and reached over to the side of the bed. She saw the small dagger in his hand and tensed. He grinned wider and pressed the tip against his neck.

"The things I'm willing to do for love...but you need to learn how to bring your fangs out. The scent of blood will trigger it. Just don't fight or think about what you're doing."

She watched in horrified fascination as he cut his skin. Blood welled and he tossed away the dagger, grabbing her hip again. The copper smell of it filled her nose, her eyes widened. Her gums tingled, nearly seemed to throb, and she opened her mouth to ask him what was happening to her.

"Whath—" She paused, her voice sounding funny, and she touched her mouth. Something sharp made her cry out and stare at her finger. Blood welled at the tip.

"Easy." He laughed. "They are sharp. Careful, or one of us will need to lick whatever you cut with them." He tilted his head. "Look at my neck, Matty love. I fed before I woke you. It's your turn."

Her gaze tore from her finger to his neck. Hunger rose, and she inched closer.

"Go with it, love."

She couldn't stop. She licked at his blood. The taste made her moan—and she bit into him.

The feel of her fangs piercing his skin created a jolt rushing throughout her body, and pure pleasure struck. She clutched at Blaron, moaning, pressing her breasts tightly to his skin, frantically rubbing against him, needing to come so badly it hurt.

"Yes," he groaned, his hands gliding down her sides to cup her ass. "Ride me."

Desire burned through Matty. She wanted him to fuck her. She pulled her mouth away, remembered to lick at his skin, and stared into his eyes. She lifted her hips and wiggled them until his shaft aligned perfectly with her pussy. She sank down on him, her body sleek with need already, and cried out as she came just from the feel of him stretching her with his thick cock. Her body quaked and Blaron groaned.

Their gazes met. "Bite me again and it will make us both come."

She hesitated. "I love you."

He smiled. "I love you too."

"This is kind of crazy. We barely know each other."

His hands caressed her skin. "We have forever to learn, and what is between us is already strong. We're meant to be together."

She moved on his shaft, moaning. "You're irresistible, in my defense."

"I can be persuasive when I'm after the thing I want most in the world, and that's you." He turned his head, offering his neck. "Take me, my brave, beautiful Matty. I'm yours."

The sincerity of his words made happy tears fill her eyes. He meant it. He didn't see her scars. He loved her, and had given her an eternal new life to share with him. She was sexy, desirable and beautiful to him. Something inside her knew, as she brushed her lips over his neck, that they'd be happy together. They had forever to get it right...and any arguments in the future promised to be very, very pleasurable.

# Lacey and Lethal

# Chapter One

Lacey held her breath. She wrapped her hand tighter around the weapon, knowing she couldn't afford to miss the target. She would only get one shot and if she blew it, it would be a deadly mistake. The wind stirred and she nearly backed away from the edge of the building. A breeze wasn't her friend.

The back door of the club swung open, hit the wall, and one of *them* stepped outside. He stood in the shadows, paused while the door closed at his back, and light flared from a small source. A grimace twisted her lips. Of course he wouldn't be worried about getting cancer from smoking a cigarette.

"Do it," a male voice whispered from the earpiece wedged inside her left ear. "Take the shot and bring that bastard down."

Her boss stating the obvious annoyed her. She'd climbed a rickety fire escape to the top of what should be a condemned building to do exactly that. She adjusted the barrel just enough to get a bead on the shadowy figure of the tall man, took aim, and pulled the trigger.

The rifle barely made a sound but she could have sworn he heard it when his gaze turned her way, as if he was curious to identify the noise.

Just before he collapsed, she glimpsed long, muscular legs encased in black leather. She shot him again in the muscle of his calf, the silvery dart visible against the black.

"Go! He's down. Move it!"

An engine roared to life and headlights blinked on from farther down the alley. Tires squealed as a van shot forward then skidded to a stop as the side door rolled open and two burly men jumped out. They grabbed the motionless, drugged man on the ground, moving fast to scoop him up and dump him inside. The driver punched the gas and the van took off.

Lacey backed away from where she'd hidden, keeping low and quiet in case the guy's friends heard the commotion and rushed out of the club. She shoved her rifle into the holster that was slung across her back. She gripped the rope she'd tied to the air-conditioning unit and jumped, praying it would hold her weight.

Her body slammed against brick but she eased her grip and quickly slid lower, leather gloves protecting her skin. She reached the ground safely, heard the roar of the engine coming at her, and turned her head.

"Shit. I hate this part," she muttered. Jeff wouldn't stop but he'd slow down. She hesitated, gauged the speed of the van and began running ahead of it, keeping as close to the wall as possible.

Fear made her heart race. The guy they'd tagged didn't live alone inside that club. If the others had heard anything, they'd be coming outside, searching for him. They could be hot on her ass and she wouldn't know it until they had her. The bastards moved lightning fast.

She turned her head and threw out her hand when the van slowed. Matt reached from the open doorway, one strong arm thrust outward while he clung to an interior handle.

Their hands clasped and he yanked hard. Pain shot through her shoulder as she was hoisted off her feet and jerked inside the van. He released her as soon as she was inside. She landed on something soft. Something large and warm was sprawled out under her.

Her gloved hand felt crushed from Matt's grip but she flexed her fingers and knew nothing was broken. The van door slammed closed and darkness reigned as the vehicle picked up speed.

"Brace!" Jeff, her boss, yelled.

The van turned sharply, the tires protesting as the van tilted toward the left. Lacey tensed, tried to grab hold of something, but rolled and slammed into the opposite wall. A heavy weight flopped over her legs. She grimaced, her shoulder aching. The van righted, picking up even more speed.

An interior light came on. She glanced at a pale Matt and a frightened-looking newbie. She looked down while removing her gloves and cursed. The guy they'd taken was facedown now, his legs tangled with hers. She sat up to stop the rifle from digging into her shoulder blade.

"That was easy." Matt grinned.

"Screw you. Next time *you* can be the one who scales down a building without a safety harness and feels like a fish being yanked onto a moving boat." She rolled her shoulder. "You'd have dislocated my shoulder if you were any stronger."

A loud bang from the top of the van startled them.

Lacey's gaze jerked to the roof and she watched in stunned shock as something sharp pierced the top of the vehicle. The long blade sliced it as easily as a can opener.

*Is that a damn sword? Really?*

89

The newbie screamed in a high-pitched girly wail as he scrambled to the back of the van. Matt kept his cool, tossing a handgun at Lacey. She caught it, leaned back flat, and began firing at the roof.

"We have a passenger!" Matt bellowed.

The sword withdrew and the van lurched wildly as Jeff spun the wheel sharply in an attempt to knock the person off the roof. Something thumped and rolled away. Lacey stopped firing, ejected the empty clip, and held out her hand. Matt threw her a fresh one. She barely caught it, slammed it home, and waited.

The long blade didn't tear through the roof again. She looked at Matt and he nodded. He gripped the side door, shoved it hard, and then dived toward the back. The door rolled open.

Lacey scrambled back against the opposite side, her gun trained on the opening—but nothing happened.

She relaxed, watching the buildings fly by as the van picked up speed. Matt crawled forward to close the door.

"I hate our job," he muttered.

"Jesus," the newbie sobbed.

Lacey held Matt's gaze. "You shouldn't have brought your brother along."

He shrugged. "We're a man down and we needed an extra pair of hands. I couldn't haul that bastard inside the van by myself. It would have slowed us down, and we just barely got out of there alive."

She turned her focus on their unwilling guest. He took up a lot of floor space. His boots were black leather, which matched his tight pants. The jacket was black leather too—one she'd probably keep. It was kick-ass, but would be extremely baggy on her much smaller frame. His hair held her attention next as she studied the long, black, silky strands that lay in a messy mass that covered his face.

"He has chick hair. It must almost reach his ass." Matt snorted. "What a wuss."

She disagreed as her gaze slowly examined his broad back, trim waist and bulky, muscular thighs. He was massive—and would be extremely deadly if the drugs wore off. Lacey climbed to her knees. She slipped her hand into her vest pocket, found another dart, and jabbed it into the guy's nicely rounded ass.

"Three?" Matt crouched on the other side of the unconscious male. "Do you want to kill him now?"

"He's got to weigh close to two hundred-fifty pounds. They don't stay down long. It's not as if we could kill him with an overdose, and I sure don't want him waking up before dawn." She shuddered at the thought. They'd all be dead within a minute if that happened. It was a confined space. He'd take her gun away before she could say "oh shit," snap her neck, and make mincemeat out of the rest of the team.

"True." Matt paled further, probably thinking along the same lines.

"I want to go home," the newbie sniffed. "This is some seriously screwed-up shit."

Matt glared at his brother. "We're at war. One of these monsters killed our mom. Don't forget that."

"What if they are following us?"

"That's why we're driving around," Matt explained. "To make certain we've lost them."

Sadness gripped Lacey as she settled down on her ass. Their ragtag group was small, one of numerous teams out there trying to stop the hidden killers who stepped out of the shadows and took many loved ones. She'd lost her sister, Beth, to one of the monsters. Vampires were a menace to humans and deserved to be exterminated.

Ten minutes later, the van finally stopped and the engine died. Jeff opened the side door to examine their catch. "Good job."

Lacey avoided his eyes. She hated her boss. Jeff was a jerk but he always came up with good plans and had a knack for discovering vampire nests. Matt climbed out and both men dragged the limp bloodsucker out of the van. She followed them into the warehouse that served as their operations base.

"I want his jacket," she called out. "Dibs."

Jeff and Matt removed his jacket and hoisted the big male onto the weight bench they'd reinforced and welded with thick steel. They chained his arms and legs and stretched him out. His feet hung over the end. Chains rattled and locks clicked closed.

"You're up, Lacey."

"Great," she muttered.

Her boss shot her a glare. "My kid has baseball practice first thing in the morning and Matt has to start his shift at five. I'm not trusting the newbie alone with that thing. It could talk him into letting it go. You have no life."

She resented the reminder. "I didn't say I wouldn't stay," she muttered. "I'll do it."

The guys left, Matt taking his traumatized brother with him, and she locked the warehouse door. She removed her weapons, the rifle holster, and her vest. She turned, studying the guy in the center of the room, grabbed a chair and dragged it closer to the bench.

The control for the skylight dangled on a long cable beside her chair. She looked up to make sure the skylight was sealed, the building secure. She always worried a vampire would track them back to base but it hadn't happened so far. A quick glance at her watch confirmed it was a few hours until dawn.

Her focus fixed on the immobile guy stretched out on the bench and she rose to her feet, curious. The last vampire they'd grabbed had been unwashed, dressed as if he were homeless, and stank. This guy was well-groomed and clean.

She hesitated, but then gently brushed his hair away from his face so she could see it. The silky black strands were thick and soft as her fingers slid through them. Striking olive features were revealed, and she gawked at him. Calling him handsome would be an understatement.

"Hello, hot stuff," she whispered.

He wasn't a pretty boy, too masculine for that with his sturdy chin, sculpted cheekbones and a plush, pouty mouth, now lax in sleep. She leaned closer and inhaled the wonderful cologne he wore as her fingers stroked his long hair. It was beautiful. Matt's "chick" comment flashed through her mind and she smirked. Nothing about this guy was remotely feminine.

*What am I doing?* She jerked her hand away and backed up until she reached her chair. She dropped her ass onto it and hugged her chest, examining the rest of the vampire. He wore a tank top, revealing a lot of skin, bulky biceps and really broad shoulders. The thin cotton shirt stretched tightly over his torso to a flat belly and trim waist. A belt buckle of a carved wolf's head secured his black belt. Long, muscular legs stretched beyond the end of the bench.

*He's got to be at least six-foot-four or five.* They'd been lucky to grab one so big. He probably wasn't old either, judging by his biker apparel. Vampires tended to choose styles that reflected the era in which they'd been turned. Even the really old ones clung to small, familiar details. If you knew what to look for, there was always something. She mentally ticked off the nine she'd killed in the past three years, and all had telling signs in their attire that had hinted at their true ages.

She glanced at her watch, stifled a yawn, and relaxed in her chair. Part of her hoped he didn't wake before the sun rose. She'd open the skylight once it did to finish him off. She longed for her bed and at least eight straight hours of undisturbed sleep.

Her gaze drifted back to him and a small part of her hoped he wasn't really a vampire. It would be a shame to take out such a magnificent-looking man. But she really had no doubt of his guilt. He was a merciless, bloodsucking killer in a sexy body.

She bit her lip, rolled her shoulders, and winced a little from the pain. Innocent men didn't hang out in vampire clubs, and she doubted the monsters would allow one of their victims to step outside to take a cigarette break before they drained him of his blood.

Lethal knew he was in trouble before he opened his eyes. His limbs were chained, his body immobilized. His last memory was stepping out the back door of the club to take in some fresh air…

The rest came to him quickly. He'd been shot with something powerful enough to take him down. He seemed to be uninjured, though, and was surprised that nothing hurt.

His heart beat sluggishly. He'd been drugged. The last time anyone had dared do that to him had been twenty years ago. His best friend had been there to save him that time.

Someone had captured him, and whoever it was would pay.

He listened for any sounds to avoid alerting them that he'd shaken most of the drug from his system.

He heard a heartbeat nearby and breathing that was shallow and slow. He peeked through barely slitted eyes. A figure sat slumped in a chair about ten feet away. She appeared to be asleep, so he openly peered at her.

Surprise jolted through him while he studied the lass. She wasn't a werewolf or a vampire, but a human. He inhaled deeply to make sure. Humiliation was a humbling experience. He'd been captured by a wee lass. His friend would laugh his arse off if he could see how tiny she was.

His gaze left her to examine his surroundings. It looked like an abandoned warehouse. The smell of sawdust teased his nose, leaving him to guess it had once been a furniture manufacturer or a mill.

He needed to escape.

He tested the restraints on his arms and legs. The chains held but made enough noise to make him wince. The lass slept on, though, undisturbed. He gathered his strength and attempted it again. Sunrise had already come. He could feel it in his bones. He strained but the metal didn't give.

Lethal bit back a curse, lifted his head, and stared down his body to see what they'd used to keep him in place. Heavy-duty chains wrapped around his arms and legs numerous times. The combination of the drugs in his system and the sun having risen left him in a slightly weakened state.

*Where is Blaron?* His friend had to know he'd gone missing when he hadn't returned to the club. They'd have gathered everyone to hunt him down. Lethal clenched his teeth to smother a growl while he glared at the lass. Whoever she was, she had no idea what kind of trouble she'd taken on. The club would pay any ransom for his return, but she wouldn't live long enough to spend it. Hell, he didn't even want it to get that far. No one could ever discover a wee lass had taken him captive. He'd never hear the end of the jokes.

He allowed the anger to build until he knew his power showed in his eyes as he concentrated on the lass. The stench of human males still clung to the bench, adding insult to injury. He'd wake the female and take control of her mind, make her release him. He'd have to place a call to help Blaron

96

locate him. It would be too dangerous to stay until sunset. Some of their wolves would have to come and move him during daylight hours.

Revenge would be sweet when he was free. His nose told him the lass was type A positive. He wouldn't kill her—he never harmed women—but she would know his wrath. He'd give her a scare she'd never forget after he took some of her blood. Then he'd send her on her way with orders to never go near the club again.

First, though, he'd have to make her bring him a phone. It would only be a matter of waiting for help to come at that point.

He rattled the chains again. Her heart rate increased as she sucked in air and her head jerked up. Lethal saw her heart-shaped face and instantly changed his mind about her fate. She reminded him of an angel.

He would do more than just take a little blood. His captor was one bonny lass.

# Chapter Two

Lacey jerked awake, alarmed, and nearly fell out of her chair when her gaze locked on her prisoner. A pair of intense dark blue eyes met hers. They narrowed, and she shifted her focus away from them to his straining biceps, which tested the restraints. He obviously worked out to get that kind of muscle mass. The thin material of his tank top didn't hide six-pack abs bunching from the effort.

"Don't try giving me the glow-eyes routine. Mind control hasn't work on me yet, and you're not going to be able to snap the chains. Others have tried and failed. You're not my first vamp." She doubted that he'd listen to her advice but she gave it anyway. "You all try that shit."

"What do you want?"

His deep voice startled her. He had a slight accent, maybe Scottish or Irish. She glanced at his eyes, his features, and the long black strands of hair that grazed the concrete floor. He obviously had a naturally bronzed complexion unless he'd very recently been turned. He sure wasn't sunbathing anymore.

"How much money will it take to get you to release me?" His voice deepened with anger. "Just name your price, lass."

She leaned forward, met his intense stare and licked her lips. She noticed that he glanced down when her tongue darted out but his gaze returned to her eyes. "You want to know what it's going to cost you for your freedom?"

"Yes."

"I want my sister back, you son of a bitch."

His black eyebrows shot up and surprise widened his eyes. "I didn't take her."

Lacey rose to her feet. "How do you know?"

"I'm not a kidnapper, and I'm not holding any women against their will."

Anger surged as she raked her gaze up and down his big body. He'd probably have killed her already if he wasn't restrained. She was tired, heartsick of the life she led, and hated how drastically her world had changed in the past three years. She hesitated before she climbed onto the bench, lifting her leg and straddling his hips.

He sucked in air, obviously surprised again, and watched her with those beautiful sapphire eyes. She put her hands on his chest, careful not to get near enough for him to lunge and bite her. She couldn't ignore the firm feel of his body under her fingers and palms.

"Do you ever think about your victims' families? The people who love them? The way we grieve when their bodies are discovered?" She paused, studying his features for any sign of remorse. "Do we even count to assholes like you? Are we just sheep to slaughter? Disposable meals to toss into the garbage when you're done feeding?"

His handsome face tensed, his lips pressed together, and wariness narrowed his eyes. "I don't know what you're talking about."

"You do." She lifted a hand off him and pointed above them. "See that? It's a skylight that is currently closed." She twisted her wrist, made

99

sure he could see the time displayed on her watch, and planted her hand back on his chest. "Dawn came about an hour ago. The weather report promised a nice sunny day."

A cold look settled into his eyes as he glared at her. Then he masked his features, hid any emotion, and she knew he understood the implied threat. The silence stretched between them as they regarded each other.

"I don't kill," he rasped. "I feed but leave them alive."

"Sure you do."

"Do you want to talk to them? My cell phone is inside my inner jacket pocket, unless you got rid of it." He jerked his head toward the floor where his jacket had been tossed earlier. "You'll also find the number in there of the manager of a medical research company we own. Put it on speakerphone and I will get him to tell you about the blood he has delivered to me. I rarely feed from live people, and the ones I do are fine. They are willing. I just take what I need, with their consent, and *always* leave them alive."

Lacey inwardly cringed. She hadn't checked his pockets. Most bloodsuckers weren't into technology. Maybe they thought it would get them caught or somehow reveal their nests. None of the others had ever had cell phones. She really hoped no one was tracing the phone. It was her first instinct to get up and smash the thing but she resisted. It would be bad to show fear, so she climbed down nonchalantly, located it, and turned it off. She would destroy the phone right after she took care of him. She resumed her position astride his body.

"I'm not stupid enough to use your phone. They'd track the signal. I know some of you hire thugs to protect you during the day while you sleep. Criminals don't care what kind of monsters they're protecting as long as the price is right."

It suddenly hit her that he was very much awake, even though the sun had risen. Their knowledge of bloodsuckers wasn't as extensive as she'd like, but one thing was clear—he wasn't some newbie vampire. Only the older, stronger ones had fought back against the teams who'd hit unguarded nests during the day.

*He's a master. Shit! We really scored.*

Her next thought wasn't as pleasing. *The rest of his nest will really be pissed that we got him...and will want payback.*

"I'm not a killer."

"You're a vampire."

He didn't respond. He didn't need to, though, since they both knew the truth. His gaze flicked to the ceiling before returning to her. "I don't kill, and I don't have your sister. I don't kidnap women and make them blood slaves."

"She's dead. One of your kind tore out her throat and tossed her broken body away." Pain squeezed her heart. "She was just a baby— nineteen—and so sweet she wouldn't hurt a fly. The son of a bitch grabbed her by her car outside the library. She was going to be a pediatrician. She loved kids and wanted to have half a dozen of them."

"Shit. I'm sorry."

He was good, she'd give him that. Regret filled his steady gaze. Some of her anger eased, but not much. She knew he wasn't the one who'd killed Beth. The vamp who'd grabbed her had been caught on camera, and he was smaller than the one she sat on. The image had been blurry—the killer had run through the parking lot, snatched her sister, and they'd both disappeared in seconds.

"I don't kill people. I know you don't believe that but it's true. *We're* people too—different, yes, and some of us are bad, but some are good."

"And you're a good guy? A nice, sweet, friendly bloodsucker?" She arched her brows and smiled coldly. "Sure." She perused his body from the waist up. "You're just a big, strapping teddy bear with fangs, right?"

"I don't harm humans."

She sat up straighter and eased her hands off his chest. She peeled her black turtleneck sweater over her head and dropped it to the floor. Her hand drifted to her hair, pulled it away to reveal her neck, and she tilted her head enough to show him the column of her throat. His gaze riveted there then drifted to her bra, her breasts, before meeting her gaze again. The blue of his eyes seemed to grow even more intense and beautiful.

"Hungry? Show me the real face of a monster, because I know you're dangerous."

His breathing changed, quickened—and to her shock, something stirred between their bodies where she sat. She glanced down, and then jerked her gaze up to gape at him.

"You get hard ons?"

"You're very attractive, half undressed, straddling me, and I'm a man."

"You're dead."

"I'm a vampire. There's a difference. See my chest rising? I breathe air…and I'm not immune to a beautiful lass."

He didn't hiss at her, his fangs didn't extend as she'd seen with other vampires—not that she'd taken the time to talk to many of them. Instead he calmly watched her without struggling. He didn't stare longingly at her throat as if wanting to feed from her, the way others had, though she knew he did too. His gaze kept drifting to her breasts.

She adjusted her position on him, feeling the hard length of his cock trapped between their bodies but trying to ignore it. It shocked her that he could even get an erection. Maybe feeding or wanting to feed was the thing that aroused them. It piqued her interest just a tiny bit. If he wasn't so attractive, she wouldn't have found that fact fascinating in the least. *Am I really that shallow?* "So you're just a guy, huh?"

"Yes."

Three years of pain, loneliness, and heartbreak weighed heavily on her. Beth's death had changed her life in every way. Her fiancé had abandoned her. She hadn't dated after being dumped, hadn't allowed anyone to get close to her, not even her team.

They'd lost a few members over the years. If someone grew careless on a job, there were no second chances when mistakes were made around vampires. Caring about anyone else hurt too much when members died.

Her gaze lingered on the sexy body under her. Beth had died because some asshole had been hungry. They just took what they wanted without bothering to consider the ramifications to their victims or their families. Why shouldn't *they* be used too?

The bitterness might be getting to her; she admitted that. It was growing increasingly difficult to get out of bed every day.

She held his gaze and his eyes seemed to actually glow. A slight tingling sensation made her a little dizzy. She'd noticed it building but it wasn't the start of a headache. It was something else. She frowned, trying to break eye contact, but couldn't.

"Easy lass," he whispered. "You don't want to hurt me. I understand your need for vengeance but there are other ways."

She didn't have the stomach or the desire to torture him for revenge. The vamp sure couldn't bring Beth back, but she would show him how it felt to be helpless and used. Vivid images of how she could do that popped into her head. They were shocking. Erotic…

*What the hell?* She glanced around, as if afraid someone else might see them too.

More images poured into her mind—of him and her. Suddenly, for some reason, it made sense.

Three years of loneliness had been hell. There was a lot she missed about having someone in her life, but one thing topped the list—sex.

She bit her lip and ran her hands down his chest to his waist, tugging at his shirt.

"Let me help you," he murmured as he arched his back.

She glanced at his face. "Shut up."

He had beautiful golden skin and he tensed, revealing those well-defined abs again. They looked much more appealing in the flesh. He was really striking, would have made a fortune as a model or male stripper, and his warm skin felt alive as she traced her fingertips over each muscle. It felt good to touch someone again, to be that close to a man, or what passed for one. She'd really missed intimacy of any kind.

She reached for his belt, unfastened it, and pulled it free from the loops. One of the other things she'd missed was exploring a man by gliding her palms over his skin, and all his wonderful reactions to that. The way his muscles tensed, the soft sounds as his breathing changed, and just…his warm skin against hers.

Memories flashed through her mind of her former fiancé. Their relationship had not survived the tears and depression she'd suffered in the aftermath of losing Beth. It had been a cold consolation to realize she was better off without someone that shallow, once he'd delivered his lame breakup speech.

"Lass, what do you really want from me?" His voice was deeper.

She met his gaze. "I'm using you. You need to know what it feels like to have someone take something from your body and not give a damn that you can't stop them."

Her fingers traced the zipper of his pants, exploring the hard outline of his cock trapped beneath. It felt pretty big. She scooted down a few more inches on his thighs, unfastened the snap of his pants, and liked the way he sucked in air as he gasped.

"Lass? Release me."

"Shut up or I'll do something painful." He was blowing her enjoyment a bit by reminding her that what she was doing was wrong. She was molesting another person and excusing her actions because he wasn't really human.

Silence reigned. She opened his pants, spread them apart, and was surprised when his cock sprang free. No underwear. Even his cock was beautiful—thick, perfectly shaped, and large. She hesitated before slowly reaching for it. She hadn't meant to take it that far, but he was too tempting. Her fingers explored velvet-soft skin wrapped around a steel-hard shaft.

It jerked in her hand as it lengthened even more. She felt butterflies in her belly. She closed her eyes while she continued stroking gently up and down his shaft, faded memories surfacing of what it would feel like to sink down on a man and take him inside her body. Her nipples grew stiff and her heart rate increased.

*Why shouldn't I?* She opened her eyes to study his face. He no longer protested and actually lifted his hips a little, arching into her hand. His breathing quickened and his face was a little flushed. She wasn't blind to the signs of passion.

He enjoyed what she did to him—but she wanted more. No way would she get him off while she suffered sexual frustration. She bit her lip, debating. The doors were locked from the inside. No one could enter unless she let them in. No one would ever have to know what happened between them. She sure as hell wouldn't confess to anyone on the team.

*Oh hell. I've gone this far. Fuck it.*

*No...fuck him.*

She released his stiff cock, swung her leg over him, stood and kicked off her shoes. She knew he stared at her but she refused to look at him. She quickly shed her jeans and underwear before facing the vampire.

His gaze lingered on her bare lower body and his cock jerked again, rising slightly from where it rested heavily against his belly. If she didn't know otherwise with absolute certainty, she'd swear he was human. She straddled him again and her ass settled over the cool leather stretched across his muscular thighs.

"I haven't had sex since before my sister's death," she admitted softly. "I bet you have no idea what it's like to go that long. Vibrators are great but not the same. Watching Internet porn while masturbating will do in a pinch...but mostly I miss the feel of touching someone else, the sensation of a real guy inside me. Dildos might look realistic, but they sure don't feel that way to me. I don't even bother to use them."

She studied his cock to avoid looking into his eyes while she babbled. She was painfully aware that she made excuses to herself and to him, trying to make it okay to take things further. It was humiliating, but she didn't care when her body hurt so badly with need. It was sad that she'd reached such a low point in her life, but at least she would give him a choice, be completely honest.

"Here's the deal. I'm going to kill you, but if you're really a man, you might want to get nailed first. A come-before-you-go kind of deal." Her fingers traced his shaft up to the crown, her thumb rubbing the rim before she found the courage to meet his gaze. His eyes seemed to be glowing again. "Are you in or out? I mean that literally."

His gaze dropped down her body. "In. I always said I wanted to go out with a lass under me, but I'll take one on top any day." He paused, his gaze piercing as it met hers. "I just want you to know two things first."

She hesitated, almost afraid to ask. "What?"

"My name is Lethal. But I don't kill humans."

"Noted." She tilted her head. "That's your real name? Seriously? Your mother tagged you with that?" She knew he couldn't miss the sarcasm in her voice.

"Morgan, but I don't use it, and haven't for a really long time. My friends call me Lethal, and I like it."

"And the other thing?"

"May I ask *your* name?"

"Lacey, and yes, that's on my birth certificate." She had a sudden, horrible thought as reality intruded. "Wait! I know vamps don't carry diseases, so you can't transmit anything through sex...right?"

"No." He looked insulted.

*Very convincing.* She believed him. Amused, she reached behind her, unfastened her bra, and dropped it to the floor.

# Chapter Three

Lethal couldn't believe his changing luck. He'd gone from being shot after coming out of the club to being restrained with a hot, naked woman straddling his thighs. She was going to kill him, but what a way to go. He studied her amber gaze, her long, streaked blonde hair that teased her rosy, taut nipples, and he wished he could reach them with his mouth.

He'd planted an idea in her mind—her wanting sex with him—and nurtured it. He'd made her see him as a man, not the monster she hated. Encouraged her latent desire, stoked her fire. But she'd resisted his suggestion that she release him. He could force the issue but the lass had spirit. She only allowed him so much leeway. It meant she was honestly attracted to him. He could relate. And, surprisingly, he wanted her to retain her power to choose this. He would just enable her to rationalize her actions.

His gaze lowered to her soft belly and womanly, rounded hips. He was grateful she wasn't some waif who starved herself. The lass was healthy and curvy in all the right places.

Her fingers played with his cock, her touch so light it tormented him, and he wished he could brace his feet in anticipation of when she sank down on him. He'd love to drive up into her and really give her a ride.

Her other hand lifted to cup her breast, squeezing the lush mound, and his passion notched higher. He'd tie her down and torment her with his mouth if he could break free. She released her breast and slid her hand down her belly, her thighs spreading more, and he wished his cock wasn't straining so hard, since it blocked his view of her sex.

He twisted his head to see around it and groaned when she ran her fingers along the seam of her pussy. She shaved it bare. Her pale flesh spread enough for him to see the pink bud her fingertips brushed, and he held back a growl. It would probably scare her away or help her change her mind if he made any noises she might find alarming.

"Move up here. My mouth can do a better job than your fingers." He'd love to lick her clit and test how wet she was with his tongue.

She smiled at him. "Right. I'm really going to ride the face of a vampire with sharp fangs. You'd bite into me and bleed me dry."

"I won't bite."

"I'm not stupid. It's tempting, but no."

She leaned away, released his cock and closed her eyes. Her head tilted back as she played with her clit. The scent of her building arousal drove him a little crazy. The desire to taste her pussy was stronger than his bloodlust. He just knew it would be so sweet, enticing, and his cock throbbed with need.

Her breathing changed to soft little pants and his thighs tensed. "Ride me, sexy. At least free my legs. Don't make me just lie here. I'll give you the best bucking of your life."

Her head lowered as she stared at him. "I'm so tempted, but no." Her hand moved away from the vee of her spread thighs and she leaned up, her hands bracing on his stomach. He tensed as she lifted her hips.

"Try not to come before I do." She stared into his eyes. "Please? I'm so close that it's not asking for much."

He wondered if men had left her wanting often. They were fools if they didn't appreciate her beauty to the fullest. "You can fuck me for hours. I'll stay hard no matter how many times I come."

Interest sparked in her eyes. "Really? So you do get off?"

"Yes, lass, I sure do."

"You have sex with humans?"

She amused him. "I told you, I'm not dead. I'm still a man."

Her hand lifted off his stomach and gently squeezed his cock. She hovered just above him. She lowered a little, rubbing the crown against her very warm, wet pussy. Lethal groaned in anticipation of what she'd feel like once he was buried balls deep.

"Don't torture me, Lacey." He wanted to get inside her.

She eased down and he ground his teeth together, his fangs lengthening at the sheer ecstasy of how tight and welcoming her body was. Sleek heat constricted around his cock as she took more of him. Her moan of pleasure became the most wonderful sound ever as she began to move up and down. Her hands slid up to his chest, braced against him, and he couldn't look away from her beautiful eyes when they met his gaze.

He was tempted to strongly enforce his will and order her to unchain him. She was wide open to him both physically and mentally now as the pleasure between them mounted. He resisted using mind control, not willing to interfere with her actions. She felt too good riding him and he wanted her a bit too much. It was best if he remained restrained. He didn't trust that he wouldn't lose all control. She was fragile, and accidentally hurting her was a possibility if he was in charge.

There were other suggestions he had no qualms about, however.

*You won't kill me. You no longer have that desire. You want to believe what I say, and deep down you know I'm nothing like the vampire who murdered your sister. You want to figure me out, and shield me from others who will do me harm.*


Lacey rode Lethal frantically, her gaze locked with his, and the glowing beauty of his eyes turned her on more. His cock was large, thick, and incredibly hard. No man had ever felt so good.

She adjusted her hand, reached between their joined bodies, and her fingertip massaged her clit. She broke eye contact with him as the climax hit, so powerful she cried out and shook from the force of it. The man under her tensed his legs, bucking his hips upward as much as he could with the chains holding him down. He slammed into her hard and furiously, groaning her name as he came.

She felt it when he did, as her vaginal muscles fluttered from the aftermath of her own release, milking his cock, and his warm semen flooded deep inside her. She panted, stunned by the intense response to his body as she nearly collapsed on top of him. She would have, but knew it would put her in range of his fangs.

*That would be really stupid.* She opened her eyes. He looked even sexier after sex. Those white fangs pressed against his lower lip, as if he'd

112

tried to muffle the sounds he made. That was disappointing. She would have loved to hear every one.

His irises truly glowed, and she wondered if he attempted to take control of her mind. She should look away. Though vampires had never been able to make her brainless with their suggestive abilities, it was possible she just hadn't come across one who was strong enough. He was a master, and none of her team knew exactly what one was capable of, what powers they possessed. They'd never caught one, and didn't know anyone who had.

She just couldn't look away, despite the risk. Part of her wondered if she'd been compromised but she disregarded it. He'd have forced her to remove the chains, not have sex with him.

He licked the tips of his fangs. "I'm sorry if I frighten you. I have no intention of biting but they tend to come out when I'm really turned on."

She shrugged and brushed her hand over his stomach, tracing the muscles there. Fear wasn't at the top of her list of things she currently felt. It was a little disheartening that the best lay of her life happened to be with a bloodsucker. It made it ten times worse that it was her duty to kill him. It was a depressing thought.

"No worries. I'm not going near your mouth so it doesn't matter."

He sighed. "I'll die a happy man now." A smile curved his lips. "I'll close my eyes when death comes, and remember how gorgeous you are...and how amazing that was."

His words stunned her. She figured he might try to change her mind about opening the skylight. Most men would be pretty smug about getting a woman off. Not this one. It made her like him a little more. *Not good.*

"Do you know anything about the vampire who killed your sister? Do you have a description of him?"

The question surprised her. "Why do you want to know?"

"I'd like you to do me one favor after you open that skylight and turn me to ash. Leave a note at that club you took me from, detailing what you know about her killer. My friends will hunt him down." He paused. "We don't abide vampires who take lives. It not only increases the danger of our exposure to your kind, but it pisses us off. Just do it quickly. They'll realize they've been compromised when I don't return and move their location."

"Why would you offer me that?"

"You gifted me with a memorable last evening. It's a good way to die."

She didn't believe him.

"Trust me, Lacey. I've imagined how I would go out of this life many a time. Most of my kind dies in battle or from the stakes of humans who kill us for sport. Family is important enough to avenge. That is honorable, and I respect that. You have a noble cause." His gaze lowered to her breasts, a smile playing at his lips. "And a beautiful body. I wish to help you fulfill your quest to take out your sister's murderer as a way to show my gratitude."

She stared at his face, looking for some hint of deception. What was his angle? Maybe he hoped she was dim-witted enough to share details with someone at that club so they could figure out how to find her. They would come seeking revenge for Lethal's death.

"I don't think so."

He frowned. "Fine. There's a rogue vampire out there attacking and killing humans, and he won't stop until someone takes him out. You have known the loss of a loved one. Why make others experience that same pain?"

She leaned forward, her hands braced against his chest again in case he lunged up to try to sink his teeth into her. With her arms locked, it would throw her back if he attempted it. She wanted to believe him, but anyone in his situation would say anything to save his own life.

"What makes you think they could find him?"

"There aren't many of us in each city. It's just a matter of having a description and setting up surveillance of anyone who fits it. They'll be there to stop him permanently the first time he goes after another woman. We weren't aware of any murders or we would have already taken care of it. We haven't been in town long, and only the high-profile cases have caught our attention. With your help, they'll know who to hunt."

*He is really good.* Long black eyelashes adorned those arresting eyes. He looked at her with such sincerity that, if she didn't know what he was, she'd have believed him.

*What if he is telling the truth?*

She bit her lip, considering that. The idea of finding Beth's killer was too tempting to easily dismiss.

"Her death ruined everything," she admitted. "I was engaged, had a job I loved and a great life. After she died, this jerk showed up at my apartment to tell me he knew what had killed her. I thought he was

115

insane—until he showed me one like you. They'd captured a vamp, and I watched as they let him burn alive in the sun. After that, I became obsessed with finding your kind, to prevent others from knowing my loss. I couldn't stomach lying to everyone I knew, so I avoided getting close to anyone after I walked away from my old life."

"Why did they even tell you?" He frowned. "I mean, what was the point? The truth would only torment you more."

"They needed help going after vampires, and my father was a Marine sniper, which was mentioned in Beth's obituary. Our dad raised us after our mother took off. He taught us how to use guns, and the picture I'd given to the newspaper showed us posing together at the firing range."

He sighed. "Did *you* shoot me or was it your father?"

"He died a year before I lost Beth. It's just me now." It was a roundabout admission. It didn't sit well with her to admit that she was the one who'd taken him down, now that their relationship had become far more intimate. She couldn't ignore that.

"Please leave the note. Don't make my death meaningless. I always believed I'd die in battle." His gaze flicked to the ceiling, where the sun awaited him when she opened the skylight. "Give me the peace of knowing my friends will go after that animal who killed your sister. It's what my friends and I do. We kill the bad ones."

She gazed into his pretty eyes, and unless he was the most convincing liar in the world, he honestly seemed to mean every word. She *wanted* to believe him. She had fried vamps before for the team, a few times actually, and she'd done it without hesitation. Just thinking about watching Lethal burst into flames, the screams of agony that would follow, and him fading into ash, turned her stomach.

She couldn't do it.

Her emotions were in turmoil. He was a killer, a vampire. Everyone on the team had suffered personal loss. For three years, she'd helped take out vamps but had never found the son of a bitch she wanted to kill most. Lethal had the resources to accomplish that, if he was being truthful.

It wasn't easy working for her boss. Jeff could be a first-rate jerk whenever anyone disagreed with his orders. He kept the team on a shoestring budget. He always stripped the vamps of their money and used it to fund the team, since it was impossible for most of them to keep full-time jobs with all the assignments he passed out. He didn't care about tracking Beth's killer, any vampire would do, and he gave her hell every time she brought up the subject.

Lethal offered her more help than Jeff ever had, yet he was facing the dawn. Could she trust him? Did he really want to help? If so, that said something about his character that she couldn't ignore.

Inexplicably, she'd had mind-blowing sex with Lethal—and she'd never been one to take that lightly. Her body and heart were connected.

*I can't do it. I can't watch his destruction. What if he's telling the truth?*

Some humans were killers, rapists, and worse than rabid animals. Others were good, kind, wonderful people. What if vampires were the same? That question would haunt her if she opened that skylight.

"Son of a bitch!"

She rose to her feet and stomped over to the table where she'd dropped her vest. She tore open a pocket and grabbed two darts. She spun, met his gaze, and slowly approached.

He glanced at her fisted hand. "Thank you, lass. It's kind of you to knock me out so I don't suffer an agonizing death." He paused. "The sex was amazing. You're a beautiful lass, and I hope you find the one who took your sister from you. If you decide to leave that note, tell them to go after him for Morgan McKay. Tell them it's an honor debt. Those words will always protect you from my friends."

She hesitated. "Why?"

"We *do* have honor. The use of my birth name will be proof to them that it's not a trap when they go after the rogue. They'll know I want him punished for what he did to your sister. They'll do it."

She wanted to believe that, but she also wasn't a pushover. The sex had been really hot, the best she'd ever had, but she'd never admit it to him. "I'm going to make the sun seem like a fun, delightful way to die if you're lying to me." She straddled his thighs again and leaned forward, planning to jab the darts into his arms.

A smile lifted the corners of his mouth as his gaze fixed on her cleavage. "I can die happy with your bonny breasts the last thing I see."

*A charming vampire. Who knew?* She almost hated to hurt him, but he didn't wince when she sank the tips of the darts into the muscles near his elbows. His eyes closed and his head slumped to the side when he lost consciousness.

# Chapter Four

Lacey experienced a bit of guilt for staring as the washcloth cleaned away the small amount of blood from the naked body stretched across the bed. She'd put a sheet over Lethal's lap but she'd seen it all when she'd stripped him of his tank top and leather pants. She'd looked plenty.

A quick glance at the bedside clock assured her that he'd wake soon. She'd run out of drugs to keep him down two hours before. She hadn't wanted to risk him coming around while she'd run errands. Her worried gaze lifted to the solid wood bedposts, and she prayed he wasn't strong enough to break them. If so, she'd find out quickly if she'd miscalculated. He'd kill her faster than she could suffer regret.

The side of her hand brushed warm skin as she washed away the last drops of blood from his extended arm where the dart had broken his skin. The marks from them had already healed. It shocked her that not even a faint scar remained.

Her vampire had a tattoo on the side of his hip, something beautiful in some strange language she didn't know. It curved along his hipbone, down to the side of his thigh. Another one graced the back of his shoulder, a sword with more strange writing on the blade. It was stunning, and whoever had inked him was a true artist. Of course the canvas they'd used was perfection. The guy had the best bod she'd ever seen.

Her cell phone rang but she ignored it. She knew Jeff would call and it didn't matter anymore. The ashes from the last vampire they'd fried were spread where Lethal would have been if she'd opened that skylight. It might fool the team into thinking she'd completed her job, but she hadn't been willing to risk it. Whoever got cleanup duty might notice a missing jar of ashes when they added the new one.

Jeff would see her as the enemy if he even suspected she'd grown softhearted. She wouldn't put it past him to torture her until he learned Lethal's location. He could be that much of an asshole. It wasn't a concern that they could trace her disposable cell. The team feared that law enforcement might discover their operation. Officially, vampires didn't exist, so her team would be viewed as dangerous crazies with guns.

The team would go to her place, not find her there, and wouldn't know where else to search.

She'd always had a secret place to hide in case one of their group was ever compromised. She hadn't told anyone about Beth's life insurance money. Jeff would have wanted the money to fund the team. The basement apartment afforded her privacy, and the auto store above it had gone out of business. She'd bought the building at a steal. No one would hear Lethal if he raised hell.

The body next to her jerked and Lethal's sapphire eyes flew open. He frantically peered around the room until he locked gazes with her. Surprise was clearly displayed on his face.

"You moved me." He paused. "You didn't kill me."

"Not yet." She lifted the damp cloth away from his body and dropped it into the bowl of warm water. "I did what you said and left a note for your friends. I guess I'm going to find out how honest you are."

She crawled across the big bed to set the bowl on the nightstand and turned to face him. He stared at her bare legs and the nightshirt she wore that fell to mid-thigh.

"I've had a busy day and forgot I needed to do laundry. My nightshirt was the only clean thing I had here." She sat back on her legs next to him. "I showered and didn't want to put on my dirty clothes. The load I washed is in the dryer."

He lifted his head and stared down his body before glancing back at her. A black eyebrow arched. "You're washing my clothes too?"

"No. I stripped you because I had to leave evidence that you're dead, back at the warehouse—make it look as if you burned. I called dibs on your jacket, but the pants were leather and probably wouldn't have totally gone up in flames with you. I torched them and left what remained on the bench with the other ashes. You're still naked though because I'm hoping it will dissuade you from attempting to escape. I know you can move fast, but someone your size streaking around would draw a lot of attention. Nothing I've got will fit you. You're really tall and big." She smiled. "I highly doubt you could even wiggle into a pair of my sweats."

He let his head drop. "Where are we? How did we get here?"

"I threw a tarp over you, backed my car into the warehouse, and rolled you from the bench into my trunk. Getting you into my hideaway wasn't so easy. I dragged you out into a wheelbarrow inside the shop to keep you out of the sun, and threw the tarp back over you. I'm amazed I managed not to dump you down the stairs since you weigh a ton. You can yell but no one will hear you." She paused. "We're below ground, there's steel covering the windows and doors, and only I know the code to unlock them. You're going to slowly starve if you kill me."

"Why didn't you open the skylight?"

*Hell if I know.* She blew out a breath and changed the subject, not willing to discuss her inner turmoil. "Are you hungry?"

His gaze flicked to her neck and seemed to slightly glow. His lips twitched but didn't part. She crawled off the bed, opened the cooler, and withdrew one of the bags. She tried to hide her aversion as she stared at him.

"Will fresh animal blood do it for you?"

He nodded, refusing to open his mouth.

"Can you drink cow blood? Sorry but I have no idea how to get human blood. It was hard enough finding this. I don't even want to tell you the wild story I had to come up with to sweet-talk the butcher into selling me some. Let's just say he thinks I'm probably the worst ex-girlfriend a guy could have to want to pull such a vicious prank."

He nodded.

Her gaze narrowed, and she realized why he wouldn't speak. "Fangs out? It's okay. I've seen them before." She glanced at the bag. "I'm not sure how to feed you. Should I put it in a glass with a straw?"

"Just bring the bag to my mouth," he rasped, his white fangs showing when he spoke. They were long, menacing things. "I won't bite you."

She hoped he meant that as she crawled closer to him and grabbed the towel she'd used on her damp hair. She settled it over his chest up to

122

his neck, not wanting any blood to spill and drip onto her bed, and carefully put the bag against his lip.

He struck fast, the sharp tips of his teeth puncturing the plastic, and she was amazed at how quickly he drained it.

She removed it when he was done and watched him. "More?"

"That's good." He licked the blood from his lower lip and fangs and kept his mouth open as they retracted, not hiding it from her this time. "Thank you."

"Sorry it's cold."

"I'm used to it. We store human blood in the fridge at the club. Just don't freeze it."

"I'll remember that." She dropped the empty bag on the towel, wrapped it into a ball and tossed it toward the bathroom. It hit the tile floor just inside. "Here's the deal, Lethal. I'm not okay with killing you if you were being honest about what you do, and if you don't kill people. I'm willing to give you the benefit of the doubt regardless of my inner voice wanting to bitch-slap me for stupidity." Her gaze wandered down his body, hesitated at the sheet across his lap, then rose. "You're not like the other bloodsuckers I've met, and it's not just because you've got a rocking bod or beautiful hair."

His eyebrows shot up in surprise.

"I'm not dead either. You're hot, you know it, and I think it would be a shame to waste you unless you're a monster. I'm going to do a little research on you, find out if a lot of people have disappeared or died around that club you use as a nest, and if not, I'll let you go. If I find a string of

123

missing persons or death reports, you're baked goods. Do we understand each other?"

"Yes."

"Perfect. Now be a good vampire and relax. Do you watch TV?" She nodded toward the corner. "Sorry it's not a big screen, but just having this place is a drain on my finances. I'm going to consider you a big serial killer if you try to escape."

"Fair enough."

She hesitated. "I'm going to check my clothes and grab something to eat. Behave, Lethal." She lifted the remote, turned on the news, and left the bedroom.

Lethal watched Lacey closely as she disappeared. He cocked his head, heard her bare feet on the carpet as she moved around the other room, and lifted his arms. The handcuffs she'd used were quality ones but he smirked. He could easily snap them. His arms relaxed.

He inhaled slowly, breathing in his surroundings, and concluded that she'd lied. She lived alone but the smell of fresh air promised freedom if he wished to escape. A sealed location wouldn't have much if there were no windows or doors easily accessible. His gaze traveled the room, saw where a cabinet had been recently moved, and he smiled. It didn't belong in a bedroom, looked out of place. He guessed it now covered a window she tried to hide from him.

The human intrigued him. His lass was a smart one. He listened to a microwave drone, then ding. He heard her sigh. The smell of a TV dinner

124

wafted into the room and he grimaced. He wouldn't feed them to one of the stray dogs who haunted the alley behind the bar, yet the sexy blonde ate it.

He closed his eyes and tested the restraints on his ankles, shifted his legs, and knew he could free himself if he wished. He hesitated. He should just leave but curiosity held him in place. He wouldn't hurt her, never would. He opened his eyes when she tried to sneak up on him.

She peered at him with a hint of fear, which she believed she hid, and hesitated outside the door. He refrained from smiling. She was damn cute and that big nightshirt showed a lot of leg. A hundred things he'd enjoy doing to her filled his thoughts. Stripping her out of the garment topped that list.

"I'm still here."

"I see." She stepped into the room. "I worried the handcuffs wouldn't hold you but they're police issue."

"You're a cop?"

She blushed. "Uh, no. My ex-fiancé was, and he kind of left a few spare ones in our apartment when our relationship ended. He forgot them in my nightstand."

Lethal detested the jealousy that rolled through him at the thought of another man touching her. "What were they doing there?"

"What do you think?" She lifted her chin. "That's why I'm hoping my bed can hold you. *He* couldn't break free, but he wasn't a bloodsucker or nearly as big as you are." She walked closer. "Do you know all the vampires in the area? Beth's killer was average height, had short brown hair, and he moved really fast."

He shook his head. "I need more than that. I'm aware of those of my kind who have set up 'nests,' as you call them, but I believe the one who attacked your sister is on his own. Loners are harder to find since they hide in the shadows and change locations often. They're like rats in the sewers. They only come above ground to feed."

"That would explain why the ones we catch always smell so bad."

He hesitated. "What was listed as the cause of your sister's death?"

"The police thought it was a homeless guy on drugs."

"That's probably why we missed it. We take note of serial killers and murders that have the same MO or mysterious circumstances. Vamps tend to have a routine when they take victims. Her death was probably considered a random crime. Your team consists of family members of victims?"

"Yes."

"That's how you've been successful in catching them. You know the details and locations of the killings." He cocked his head. "What led you to my club?"

"One of our guys dated a girl who talked about going there, and she suddenly came down with a bad case of anemia. He put it together."

He grimaced. "I see. I'll have a talk with some of my members about taking less blood." His chest expanded as he took a deep breath and blew it out slowly. "What else do you know of your sister's killer?"

She cautiously sat at the end of the bed. "I have a copy of the surveillance video from the library. My ex got it for me before he decided to leave. You could watch it. Maybe you'll recognize him. I left a copy at the club for your friends." She chewed on her bottom lip. "Were you telling the truth? Just be honest. Please? Will they go after him for real?"

"Yes. We call them rogues. The days of killing for feedings are long past and it's barbaric. They risk exposing us all when they take human lives, and obviously that isn't something we want." He paused when she didn't appear to believe him. "The last thing we need is police investigating excessive numbers of missing persons or deaths. We live in secrecy, keep a low profile, and that's how we survive. Otherwise we'd be hunted to extinction."

"You honestly don't kill people when you feed?"

"I don't. There's no need."

"I bet." Her gaze ran down his body and she frowned, obviously not liking his answer.

"The women who visit our club are willing, and I don't hurt them. They all walk away healthy and very much alive. The woman with anemia should convince you of that. She would be dead if we killed everyone we took blood from."

"Do they know what you are?"

He shook his head. "I can seal a bite mark with my tongue. I distract them and they never even realize I'm taking blood. They just think I'm nibbling on their bodies."

127

He noticed how her lips compressed into a tight line. She tried to appear nonchalant but failed. He wondered if it bothered her that he took blood unbeknownst to his donors, or if she might not like the idea of him with other women. He hoped for the latter. A little jealousy implied she might like him enough to offer up her neck.

"It doesn't hurt?"

"No. I'm told it's pleasurable." His cock stirred, thinking about Lacey in his arms while taking her blood. "It's been a while since anyone has fed off me. But I don't remember it being painful."

"Let me guess. A woman turned you?"

"Yes."

"Big shocker."

He forced a smile. "I believe that's a compliment, Lacey."

"Where is she? Will she try to find you?"

"No." He pushed back the memories that always angered him.

She studied him closely and he figured anything she thought up would be worse than the truth.

"She turned my friend and me the same night. She wanted two strapping men to protect her, and we did for a long time, despite not liking her. We'd have to take her down for being rogue if she were alive today. She enjoyed the kill far too much."

"She's dead?"

"Yes. We didn't approve of her feeding habits so she hunted without us. She chose the wrong man to feed from and he killed her."

"Did you murder the guy for dusting her?"

"There's no censure for men wanting to survive. He was justified in his actions."

An uneasy look crossed her face. "I need to run some errands. Will you behave?"

"I will."

She fled the room and Lethal frowned. She'd given him a strange look before she'd left. He could hear her bumping around in the small apartment before a door creaked, light footfalls followed, and another door closed in the distance.

She'd really left.

A cell phone rang from the floor and Lethal was surprised, realizing she'd forgotten it. He glanced above his head, noted how he could break the bed loose without it showing, and easily freed the chain securing his wrists. He kept a keen ear out for her return.

A check of her cell phone revealed she'd missed a total of four messages from someone named Jeff. He seemed to badly want to get in contact with Lacey.

Anger surged. He just *bet* the human wanted Lacey, with her pretty eyes and tempting body. Too bad he wouldn't get her. He grinned when he realized she was in the habit of erasing all her outgoing calls.

He quickly placed a call to the club, still on alert for any sound, and smiled when one of the wolves answered with a cautious "hello," probably due to the unfamiliar number.

"It's Lethal. I'm fine, but clear out the club. It's been compromised. We'll move to the forest location."

"We have teams searching for you," Mark growled. "We're tracking your scent all over the city. The female's too. It was smart of you to send her with the note to give us her scent."

Rage burned. "Did she write that I owe her an honor debt?"

Mark paused. "We believed you'd been tortured to get you to say that. The club has been cleared of vamps and we have teams waiting here for an assault if anyone breaches it. We'd planned to torture your location from them."

"Keep the club clear but call off the hunt on the woman, damn it! There will be hell to pay if anyone so much as bruises her."

"Yes, sir." Mark cleared his throat. "I'm sorry."

Frustration rose. "Call off your pack and tell everyone she's under my protection. I pay you guys the big bucks, and I expect you to do your jobs right. Call Chase next time before you fuck up. Your alpha would never make this mistake."

"He's hunting that rogue mentioned in the note left at the club. He took off right after it was discovered."

"And did he order you to track the woman?"

"No."

Some of his temper soothed. "Do as I said. Call off the hunt on her. And grab a pen to make a list of some items I want in my bedroom by tonight."

"Yes, sir. Tell me what you want."

# Chapter Five

Lacey worried that she'd been gone too long. Had Lethal managed to break free? She really hoped not. She'd had to visit the library. Then she'd thought two scary men had followed her out onto the street, but one of them had gotten a phone call and suddenly they'd disappeared. She'd avoided going straight home to make certain she wasn't being tailed.

She reached under the lip of the kitchen island and pulled the hidden gun from the holster. It was loaded, the safety off, as she tiptoed into the bedroom. Bare feet peeked out from under a sheet as she peered around the corner into her bedroom. She relaxed.

"Sorry that took so long." She rested the gun on top of the shelf in the hallway and stepped into the room.

He shrugged. "I'm just lying around."

"Cute."

He smiled, devastating her with how handsome he looked when he did. "This is the most rest I've gotten in years. I should be thanking you. My only complaint is that I have an itch on my lower stomach that's driving me crazy."

"Sorry." She kicked off her shoes, climbed onto the bed, and tried not to gawk at his tantalizing chest. "Where is it?"

"Lower right side above the sheet."

Her fingernails raked his skin, and he shifted his big body to put them right where he wanted them. It was an intimate thing in Lacey's mind but touching Lethal wasn't a chore. She met his gaze and stopped scratching.

"I did some research while I was gone. There have been some missing-person reports and murders in the news, but not near your club. They're in the vicinity of where Beth was taken and killed."

"You told my friends where she was kidnapped, right?" His amusement faded.

"I did."

"It sounds as if there's a predator vampire who's been marking his territory. That will help them track him if he's still sticking to the same hunting grounds." He paused. "Are you all right?"

"Yes. I just really wanted to kill that bastard myself."

"I understand vengeance, but it's best if my people handle this rogue. No offense meant but he'd be faster than you."

She smiled. "I took you down, didn't I?"

"From a distance, with a dart gun. You get a lot of credit for that."

She hesitated, thinking about that sword tearing through the top of the van. They'd almost been killed for grabbing Lethal. "I said I'd let you go if I believed you weren't killing humans." She liked to keep her word but her heart sped up a little as fear kicked in. "Are you going to kill me if I do that?"

"No." Sincerity shone in his eyes. "You haven't harmed me."

He might have some issues with her using him as a boy toy. His ego was probably as large as his impressive frame.

"Here's the plan. You're going to stay one more night with me and twenty minutes before dawn, I'm going to unhook one side of your handcuffs before I leave you the key and run like hell. I still have your shirt, wallet, and jacket. Your boots were left in the warehouse." She paused. "I bought a faded pair of jeans and flip-flops from a secondhand store that I think will fit you. You won't chase me because you'll have just enough time to find somewhere safe to be when the sun comes up after you get dressed. Being arrested for indecent exposure would suck for you. I doubt you'd get bailed out before that annoying sun rose."

A dark eyebrow lifted. "Good plan."

"I thought so. I won't be coming back here for a long time, so don't bother looking. I'm smarter than that. It would be a waste of your time to try to track me through the false name I used for this place."

"That's nice of you to share with me, but I don't plan to go looking for you."

*Ouch. Thanks for letting me know the sex meant nothing.* "Good," she replied, surprised that she felt a little let down.

"Will you and your friends come after me and mine again if we stay at the club?"

"I don't control them, Lethal. I won't ever try to hurt anyone there again, but I can only speak for myself. It's best if you ditch it and find another location. I think the team believes you're dead, but they'll want to take out the rest of your nest."

"Damn. I love my club." He hesitated. "It's not a nest. I hate that term. I don't go around turning humans into vampires. They're annoying as hell."

She arched her brow, curious what that meant.

"Newly turned vamps are very dependent upon their makers. They tend to follow them around like puppies. They fight amongst themselves to be the favorite."

"You're a master though, right?"

"I'm powerful."

"Who're the vampires you hang out with at the club, if they aren't ones you made? You said the woman who turned you is dead."

"My friend—the one who was changed the same time it happened to me—and I own the club together. We cater to other vampires for a high price."

"You're selling humans?" Her gut twisted.

"No. We just give vampires a safe place to hang out and feed. It's equally safe for the humans who enter my club. There's no killing allowed and they must be willing."

"You said women don't realize what you do to them, so how can they agree?" She had him there and knew it.

His eyes narrowed. "It stands to reason that if they are willing to have sex with someone, they don't mind sharing body fluids. They just don't expect it to be their blood."

"Good point."

"I'll miss the club."

"I'm sorry." Lacey glanced around the room. "I know what you mean about hating to lose access to a place you like. This was my hidden retreat when I wanted to disappear. I'm going to have to avoid my team in case they weren't fooled by the ashes I left behind. I didn't have a second safe house set up."

"You're safe here, Lacey."

The soft tone of his voice drew her gaze back to his.

"I won't ever hurt you, and I *can* speak for my friends. None will come after you. Give them my birth name, if you ever run into someone of my nature who wishes to do you harm. They'll never touch you."

"Morgan McKay?"

He nodded. "Though I don't go by it anymore, everyone knows who I am. You tell them we're friends."

"Why would you offer me the protection of your given name?"

He glanced down her body. "Let's just say I'm fond of you."

Her nipples grew taut at the husky tone of his voice and the way his gaze lowered, taking in every inch of her. If that wasn't enough of a clue to where his mind wandered, the way the sheet began to lift over his lap was. She licked her lips and watched as his cock swelled under the thin material.

"We should have a proper goodbye," he rasped. "Will you at least unfasten my ankles this time? I won't hurt you, and I'm happy to be of service if you're thinking of riding me again."

She was torn. Part of her wanted him so much she ached in places, but it was a bad idea. She'd already grown a little too attached to him, and knew that having sex with him a second time would only make it worse.

One sweep of her gaze down his sexy body stretched out over her bed was motivation enough though. *What the hell.*

Lacey scooted away and dug into her jeans for the handcuff key to release his ankles. "This is crazy but you're worth a little risk."

He grinned. "I'm grateful to hear it."

She hoped she was right about him not being dangerous. She glanced at the scratch-free bedposts, which told her he'd meekly lain there without fighting. An evil bastard would have fought hard to break away and kill her. Lethal had given his word and he'd kept it.

Some of her fear eased and she realized how much she wanted him. Who knew how many years it would be, if ever, before she got the chance to have sex again? Other men sure wouldn't be as handsome or as well built as Lethal. He wasn't someone a woman would forget.

She freed his legs and began to strip. When she stood naked, she gripped the sheet and pulled it off him completely. The raw masculinity of his sculpted, powerful body turned her on more than other men had ever done when they'd kissed her. Seeing Lethal made her ache for him before they even touched.

"You can climb up here and settle that beautiful femininity over my mouth." He licked his lips, his fangs extended. "I won't draw blood. Hurting you is the last thing I want."

"Really tempting, I won't lie, but again...not happening. You might not mean to hurt me, but those fangs look pretty sharp."

"Just hold very still while I use my tongue."

Passion flared at the idea but she shook her head. "I would wiggle around if you're any good at it, and if you aren't, that would disappoint me."

"You could release my arms and I could be on top." He stared at her pussy. "I'll pin your hips under my mouth and hold you still to enjoy the tongue-lashing I want to give you. I'm *very* good."

Wetness dampened her thighs. "You're dangerous, Lethal."

"Not to you."

"Tell it to my body. You keep talking that way and I might just come before we even get started. Damn, you talk a good game. Plus you're hot, but you know that."

He spread his legs, his cock jutting upward, and his muscular arms tensed as he positioned his body higher on the bed. "I won't bite. Climb on, Lacey. Lean over me until your nipples rub against my chest, and my lower belly can rub you instead of your finger."

Lacey was on the bed before she could rethink it, the promise of another amazing bout of sex with Lethal just too much to resist. She hesitated a moment, a little taken aback at her eagerness, before dropping to her hands and knees, her face hovering above his cock.

"You're perfect everywhere." She studied him in great detail. "I never thought I'd admire a guy's dick, but not only are you big, you're just pleasing to the eye."

He softly groaned. "You're breathing on me and it's torture."

"I remember how you said you could go hours. Was that true?"

"I wouldn't lie to you."

"Fast recovery?"

"I'll stay hard."

"Too bad you're a vampire. I think I could fall in lust with a man like you, Lethal. I almost wish the circumstances were different." She smiled and opened her lips.

She lifted a hand from the bed and gripped his shaft as her tongue circled the outer rim of the crown. His body tensed, and he whispered her name in a sexy way. It incited her to wrap her lips around him and take more of the thick length deeper inside. She moved slowly, testing his girth and swirling her tongue everywhere she could.

"Fuck," he groaned. "You've got the hottest mouth. It's pure heaven."

She moaned around him, knowing he'd feel the vibrations, and his cock twitched in response. She took him deeper, to the back of her throat, not an easy feat with his size, and moved faster up and down.

"Swing around and spread those thighs around my face," he demanded, panting. "Give me what I want, Lacey. I'm dying to taste you. You smell so damn good."

She shook her head, letting him know she wasn't about to become his blood donor, while at the same time trying to bring him closer to the edge. Her fingers stroked his shaft in rhythm with her moving mouth. His groans and the way his hips slowly rocked told her he was close. She kept sucking and licking him until Lethal inhaled loudly and the taste of him filled her mouth as he came.

Lethal was different in even that. The flavor of his spent passion was something she could easily enjoy. She milked him until he stopped coming, his moans subsided, and she slowly released him from her mouth. She lifted her head and met his glowing eyes. It took her breath away to see the satisfied look she'd put on his face.

He cleared his throat and lifted his head. "I take it you wouldn't consider dating a vampire?"

She smiled. "No. I can't see that working out long term, but having sex is another matter. That was a little body worshipping. You've got one that deserves it."

Her gaze dropped to his well-defined abs and she released his cock to splay her hand on his hip, knowing he could take her weight as she put a leg over his and inched up his body. Her lips and tongue found hot skin as she kissed her way over his lower stomach, up to those ridged muscles, and only hesitated at his ribs because his stiff cock dug into her belly as she stretched across his body. She looked down.

"Damn, you're perfect."

"Not quite. I can be an ass."

She chuckled. "That's just a man trait."

She began kissing his body again, intent on straddling his lap to ride his cock, when a noise startled her. The *popping* sound was close, loud— and her head jerked up in time to see Lethal pull his wrists apart when he snapped the chains.

Terror engulfed her as her gaze flew to his, locking on his beautiful eyes. *Oh god!* Her life was over.

If he could get free that easily, he'd been playing with her since he'd woken that first time, restrained to her bed. He would rip out her throat. She imagined the agony and envisioned herself screaming as she died.

Lethal softly cursed. "I won't hurt you but I can't take any more. You're torturing me. Don't look at me that way. *Think.* I could have gotten free at any time."

Lacey was beyond rational thought. She tried to lunge away from him, the gun in the hallway her only chance of survival if she could get to it.

The vampire had superhuman speed and strength though. She cried out when strong hands grabbed her. She hit the bed hard and then one turned-on vampire had her at his mercy when he pinned her under his big body. Their gazes held.

"Damn it, lass," he rasped. "Don't be afraid."

"You were playing with me," she accused.

"You were actually the one playing with *me*." He smiled. "Now it's my turn."

"Are you going to kill me?" Lacey hated the catch in her voice.

"No. I'm going to make you scream." Lethal winked.

Tears filled her eyes and she wondered how badly it would hurt when he savaged her with his fangs.

He cursed, broke eye contact, and lifted. It surprised her when he released her—but then he dropped back down, shoved her legs apart, and lowered his head.

His mouth fastened on her clit immediately. The shock of it made her gasp, and she grabbed his long, silky hair.

She tugged but couldn't budge him. She felt his fangs against her inner folds and froze. She was terrified he'd sink them into her sensitive flesh and feed from her there.

Instead, a firm, hot tongue stroked her clit. He lashed it with rapid strokes. Pleasure engulfed her. He sucked, licked and rubbed against her, nuzzling his mouth tight to her pussy. Fear faded quickly into desire.

"Oh god," she moaned.

Lethal's oral skills were amazing. Ecstasy should be his name. He knew exactly how to work her with his mouth, playing with the bundle of nerves, manipulating them until raw pleasure turned into a screaming orgasm that left her gasping, her head thrown back, her eyes closed.

He released her clit and blew hot air over it. She shivered.

"So pretty and pink. So damn tasty." His tongue brushed her clit again, swiping it as if she were ice cream. "So you could never care for someone so different from you? Is that what you're saying?"

Confusion clouded her already hazy mind. "What?" He was playing some kind of cat-and-mouse game with her.

"You heard me. You said you wished for different circumstances. You could care for me if you allowed yourself to see me as a man."

She held still, letting his words sink in. It wasn't so much what he said, but the tone she heard in his voice that gave her hope that he wasn't a bad guy after all. Maybe he was as lonely as she was. Maybe he liked the sex enough to want to keep her around for a while without having to hide what he really was.

It had to be tough to keep a steady girlfriend in his life. The whole biting without someone figuring out he was a vampire would be difficult. They could hypnotize most people with their glowing-eye thing. Did he make women forget him the moment he was done?

She tilted her head to stare at him. "You're a vampire and I'm not. It would never work long term."

He licked his lips. "You can't deny the strong attraction we have or the scorching sexual chemistry. You're attracted to me, and I'm quickly becoming obsessed with you."

She was glad to be flat on her back. "I can't believe we're having this conversation. You should be eating me right now, and I should be screaming in terror."

He chuckled. "The eating and screaming part already happened but you've got nothing to fear. For the past few hundred years I've not really lived…until I met you. You're a hunter—and you caught me." He smiled. "Now *I'm* the hunter, and I've caught you. You know what that means, don't you?"

"No clue. We're both fucked up and confused because we want to have sex together and it's really good?" His words sank in. "How old are you?"

"Much older than I look, but it's just a meaningless number. I feel much younger than I actually am."

"You dress modern. I've never seen that before from your kind. At least, not in my experience." It astonished her that he'd been around a few centuries but it explained his mad sex skills. He'd had time to really learn how to please a woman. She knew masters were old, but she'd figured a century at most. The oldest vamp she'd ever captured had been from the nineteen fifties.

"Some vampires can't adapt to the changing times, but I have. I'm very attracted to you." He grinned. "I think it started when you straddled my lap and showed me your pretty breasts." He stared at them. "I'm going to suck on them soon, and you're going to love it." He met her gaze. "I figure it will take a few hundred years or so to do all the things we can think up."

"A few hundred years?"

He chuckled. "It's a saying."

She gaped at him, trying to make sense of his words. He was acting crazy. The drugs should be out of his system by now—vampires shook them off fast—but something was seriously wrong with him. He wasn't acting the way she thought he would.

"Are you having a bad reaction to the cow blood?"

"No. It was kind of nasty tasting but I can survive on it fine."

"Maybe you should go home and have some human blood." She hesitated. "Please don't take mine. I could have killed you but I didn't." Reminding him of that seemed imperative.

# Chapter Six

Lethal resisted laughing. Lacey was too damn cute. His heart softened even more toward her as she stared at him with concern. It saddened him that she doubted his sincerity. He'd have to teach her that he could be trusted.

She did make him feel alive. Time tended to blur into monotony at his age. Humans bored him mostly, especially the ones he fed from. It might have something to do with the fact that they were unaware of who he truly was, what he was, but Lacey was aware. He was also highly amused by her in every way.

She studied him intently, and he could almost see her mind trying to figure out why he'd want to keep her. It made her even more appealing. A woman this attractive usually tended to be vain. Not Lacey. He smiled, knowing she was the one for him. It was just a matter of convincing her of that.

He crawled up her body and pinned her beneath him. "You're mine, but you just don't realize it yet."

She hesitated before gently touching his forehead. "You don't feel feverish. I'm worried, Lethal. You're talking crazy."

"You said you don't have any kind of life and haven't for a while." He paused, watching for any hint to her emotions. "Have one with me. It'll be fun. You can still kill vampires if you have a mind to, but you will be fighting at my side from now on. I won't allow you to go out on your own to kill rogues. Nothing is going to happen to you. I'll protect you and plan to cover you a lot." He chuckled. "Spread your thighs wider. I plan to cover you for a few hours at least."

"You want to fuck me now?"

"Dying to," he rasped. "Kiss me."

"Not with those teeth you're sporting. Tongue piercings aren't as hot on women as men. At least not from my perspective."

He laughed, unable to resist her charm. She was feisty and smart, two things he admired. "I didn't nick that sweet pussy of yours. Kiss me. I'm dying to taste you."

She didn't comply. "I really think you're having a bad reaction to something. Do vampires have doctors? Maybe we should call one."

"Is it so difficult to believe I would want to keep you?" He grinned. "You kept *me*."

"I couldn't kill you if there was a chance you were good. I've known some monsters in my time who were totally human. It just stood to reason that it might be the same in your world. Good and bad bloodsuckers."

The last smidgen of doubt left Lethal as to why he was so drawn to her. The lass was ideal for him. "I know the perfect cure for what ails me."

"What?"

"You spreading your thighs and letting me inside." He softly growled. "I need you, Lacey. Only you. Stop worrying about me harming you and live for the moment."

"For the record, this isn't what I expected if you broke free."

"Noted. Now open up for me, lass. I want you, and you want me."

"What the hell." Her fingers slid into his hair. "We've done everything else. I still think you're having a bad reaction to the blood, but I'm just glad it makes you horny instead of violent."

"We haven't quite done everything. Agree to stay with me." He could think of a hundred things he'd like to do to her, with her, and have her do to him. She would balk at first at some of it but he was certain, once she got over her aversion to blood, she'd see the pleasure in sharing some with him.

"Tonight?"

"Every night."

"You're high on drugs or cow blood. You don't mean that."

He laughed. "I'm high on happiness and living. You're a breath of fresh air, and you make me content. You live on the edge already as a vampire hunter. Take another risk. What do you have to lose, Lacey, love? Lonely nights with a vibrator? I'm much better, and I don't need batteries. You're hanging out with people you don't trust. You said you can't speak for your team, which implies you aren't close to them." He settled over her, pinning her more firmly under him. "You and I, we're as close as two can be. It will feel right if you'll just release your fears. I'd never hurt you."

"I barely know you but you're acting as if you want us to live together. Every night is pretty specific."

"We fit together." He shifted his hips, his cock pressed against her pussy, and he began to stretch her vaginal walls with his thick shaft. She was pure heaven as the tight fit of her pussy squeezed around his dick. "Perfectly."

She moaned. "That feels so good."

"Say yes."

"You're already halfway in." Her hips bucked, trying to urge him to drive all the way inside her body. "Give it to me."

He planned to. "Lacey?"

She stared into his eyes. "Lethal?"

"I won't let you down. Whoever that human was, he was a fool to let you go. I'd never make such a mistake."

He didn't want to frighten her by explaining what he was about to do. She might fight him. As much as he wanted her trust, keeping her at his side meant more. The two needs conflicted, but a sense of urgency to bind them together had taken hold. Part of it was instinct once he'd decided she was his, combined with his pending loss of control. Lacey had his blood almost boiling with the desire to stake his claim.

She'd forgive him once she got over her anger. He had to believe that. There was no way he'd risk anyone mistaking her for anything less than what she was—his.

She wrapped her legs around his waist, hugging his hips with her thighs. "You're big but I think I can survive. Give me your best." She squirmed, a pleading look in her gaze, telling him she wanted him as much as he did her.

"Agree to be mine and to stay with me." Guilt pricked him, but he hadn't survived so long without taking what he wanted and fighting to keep it. "I'll never harm you. At least not beyond the next few minutes."

"Okay. We'll try this dating thing if that's what you really want. Just quit stalling by committing sexual torture and you can spend every night with me if you get me off."

She mistook his warning of pain as one of possible rough sex. He chuckled. "Not a problem. I'm going to learn every inch of you and how to bring you untold pleasure every day."

"You mean *night*."

He went for her lips, kissing her smart mouth. Lacey moaned as his cock plunged into her deep. Her vaginal muscles clenched around him and he began to fuck her in earnest, every thrust of his cock bringing her closer to climax. His mouth mimicked his hips, his tongue stroking her tongue, and she cried out when he purposely nicked her with his teeth.

Lacey's blood was sweeter than he'd imagined—actually sweet. His provocative lass really enjoyed sugary treats. There was a lot he learned as he kissed her, coaxing her to bleed a little more by sucking on her tongue to draw it out. He'd have preferred to take it straight from the vein but she'd fear that. It almost drove him over the edge and his balls tightened in anticipation of coming.

He ran his tongue over his sharp tooth, the bite of pain just adding to his pleasure. Their blood mingled as he continued to kiss her. She moaned but didn't jerk her head aside and pull away. She had to taste it, but didn't seem to mind.

149

The bonding began as he opened his emotions and allowed his hormones to do their thing. He fought the strong urge to rip his mouth away and bite into his wrist to feed her from his vein while sinking his fangs into her throat. He wanted more of her in every way. It would seal the bond forever.

*Not yet*, he ordered himself. *She's not ready. This will have to do for now. Anyone near her will know she's mine with my blood in her system. Patience.*

Lacey shouldn't have been surprised when Lethal ended up biting her tongue and sucking on it. It was bound to happen if she kissed a vampire. The pain eased and the erotic sensation of what he was doing to her made her unconcerned that the coppery taste of her blood filled her mouth. He slowed the pace, she moaned in protest as the pleasure eased just enough to keep her from coming, but he kept kissing her.

The taste of blood mingled between them. It was actually kind of hot. Lethal was a master at taking her right to the edge of climax before easing back. She frantically kissed him, trying to convey how badly she needed him. She clawed at his shoulders, digging her nails in. It seemed to excite him as he fucked her harder, faster, until Lacey jerked her mouth from his to scream from the intensity of the orgasm.

Something wet ran down the side of her mouth as she panted. It was warm as she rested her cheek on the mattress. Lethal's body shook above her, in the throes of finding his own release as he came deep inside her. She loved how she could feel that with him.

"Sleep, love." He lowered his head and brushed a kiss on her throat. "We start our new life when you wake."

"I'm okay. That was amazing but I'm not going to conk out on you. I'm *so* not a guy. If you need a nap, at least roll over first. Don't trap me under you. Of course, I can't swear I won't find a marker to write on you if you pass out. I'll be bored and that's never a good thing."

He chuckled. "I believe you would."

She dropped her hand away from his shoulder and reached for the side of her face, bothered that she might be drooling and wanting to wipe it away before Lethal noticed. Her fingers touched something slippery and she pulled her hand back to stare at them.

Blood. A lot of it. Too much. She turned her head, staring up at him in shock. That wasn't just from a nick to her tongue. "You fed from me?"

"We fed from each other." He hesitated. "I gave you some of my blood."

Horror flashed through her. "What?"

"It was necessary."

She struggled but Lethal was too heavy. He spread his knees wider and gripped her wrists, pinning her under him.

"Get off!"

"Lacey," he crooned, "calm down."

*Is he kidding?* "What did you do to me? Oh my god. Did you turn me into a blood slave? Will I have to go around saying 'yes, master' like the

151

goons in those old vampire movies?" Tears filled her eyes as she continued to struggle. "Damn it! I trusted you!"

"I marked you."

She wished she could touch her neck but he refused to let her go. And what if he'd bitten her while he'd been going down on her too? She assumed she'd have felt his fangs sink into her skin but what if she was wrong about it hurting?

"You bit me?"

"No. I shared enough of my blood that anyone not human will smell me on you from at least ten feet away."

"Why?" Panic quickly set in. "You can't turn me into a brainless minion. I'll fight it."

"You watch too many movies."

Her strength suddenly waned and she gave up struggling, going still. "You didn't ask me if I wanted your blood. What will it do to me?" A terrible thought entered her mind. "You're not changing me into a vampire, are you?"

"Not yet."

That answer wasn't comforting in the least. "Lethal? What will your blood do to me?"

He frowned. "It tells others that you're mine. No one would dare harm you."

"You said to use your given name and I'd be safe."

"What if they don't give you the chance to talk? Rogues are out there." He leaned in closer. "Did the one who took your sister have a conversation with her first?"

The reminder was grim. "No. He just grabbed her and was gone in a flash."

"Exactly. Even my enemies wouldn't dare touch you. They'd know it would be a death sentence. I'd track them to the ends of the earth if that is what it took, and they'd pay dearly for it. No one is that foolish."

Lacey forced a few deep breaths. "You could have asked first by explaining it to me. You didn't."

"I'm sorry for that. I was worried you'd say no."

"I would have. What are the side effects? Don't tell me there won't be any. I'm not an idiot. I've seen what you can do and there's no way your blood won't affect me."

"It will heal you. Does your tongue hurt where I nicked it?"

She ran it over the roof of her mouth, not feeling anything unusual. "No."

"Small doses of my blood over time will keep you from aging. It will make you feel stronger. I've heard, in some cases, the sense of smell and eyesight sharpen as well."

"You heard? You don't know for sure but you did this to me? What am I? A guinea pig?"

"I've never marked a lass before." Broad shoulders shrugged. "It doesn't matter. I plan to change you over when you're ready."

"I don't want to be a vampire."

"I want you stronger, Lacey. I need you to be my equal."

"What does that mean?"

"I told you, I don't create vampires. It's made me more powerful than others my age who have continuously shared their blood. Anyone I turn will be stronger than a newly sired vamp. I want you to be difficult to kill. You're too fragile as a human."

"You said I'd be safe since I have your blood."

"From others of my kind. What if you were hurt while you're away from me during the day? I couldn't reach you, Lacey. My blood in your system will help but massive injuries wouldn't heal. You could die."

It was kind of sweet in a morbid way. She had to give him that. "I can't ever drink blood. I'd make a horrible vampire. It's not only gross but I've spent three years hating bloodsuckers. Never once have I ever considered wanting to become one."

"You'll need to feed, and you'll crave blood once you're turned. I promise it's enjoyable."

Her mind ran over the possibilities and her jaw clenched. "You have to feed too."

"Yes."

Anger surged. "I see. This is your way of having an open relationship with me, isn't it?" Confusion clouded his gaze. It pissed her off. "You want to date me but you know I'll have a problem with you touching other women. One human donor wouldn't be enough, would it? Even if I allowed you to take my blood, you'd need more. You'll turn me into a bloodsucker so I can't complain about your feeding habits. No thanks. I told you this couldn't work. I'm into monogamy. Get off me. Your clothes are in the other room. Get dressed and leave now. Thanks for not killing me. We're even."

His mouth pressed into a tight line. "Date?" He scoffed. "I'm offering a lifetime commitment—you will be mine, as I will be yours. I would never toss up a lass's skirts...unless *you* were in them."

"I don't wear skirts."

"You know what I mean. You're all I want." He looked sincere but it had to be some kind of trick.

"Whose blood will we drink then? Can two vampires sustain each other?"

"No. We'd have to drink it from bags as well."

"You said it tastes nasty."

"I said *cow* blood does, and it was cold. I buy warm, fresh blood from my sources. We'll drink from those and from each other." He paused. "Taking blood from donors isn't always about sex, my naïve lass."

"Aha!" Suspicion narrowed her eyes. "Here it comes. You're paving the way to excuse you sucking on the necks of other women. See? It can't work between us."

Irritation crinkled his eyes and mouth. "You're being sassy."

"I'm being honest."

He sighed loudly, shaking his head. "I won't cheat. Is that clear enough?"

"Define your version of cheating. You *are* pretty old. Nowadays women don't accept a double standard."

The soft growl surprised her before he leaned in closer until their lips brushed. "It's the same as yours, lass. I won't be touching another woman. You won't be touching another man. Now go to sleep."

"I'm not tired."

He backed up a little to study her face. "You should be."

It wasn't late. "I'm not."

"You should feel exhausted."

"You mean because of the sex? It was amazing but I told you, I'm not going to snooze afterward. That's a male trait."

"I gave you my blood. It should have hit your system. You'll pass out for a few hours."

"You had no right to do that." It made Lacey angry all over again that he'd tricked her.

He suddenly rolled away, getting to his feet in one swift motion that left her gawking at the display of his speed as he paced naked at the end of the bed. "Of course you can't be normal. No, not *my* bonny lass."

She sat up, drawing her knees to her chest to shield some of her nudity. "You're mumbling."

He paused, flashing his glowing eyes. "I had plans."

"What kind?" She didn't like the sound of that.

"You're mucking them up."

She wasn't sorry, but it did make her nervous enough to slide off the side of the bed and inch toward her clothes. "I think we should get you to a doctor, Lethal. You're acting crazy again. I think it's some kind of allergic reaction to something in the blood I brought you."

He growled again, his gaze turning electric blue as his eyes shone even brighter. "Sleep," he demanded in a deep voice.

"That hypnosis shit doesn't wor—" Her knees gave way and she would have crashed to the floor if strong arms hadn't caught her.

"You've got my blood in you now." He chuckled. "You are highly susceptible to my suggestions."

She didn't even have enough time to be afraid before everything turned black.


Lethal carefully put Lacey back on the bed. He took the time to cover her with a sheet and gently brushed back the strands of hair from her cheek. "Ah, I'm gonna enjoy this rare moment, lass." He straightened and located her cell phone. The call he placed was answered on the third ring.

"Any luck yet, Chase?"

"I have some leads. I heard about what my pack did. I'm sorry. They didn't get within twenty feet of the female."

"Good thing."

Chase hesitated. "She's important to you?"

"Very."

"Understood. What do you need?"

157

"A pickup would be great. I'm bringing her in."

"Oh."

"Is there a problem?" Lethal strode into the next room and found a neat pile of folded clothes.

"I just thought you liked this woman, since you gave her your name to use. Blaron figured the same. We were hopeful."

"What does that mean?" He bent, using his shoulder to hold the phone while he put on the faded jeans. They were comfortable and freshly laundered.

"You've kind of grown cold in the past few decades." Chase sighed. "This is a revenge thing then? You didn't want anyone else to make her pay for taking you?"

"It sounds as if you and Blaron were doing a lot of speculating."

"We care," Chase admitted. "We worry about you. It's what friends do. We also had some time on our hands since you disappeared. It's been a long day."

"I'm grateful you are my friends. She is special, but the lass is a little stubborn. I knew she'd put up a fight. My blood is going to keep her down for a few hours so I'd like to get her somewhere safe. She works with a team of human hunters but she doesn't trust them. I don't think they can find us but I want her where I know for sure they can't get to her."

"*You* with a stubborn woman?" Chase laughed. "Imagine that. I knew she'd have to be something to pry your given name from your lips. Want to share how she did that?"

158

"Shut up and come get me. I assume you've been tracing the call to find my location?"

"We were prepared after the first time you made contact. We'll be there soon. They located the closest cell towers and we've triangulated the area of the address. Leave the line open and we'll signal when we're there. I persuaded the police to be helpful to our cause. They won't remember doing it tomorrow."

"Thanks." He set the phone face up on the table and dressed.

"Lethal?"

He lifted it again, his keen hearing picking up the sound from the phone. "What?"

"Do we need fresh blood on hand? Did you turn her?"

"No." Disgust rose. "She's not ready for that yet."

"Yet?" Chase sounded surprised.

"You suspected."

"I was half joking and fishing for information. Shit. Okay." Chase suddenly laughed. "Blaron will want to come with. You know that, right? We're both curious to meet the woman who finally snagged you." He paused. "We also want to know the details of how you were taken."

"I told you she works with a team of humans." He wouldn't admit Lacey was the one who took him down. They'd never cease teasing him. It was better to allow his friends to assume he'd faced off against a group. "Just get here."

"We're preparing to roll."

159

Lethal placed the phone down again and returned to the bedroom. It only took moments to retrieve a washcloth and clean away any traces of blood from Lacey's face and neck. He returned to the stack of clothes, chose a couple of items, and dressed her carefully before gently hoisting her over his shoulder. A sense of urgency filled him to get her out of the apartment. A tinge of danger lurked, and he hadn't survived as long as he had without listening to his instincts.

He paused outside her bedroom door after flipping off the lights and took the loaded gun she'd left there. He checked the safety, half listening for any sound from outside. The high windows were closed and covered by curtains. He grinned. She'd bluffed about having him sealed below ground, just as he'd suspected.

An engine passed close before all sound died. He cocked his head.

"This is it," an unfamiliar voice stated after a van door slid open. "She put it in her mother's maiden name."

"Fuck," Lethal growled, quickly locating the stairs out of the apartment. The humans Lacey worked with had found them.

He held Lacey firmly over his shoulder by gripping her thighs. He kept his other hand free to use the gun. He left the phone where it lay; he couldn't wait for his men—he would go to them.

Lethal heard more voices and counted four approaching human males. They weren't very stealthy. He glanced around the abandoned auto store— signs on the wall told him what it had once been. He spotted the attic access high up on the right corner and ran toward it. He bent, tensed, and leapt. Having Lacey's added weight wasn't a concern, but he worried when he

160

landed on the rickety metal of the stairs. The sound was loud, and he knew the humans heard it when they became silent.

He didn't have time to waste. He kicked the door hard, snapping the lock, and rushed up the ten steps. There was one more door he broke through before he breathed fresh air as he glanced around again. More buildings were nearby.

He only hesitated for a second while he shoved the gun into the waistband of his pants and adjusted Lacey in the cradle of his arms to cushion her. Then he ran full speed toward the edge on silent feet.

The twenty feet he sailed over wasn't a great distance, but he was extra careful nonetheless, since the woman in his arms was so frail. Regret was strong that he hadn't turned her already. He didn't pause after landing, just kept going, jumping across a few more buildings.

Gunfire erupted from the street, but the increasingly distant sound only assured he'd made a clean getaway. He didn't want to fight while Lacey was helpless. The humans must have resorted to shooting out the locks to gain entry to the building.

He paused a block down, knowing the direction his men would come from. It was only a matter of minutes before he saw the windowless cargo van with the familiar catering logo.

He glanced around to make certain no humans were in the immediate vicinity before he tucked Lacey's head against his chest and jumped. Soft grass cushioned his landing and he stepped out into the street so they couldn't be missed.

The driver hit the brakes and Chase's eyes widened.

"We had company," Lethal called out.

The back door slid open and a tall blond wearing a kilt climbed out. "I'm glad to see you."

"It's good to see you too, but couldn't you have worn pants to my rescue? Were you gonna flash your hairy thighs to distract them while Chase got me out?"

Blaron laughed. "I would have if it worked to save your arse." He peered at Lacey. "This is her? That wee lass captured you?"

"Shut up. Let's go. Her team found us, and I'm sure they've realized by now that we're gone. They'll be leaving there soon, and I don't want to make it easy for them to locate us again."

He crawled into the van on his knees, ducking his head, and glanced at a few of the werewolves sitting on the floor in the back. "Any of you touch her and you're dog biscuits."

Blaron climbed in and closed the door. "Let's go, Chase."

"Where to?"

Lethal hesitated. "The club. We have to take care of these hunters and they'll be coming for us anyway. We don't want to disappoint them."

Chase eased off the brake and the vehicle rolled forward. "Isn't she going to be upset if we kill them?"

Lethal settled more comfortably with Lacey on his lap. "They weren't coming after us just to say hello. I heard them talking while they were surrounding the building. They're pretty angry that she attempted to fool them into believing she'd dusted me. The one called Jeff had a surveillance camera hidden where I was kept."

162

He inwardly winced, determined to find all video the bastard might have of his Lacey, naked, astride him. Nobody but he would see her beautiful breasts bounce while she rode him. "The humans need their memories wiped—or they need to die."

# Chapter Seven

"Wake up, my bonny lass," a sexy, masculine voice crooned next to her ear. Hot breath tickled her skin before a gentle kiss brushed along her neck.

Lacey opened her eyes to stare at a white ceiling. She flattened her palms against Lethal's solid chest. She fisted a handful of his tank top as she focused on his blue eyes.

"You dick."

He grinned. "Aw, that's my sweet lass. Tell me how you really feel."

"You blood-drugged me." There wasn't a thing wrong with her memory. "Where are we?" She looked past his face again, studying the ceiling. It wasn't her apartment. She was almost afraid to turn her head.

"We're at my club."

Her heart lurched. "Why?" Had he lied to her? Was he going to toss her to his other vampires to drain dry? It was the worst scenario she could come up with on short notice.

"I told you, I'm fond of the place. I wanted you to see it."

She didn't believe him. "Lethal?" Her grip on him tightened even more. He was bent half over her and she was lying on something soft that kept her slightly upright. "What are you planning?"

Irritation narrowed his eyes. "I don't know how many times I've got to say it. You're safe."

"Not quite," a deep male voice stated. "Her friends could show up at any time."

Lacey jerked her head to the side and gawked at the tall blond man wearing a red kilt. He wore a belt with a sheathed sword and a black tank top. A long braid trailed over one broad shoulder, down his chest, to almost the hilt of the weapon. His accent was a little thicker than Lethal's, but she guessed they were from the same place. It meant he must be the friend she'd heard about.

She was in a room with not just one master vampire—but two.

"That's Blaron," Lethal rasped, still watching her intently. "How do you feel?"

She had to force herself to look at him. "Angry."

"Besides that? Do you feel stronger?"

"I feel betrayed. You lied to me."

He flinched. "I'm sorry. I told you why I had to do it."

"You tricked me into taking your blood, and I told you the club wasn't safe."

"Your friends showed up at your apartment."

That news sank in. "How?"

"You used your mother's maiden name. Ring any bells? At least that's what I overheard before I got us out of there."

"They aren't my friends." She had hoped Jeff wasn't smart enough to figure out how to track her. "They're my team members. I take it they didn't buy the scene I left behind to fool them?"

"There was a hidden camera in the warehouse."

The blood drained from her face as she realized what that meant. *"Oh shit."*

"I'll find the footage if they kept it," he swore.

"What is on it?" Blaron inched closer.

"None of your business, Mr. Sword," she snapped, her gaze silently pleading with Lethal not to answer his friend. "What if they upload it to the Internet? Your teeth..." She glanced at his mouth, remembering how his fangs had shown while they were having sex. "We can't let them do that. They might think it's the proof they need to show the world you exist."

He had the nerve to grin. "I'm more worried about how much of *you* is shown. Humans will just think it's some kind of vampire fetish video. They are very popular with your kind. It seems we're considered romantic in some movies."

"It's not funny."

"It kind of is." He winked. "It was hot. I bet it would get a lot of hits."

"Damn," Blaron chuckled. "Don't tell me you and the lass were filmed with your pants down."

Lacey blushed. "You've got to find it and destroy it."

"I will." Lethal eased back onto his knees. "Are you hungry? I ordered food for you."

She had to release his shirt to sit up, thankfully noticing that he'd dressed her in an oversized T-shirt and sweatpants. They didn't match but she wouldn't complain. She'd been naked when she'd passed out.

Her gaze wandered around the room. It was a large office with a few desks and she was on a black chaise lounge.

"You keep food in a vampire club? What? Cookies? Maybe orange juice if women pass out after you take their blood? That's sweet." She knew how thick her sarcasm sounded.

Lethal laughed, rising to his feet. "No. Real food. Our security team enjoys a hearty steak now and then, so I had them prepare one for you with all the fixings." He waved to one of the desks. "Eat. You need to keep up your strength." He extended his hand to her. "We're waiting to see if your vampire hunters come here."

She accepted his offered hand, feeling slightly weak. It was probably a side effect from the blood he'd given her, she surmised. He pulled her to her feet and a wave of dizziness hit. She swayed but Lethal was there, holding her close with one arm wrapped around her shoulders. Then he shifted his hold and just swept her into his arms.

"You need food." He sounded angry. "You've got to take better care of yourself."

"Easy," Blaron said. "She's taking all this better than I'd expected. She didn't wake screaming from being here. No need to snarl at her."

"She's too fragile." Disgust was clear in Lethal's voice.

"She's human, not an invalid."

Lethal gently set her in the chair and pushed the plate closer. She was stunned by the massive platter-size meal, and her stomach did rumble as she inhaled the appealing aroma of a perfectly cooked T-bone steak.

He stepped back. "Eat it all, love."

Lacey opened her mouth to tell him how much she hated being given orders, but changed her mind. She was starving. She reached for the silverware, almost surprised that they'd given her a sharp knife. Lethal stayed at her side but focused on his friend.

"Don't you have something else to do, Blaron?"

"Not really." The vampire rested his hand on the hilt of his sword. "The club is closed while we play bait for the hunters. Chase took a few of the pack with him to hunt the rogue. It's just a waiting game now to see if they'll come after us at night or during the day."

Lacey cut the steak into bite-size pieces. "They'll hit after dawn if they come." She peered up at Lethal. "You're going to kill them? They aren't bad people. They've had loved ones taken from them. They don't know there's both good and evil in Bloodsucker Land."

He frowned.

"Two of them lost their mothers. My boss lost his brother. They were murdered by vamps."

"Did she just say 'Bloodsucker Land'?" Blaron looked appalled.

"You get used to her slang." Lethal sighed. "We won't kill them if we don't have to. Blaron and I will try to get into their minds and wipe them. Chase might be successful if we fail. He's pretty powerful. His father was almost a thousand years old when he sired him."

She almost choked on the steak she was chewing. She swallowed. "There are vamps that old?"

"Aye," Blaron answered. "To be sure. Of course, that one ain't gonna be around much longer." He grinned at Lethal.

168

She glanced between them. "What's going to happen to him? Do you eventually die of old age?"

"No." Lethal took a seat on the corner of the desk. "He abused Chase as a boy by taking his blood as if he were a convenient snack whenever the mood struck. The bastard thinks he can use his son as an assassin when he wills it. He's in for a surprise the next time he comes after him."

Blaron's sword scraped as he pulled it from the scabbard and waved it in the air with a slashing motion. "We look after our friends." He pointed it at the floor.

Lethal nodded in agreement. "We three stand together."

"So Chase is another vampire?"

Someone knocked on the door and a pretty woman entered. "Is there anything else you need?"

"No thank you, Mora. You can leave for the night. We don't wish you to remain here if there is a fight." Lethal's tone had softened. "Be safe."

The other woman smiled at him. The green-eyed monster roared inside Lacey. She glared at Lethal until the door closed and he happened to glance her way. His smile disappeared.

"Is Mora one of your donors?"

Blaron whistled. "I'm going to take a stroll around the club. I'll leave you to explain what Mora is to us." He fled the room.

"No."

"You've never taken her blood or anything else? Lifted her *skirts*?"

"She's got a mate."

"Mate?" She pushed her plate away. "What does that mean?"

"She's a half-breed werewolf. Being mated means she's committed to a wolf. He's the same with her. And I don't take blood or sex from the pack that works for us."

Lacey set down the knife and clenched her hands in her lap under the desk. "Werewolf?" She must have heard him wrong.

"Aye."

"Don't do that cute accent thing. Werewolves exist?" She was glad she was sitting down as she quickly reassessed the situation. "You have a pack of werewolves protecting you while the sun is up?"

"Yes. We pay them well and they keep us safe."

"She looked so normal."

He arched his black eyebrows. "What did you expect? A lot of facial hair while they're in human form? Perhaps they wear collars or bark instead of using words?"

"No. I'm just...we suspected they might be real but you just confirmed it. And your voice changed when you spoke to her. I thought maybe...you know."

"She was once a lover?" He smiled. "She's just timid. We keep in mind not to move too fast or do anything to startle her. Chase is soft on her."

"He likes her but she has a mate? That sucks."

"He isn't attracted to her. She's weak in the pack and he's very protective of the half-breeds. Wolves are naturally aggressive, so he makes

170

it known that anyone who causes them harm will answer to him. We tend to agree. Mora is gentle of heart and fiercely loyal to Chase."

"But not to you?"

"I'm not her alpha, but she respects us."

"Alpha? You mean Chase is a werewolf? You said his father was a vampire."

"He's both."

"Wow." She picked up her fork. "Okay. There's a lot I have to learn. I didn't even know vampires could have children."

"It's complicated. I'll explain it sometime."

"Do you have any kids?" She silently hoped not. That would mean there was a woman out there with a previous claim on him. She also was suddenly fearful of getting knocked up. "What about me? We didn't use protection."

"I have no children, and I can't get you pregnant."

She blew out a relieved breath and took another bite. "So what's next?"

Before Lethal could reply, the door was thrown open, striking the wall. Blaron stormed inside, gripping his sword. "We have uninvited guests. They are sneaking down the alley."

Lethal slid off the edge of the desk. "Shit. They're attacking before dawn. That's brave."

Lacey rose to her feet. "My team?"

Blaron held her gaze. "At least twelve humans, and they are armed with assault rifles and crossbows."

She gripped the edge of the desk. "Jeff must have called in a few of the other teams."

Lethal growled, glaring at her. "What other teams?"

"We usually work in small groups of four or five people, but there are a few teams spread throughout the area. Sometimes we'll join forces if it's a big nest."

"You could have warned me."

"I *told* you not to come back to the club!"

"Argue later," Blaron demanded. "We didn't expect so many. We need to go to battle. This ends now. I refuse to be hunted."

"Don't leave this room," Lethal snarled at her. He bent near another desk and came up brandishing a sword of his own.

"Are you both crazy? You need guns!" They wouldn't stand a chance against a hail of bullets.

The vampires left her in the office, slamming the door behind them without comment. The loud sound of scraping metal alerted her. She crossed the room and tested the door. The handle turned but it wouldn't open. It was solid, and no amount of tugging worked. She was locked in.

She slapped her palm on the hard surface. "Damn it!"


Lethal felt highly irritated. "Teams. Plural."

172

Blaron glanced at him as they climbed the stairs. "Your human said we weren't safe. She didn't lie."

"I thought maybe a handful of them would come."

Mora waited at the top of the stairs as they entered the main floor of the club. Lethal was furious when he saw her there, holding a gun, ready to defend them. She hadn't gotten out in time. Chase would be bad tempered as hell if she got hurt. He paused long enough to give her orders.

"Go guard the office. Don't unlock it or enter. My lass has a temper." The basement would be the safest place for them both.

She nodded and fled, ducking under his arm as he held the door open.

Blaron grinned as he secured the door and locked it. "What position do you want to take?"

"Up." He pointed at the rafters. "They always assume we lurk in the dark. Let's not disappoint them."

"You really want them alive or were you just attempting to spare yourself a fight with your human?"

He sighed. "Some will die, but let's try to avoid it as much as possible."

Blaron leapt first, landing quietly above. He pulled a cell phone out of his kilt. "I'll tell the wolves."

Lethal crossed to the bar then joined his friend in the rafters. It was dark, the lights off. The humans wouldn't see them if any made it past the guards.

The distant sound of a grunt reached his ears. It had begun. His fangs elongated as he peered across the space at Blaron.

"It's done. I told them to avoid kills if possible," the other vampire whispered. "They aren't happy."

"Nor am I."

The sight of Blaron's white teeth flashing in a grin irritated him.

"What?"

"You're getting soft. Perhaps it's time to change your name to Lenient."

"Fuck you," he hissed. "You're one to talk. Your Matty has two kittens. You used to call them the devil's spawn."

"They're to keep her company while I'm at work." He shrugged. "They stopped hissing at me. Cute critters if they were minus the claws. They tore up the curtains. They make the lass happy though, so I just bought new ones."

It was Lethal's turn to smile. "We could use some softening from a woman's touch."

"Aye," Blaron agreed. "But after we deal with the hunters." He cocked his head. "Hear that?"

Lethal gripped the hilt of his sword. "They believe they are sneaking in the back. The lucky fools have no idea we'll try to spare their lives."

# Chapter Eight

Three humans holding crossbows crept along the far wall by the dance floor. Scuffling sounds came from the alley as the wolves subdued the rest of the hunters.

Blaron jumped first, landing just feet away from two of the trio that had made it inside. His sword flashed in the dim light as it struck wood, smashing one of the weapons. He used his free hand to knock the second human away.

Lethal landed behind the third human, who was attempting to shoot Blaron with a stake. The human didn't seem aware of his presence until he cried out as the weapon was torn from his grasp. Lethal struck the man in the face hard enough to knock him flat, then pounced, pinning him.

He allowed his fangs to show as he hissed, enjoying the instant horror that transformed the human's face. One glance assured him Blaron had the other two subdued. He returned his focus to the hunter under him.

"You thought it would be easy to invade our club?"

"Fuck you," the human grunted.

"You're the one who's fucked." Lethal cocked his head and heard some of the wolves talking nearby. They wouldn't be so relaxed with their conversations if there was still any threat present. "Your hunters have been dealt with." He lowered his face, his eyes glowing. "Who is in charge?"

"I am." The man was terrified but he didn't plead for his life.

"What is your name?"

The guy sealed his lips, refusing to answer. Lethal put some power behind his glare. "Tell me your name."

"Jeffrey Pars."

*Jeff.* "You are Lacey's team leader?"

The male attempted to resist the power of his gaze, but couldn't. "Yes."

"What did you do with the video from the warehouse? Tell me where to find it. How many copies are there?"

"Just one. It's on a file drive in the glove compartment of my car."

"Where is your car?"

"Two streets over. Red Mustang."

Lethal growled loudly. A moment later a wolf appeared. He ordered him to retrieve the drive from the vehicle and the wolf took off at a run. Lethal glared down at the hunter again. "Does anyone besides you and the hunters with you know about this club? Have you told them Mooning is a run by vamps?"

"No."

"That's lucky," Blaron sighed.

"Were you able to get inside the heads of the other two? I hate running across humans with a natural immunity to mind control."

"Notice how quiet they've been?" Blaron frowned. "It amazes me that they're hunters at all. They are clearly shitty ones, since only a glare silenced them,"

"They hunt from a distance." He'd never forget how he'd been shot—but Lacey wasn't going to work for Jeff anymore. He'd make sure they didn't take down any more vampires. "Let's just wipe their minds."

"These are hunters," his friend reminded him. "They probably have a lot of stuff around their homes as reminders of what they do."

"True." A mind wipe could fail if something triggered distinct memories.

"We'll need to ask your human."

He really wanted Lacey kept out of it, but then again, now she'd have proof that he'd kept his word by not killing her team. At least...he hoped they'd all survived. He should have asked the wolf who'd come, but his priority had been securing any video of him and Lacey in that warehouse. He kept hold of Jeff as he hauled him up to his feet.

"I'm going to take this one to see Lacey. Round up the survivors and bring them all in here. We'll handle this situation even if we have to question each one, make a list of anything that might trigger their memories, and send the wolves to destroy it."

"What if they've told their friends or their women?"

Lethal bit back a curse. "We'll have to wipe a lot of minds."

"For sure." Blaron didn't sound any happier at the prospect. "What a mess."

He couldn't agree more.

"It's probably for the best we aren't killing them all." Blaron chuckled. "Despite my instincts prodding me to."

"The old days." Lethal could remember how satisfying it had felt taking out an enemy. "We've evolved though."

"Aye. A shame, isn't it?"

Lethal flashed him a toothy grin. "I plead the Fifth. I'll be back." He spun the human, holding him by the back of his neck and pushed him forward.

Blaron unlocked the door to the basement and opened it. "Good luck."

"He's alive. That will score me some points."

The human struggled but was no match for Lethal's strength as he forced him down the stairs. Mora lowered the gun when she saw that the hunter was controlled by Lethal.

"Let me in there and then go home. Things are calm upstairs."

She removed the bar across the door that had kept Lacey locked inside and pushed it open. "Thank you."

He winked and shoved the hunter through the door, into the office. Lacey was standing in the middle of the room, holding the knife. She relaxed only slightly when she saw him but her focus returned to the human he held.

"Jeff." Her tone was soft.

"You backstabbing bitch."

Lethal's temper flared as he snarled at the hunter. "Don't call her names." He wanted to break the jerk's neck but refrained.

Lacey was stunned to see Jeff, but she wasn't surprised by his accusation. Lethal stood behind him, his fingers wrapped firmly around her boss's throat. They wore similar furious expressions. She lowered the knife and placed it on the edge of the desk.

"I didn't kill him. We're going to interview them to see what we need to do to make sure their memories don't return."

"I don't understand." She looked at Lethal for clarification.

"Any triggers they might have around their homes or anywhere they frequent could prompt flashbacks. We don't want them recovering memories."

"That could happen?"

"Yes." He didn't look pleased either. "Hunters keep souvenirs and other possessions that are a constant reminder of what they do."

She bit her lip, thinking about it. "Why don't you just make them think that they were paranoid and a bit crazy but they're getting better? You know? Like they made up vampires but now they know the truth. Make them believe you don't really exist."

Lethal smiled. "It could work."

"Damn you to hell, Lacey!" Jeff spit out. "We trusted you."

She stepped closer. It was doubtful he'd listen to reason but she wanted to try. "These aren't the vamps who killed your brother or my sister. Not all of them murder humans. You're still alive, right? Why? Think about it. Mindless monsters would have taken you out. You wouldn't be standing here right now. You'd be dead."

He glared at her.

179

"They are people, Jeff. Some are good, some are really bad. I'm not so blinded by Beth's murder that I'm willing to annihilate an entire race for what one of them did. We got it wrong. Can you understand that? They hunt murderers too. We're on the same side."

"Bullshit. They got to you."

"You've known me for three years. Can't you just think about what I'm saying? No one has gotten to me. I just listened to reason."

"Your sister would roll in her grave."

"No. She wouldn't. Beth wouldn't want me to blindly hate them all for what a single one of them did to her. Don't tell me anything about my sister. She had a big heart and would be proud that I'm not living with bitterness anymore."

"Sir?" The male voice came from the doorway.

Lethal turned his head. "What?"

"Ten of them survived. One shot himself in the head. We couldn't stop him. He died from the injury. I apologize."

"It's all right. Thanks for the information, Danny. Take all of them to the dance floor. I'll be up with this one in a moment."

"Yes, sir." He disappeared through the door.

"Did you hear that?" Jeff spat. "It's all right that one of ours is dead. These are the bastards you're working for now."

"I also heard that he shot himself. He was probably scared." She hated that a life had been lost but she wasn't going to blame the vampires or werewolves for it. They could have killed everyone but hadn't. "It's horrible, but they didn't pull the trigger."

"You turned your back on your own kind, for *them*."

Jeff refused to listen. She could see he'd already made up his mind that anything she said would be tainted somehow. He honestly believed she'd betrayed the team and had become a player for the other side. She wasn't surprised. It had been a lot for her to take in, too, and she'd seen more, had more time.

"I'm sorry you don't believe me." She looked at Lethal. "Go ahead and take him upstairs. Nothing I can say will do any good." She paused. "Thank you for not hurting anyone."

"It matters to you, so it matters to me. I'll try your suggestion when I get inside his mind. I'll plant the thought that they should get rid of all reminders of their past fantasies that vampires are real."

"I won't forget!" Jeff swore. "I'll come back and destroy every damn bloodsucker in this nest!" He lifted a hand and pointed at Lacey. "I'll get you too, bitch. I'm going to enjoy hearing your screams."

She started to speak, tried to think of something that would get through to Jeff, but stopped. She was done trying to talk sense into her old boss. Her gaze lifted to Lethal. He seemed to understand as he turned Jeff around and forced him toward the door.

They had almost reached it when Jeff suddenly dropped to his knees, knocking Lethal off balance.

Lacey saw her boss grab for his ankle. Her eyes widened when he pulled a gun.

Lethal snarled and tried to grab it but Jeff had surprise on his side.

Three loud shots filled the office and she saw the flashes from the barrel. It was horrific watching the man she loved fall backward. Blood flowed from his chest where each bullet had stuck—one of them directly over his heart.

"Lethal!" She ran toward him.

He hit the floor and grabbed his chest. Jeff rose and pointed the gun directly at Lethal's face, ready to unload the rest of the clip at close range.

Lacey tackled him before he could fire again. The bullets probably wouldn't kill Lethal but they might really hurt him.

She slammed hard into Jeff. They crashed to the floor and pain tore through her side as another loud explosion came from the gun. She fought, attempting to wrestle the gun from his fingers even through a haze of pain. She was horrified. She'd been shot.

Both her hands clutched the wrist holding the gun—she couldn't stop him from using his other hand as he withdrew a stake from his belt.

Lacey caught sight of it just before he plunged it into her chest.

She screamed in agony.

"Lacey!" Lethal bellowed, his deep voice thunderous.

Jeff was torn away and a loud crash sounded. She turned her head in time to watch him slump to the floor after slamming into one of the desks, his neck at an odd angle. Her view of him was obstructed as Lethal crouched over her, still bleeding heavily.

The horror in his eyes told her the truth of her grim situation. She glanced down, the pain quickly fading as shock set in. The thick piece of wood was embedded in her chest. Her gaze lifted to Lethal.

"He thought I was a vampire. What a fucking idiot."

"Lacey." The hands touching her trembled. He hesitated to touch the stake. "I need to pull it out."

"Go ahead."

It hurt worse coming out than it had going in. She almost blacked out but the hand pressed between her breasts, applying pressure to the gaping wound, caused enough pain to keep her conscious.

"Some of your blood will heal me, won't it?"

Tears filled his eyes as she stared into them.

"Shit. You cry red. That's not good."

"This is too traumatic." He glanced down her body, paling. "You're shot too."

The dull throbbing in her side assured her of that. "I'm going to die?"

"No." His voice deepened as he leaned in. "I won't let you."

She felt weaker, colder, and knew her life was slipping away. "Will...you feeding me...some blood...fix all this?"

"No." His free hand lifted. "I have to turn you."

"You're sure?"

"I'm not letting you die. This injury is too severe to fix with a little blood, Lacey."

Footsteps pounded toward the doorway and Blaron suddenly appeared. "What happened?"

"Make sure he's dead."

She hoped the son of a bitch *was* dead. He'd staked her. As if shooting her wasn't enough.

"Fuck." Blaron rushed across the room to check on Jeff. "He's dead."

"We're going to need fresh blood. Hurry!"

She concentrated on Lethal. Even with red tears filling his eyes, they were pretty.

"Lacey? Say yes."

He would turn her into a vampire or she'd die. She wasn't ready for that choice—death or being a bloodsucker. Sometimes hard choices had to be made though. She made hers.

"Don't let me go."

"Never."

He bit into his flesh with so much force that she flinched. The sound reminded her of biting into an apple. There was no time to ponder that though as he shoved his bleeding wrist against her mouth.

"Drink, my love."

The coppery taste flooded her tongue and she swallowed. Lethal curled around her and lifted her onto his lap while keeping his wrist firmly against her mouth.

"The bullet needs to come out," Blaron whispered.

"Wait until she passes."

She really hoped that didn't mean what she thought It did. She was drinking blood to *avoid* dying.

"That's it, Lacey. Fight to live." Lethal rocked her.

She wouldn't give up.

"I'll go get more blood to replenish you and the pack doctor to dig out the bullets."

She wondered if she'd been shot multiple times, then remembered that Lethal had been shot too. She worried about him but struggled to stay awake. Exhaustion hit her hard and fast.

"Do it," Lethal rasped.

She wondered if he was telling her it was okay to fall asleep or if he was talking to his friend. In the end, it didn't matter. She passed out.

# Chapter Nine

"Wake up, beautiful."

Lacey knew that deep baritone, and her body responded as instant desire spread through her. She opened her eyes, confused, and stared into an amused, familiar, handsome face. She tried to reach for Lethal but something held her. She stared at the silk binding her wrists to a headboard. Her legs were not tied.

"Are you kidding me?"

"You're not a morning person, are you?"

"Am I really a bloodsucker?" She ran her tongue over the smooth line of her upper teeth and shifted her naked skin against the silky sheets on the large bed. "I don't feel any different."

"You're a vampire." He paused. "You had me scared that I'd lose you."

"Me too."

That got a smile out of him. "Everything healed. You don't even have a scar."

She lifted her head and looked at the smooth skin between her breasts. The memory of being staked wouldn't fade as quickly, if ever.

"Wow." She remembered that Lethal had been shot and studied his bare chest. "You don't have any marks either."

"Blaron gave me blood after our doctor dug out the bullets. We can heal around them but it's best if they are removed."

186

"Did you drink it from bags or a person donor?"

"Bags. I told you, the only one I'll sink my teeth into from now on is you."

"I'm really a vampire? I thought I'd feel cold or dead."

He chuckled. "No. You're warm and you're my beautiful lass still. You're just stronger."

"And allergic to the sun."

"Yes." He sobered. "I'll make it up to you."

"*You* didn't stake or shoot me. Jeff did that. No need to apologize or feel bad."

"I'm sorry he's dead."

"No, you're not. It's okay. I was kind of over it after he buried a chunk of wood in my chest. I wasn't feeling the love, you know?"

Lethal grinned. "That's my sassy lass."

"Were you worried my personality would change once I was a vamp?"

"No. I just hoped you'd wake remembering you agreed to become one."

"Is that why I'm tied up? You were afraid I'd be angry? You saved my life."

"That's not why. I'm still a lot stronger and faster than you, so you couldn't hurt me. I always will be. Remember when I woke tied down?"

She stared at him, leery. "Yes."

"I took it well, didn't I?"

"I didn't turn you human, so it's not quite the same."

"True. At least there's no big skylight above our bed." He pointed up. "Just a chandelier."

She glanced up at it. "Really? Where are we? In a dining room?"

He chuckled. "I brought you to our home. I wanted you to wake in it. I bought the house already decorated and this is the master suite. You can change anything you like. I don't care what surrounds our bed as long as you're in it."

He sat on the edge of the mattress, wearing just a pair of silky boxers. Lacey studied them. "I like you better in leather, jeans or nothing."

"I live to make you happy now."

He stood and removed the boxers, turning to face her with a hard-on that was not to be missed. She lifted her gaze to his.

"You're definitely up this morning…or should I say evening?"

"Our day starts when the sun goes down."

"Shit. You mean every day we're going to be dead when the sun is up?"

"No, but we tend to sleep during the day. That pesky sun limits our mobility when it's shining." He stepped closer to the bed, interest sparking as his heated gaze roamed her bare body. "I can't decide what part of you I want to touch first."

"My wrists, when you untie me."

He laughed, climbing onto the bed. "I wasn't a smartass when you had me tied down."

"I'm special that way."

"Yes, you are." He stretched out next to her and slowly brushed his hand from her hip to her collarbone. "I need you, Lacey."

"I see that. You're pointing without the use of your hands."

All amusement fled as he stared at her. "I really mean it. I *need* you in my life. You make me happy, and I've fallen in love with you. Tell me you don't feel the same and I'll call you a liar. You say it in the way you look at me and the way we touch. You attacked a hunter to save me from his bullets. You could have died. Tell me if you've ever felt more alive and happy, even when you're calling me names."

She bit her lip, thinking, and knew what he said was true. She just wasn't willing to admit aloud yet that she had fallen in love with him. They were vampires and they'd live a long time together. The guy knew he was handsome and great in bed, so she figured he should work to get her to say it. She didn't want to be too easy. The thought amused her.

"I'm prepared to seduce you."

That piqued her interest and her body started to ache in anticipation. "Really?"

He smiled. "For as long as it takes. You're stubborn and I'm it for the long haul. Forever."

"This is kind of nuts. We haven't known each other that long, yet here we are. Talk about a strange relationship."

"Ever heard of sane love?"

"Point made."

"Be honest with yourself, *and* me." His hand traced the underside of her breast. "You love me a little, don't you?"

189

She stared into his eyes and it shocked her to see unease. He was afraid she'd say no. He really meant it. He loved her. She no longer wanted to keep quiet.

"I do. I love you, Lethal."

His tension eased. "I'll convince you that you need me in your life as much as I need you. I have a long list of ways to seduce you until you believe it without question."

"Really?"

He grinned. "Oh yeah. I had a werewolf go shopping for us to ensure your pleasure. You said you like sex toys. I am willing to do anything to prove that I'm the man who can make you happy."

"You're never going to let me forget what I said when we met, are you? So much for being a gentleman." She grinned, enjoying the verbal sparring. Life wouldn't be boring with Lethal.

"No." His hand caressed her skin. "You like me just as I am. What do you want me to do to you first, Lacey, love? Name it."

"Can we start with your mouth? I love that thing you do with your tongue."

"It's a given. I love the taste of you but first you need to feed. I don't want you passing out on me. If you refuse to drink blood, fair warning, I had the werewolf buy a marker." His eyes sparkled with humor. "Don't think I forgot that either. I'd love to write 'mine' all over my favorite areas of your body. You'll take blood from me or risk waking covered in ink. We'll get you drinking bagged blood much, much later."

"You're killing the mood. Gross."

"You enjoyed kissing me."

"We're exchanging blood that way again?" She could do that. She loved kissing him.

"Nope. I'm going to fuck you hard and deep while you bite into my neck. Your fangs will slide out naturally. It won't hurt. You're going to come so hard you see stars when you taste my blood now."

"Okay. I'm game as long as I see stars instead of that ugly-ass chandelier. That's got to go. I'm on top next round."

Lethal laughed. "You got it, love."

"Untie me. I don't want to do this without my hands. I love touching you." She wondered if he'd refuse.

Lethal pinned her under him and she spread her thighs to accommodate his hips. She wrapped her legs around his waist and arched her back to flatten her breasts against his chest while wiggling her ass, hoping he'd enter her. The firm feel of his cock touching her was torment. She wanted him inside badly once he'd stretched out over her. The hot press of his body against hers, his clean scent, drove her a little insane.

"Slow down."

"I'm really turned on. Is this a vampire thing?"

"Yes. It's a little bit bloodlust and just heightened passion."

"Help a girl out then. Untie me."

"Not yet."

"Why not?"

"I just healed."

"What does that mean?"

"You'll shred my back. I don't mind but this is our honeymoon, in a sense. I drank enough blood for both of us and don't want to waste a single drop."

"Tease."

"How so?" He chuckled.

"First you say you want me to draw blood, now you're telling me you don't want me to scratch you up."

He lifted a hand to his neck. "Ready, my love?"

"You're going to twirl your hair?"

He laughed and tossed it over his shoulder, exposing the area under his ear. "Just go with your instincts."

She should have flinched, watching someone use his fingernail to carve a bloody line in his skin, but the second he did it, a wonderful aroma distracted her. The sight of red had her licking her lips and her belly clenched. Strong desire hit. It was confusing, which she wanted more—sex or to taste him. Her gaze was riveted on the fresh cut.

He leaned in closer, keeping his head tilted. "Taste me."

It was an offer she couldn't refuse even if she wanted to. She lifted her head and licked the spot. A moan came from her as her gums tingled, her entire body seeming to ignite into flames. She sealed her lips over the wound, sucking. He was better than chocolate at the moment, so sweet and delicious. So hers.

"Bite me," he rasped, his lips against her ear.

She didn't think, just did as he demanded. The feel of her new fangs piercing him was incredibly erotic and euphoria had her flying as high as a kite. Emotions slammed into her—all good.

He shifted his hips and his thick shaft penetrated her pussy, driving in deep. Lacey screamed against his throat as she climaxed so hard her body convulsed. Lethal growled, his fangs sinking into her neck. Their bodies locked together as she squeezed him with her legs, his hips slamming into the cradle of her thighs as he fucked her hard and deep. His arms slid under her shoulders, gripping her and keeping her in place.

There was just the two of them surrounded in bliss. She wanted to wrap her arms around his neck and hold him just as tightly as he held her but the restraints kept her arms above her head. Another climax hit, more intense than the last one. She was pretty sure she snarled—an inhuman sound. Lethal definitely growled in response. It barely registered in her sex-hazed mind that the headboard was slamming into the wall.

Lethal suddenly released her throat, his tongue lapping where he'd bitten, and she screamed again. That minuscule touch was enough to send her over the edge again, her clit throbbing as if he were teasing it instead. The taste of him was suddenly gone and she realized her fangs were no longer embedded in his skin.

"Lick it," he panted. "Seal the wound."

She ran her tongue over his skin, the blood so good she wanted more. He jerked back a little though, out of her reach, and drove into her even faster. She threw back her head, crying out his name as she came again.

Lethal tucked his head, his lips against her ear. "I can't hold back anymore, love."

The sensation of him filling her with his semen was pure ecstasy. She could feel his pulse, every twitch of his cock inside her, as her vaginal muscles clenched around him.

"Yes," he rasped.

They lay entangled, Lethal pinning her tightly, her legs still locked around him. Her heels dug into his muscular ass as they recovered, both breathing heavily until their rapidly beating hearts slowed.

"Look at me. How did you like taking my blood?"

"I'll let you know once I remember how to open my eyes and talk at the same time. Is the top of my head still there? I think it might have blown apart."

He laughed. "You're whole."

She peeked from beneath one eyelid. "Are you sure?"

"Positive."

"Oh wow."

His eyes were glowing. "Now for the sex."

"What would you call what we just did?"

"Feeding."

"You were inside me and we both came. Technically, that's sex."

"That was the warm-up." He released her shoulders, lifted up a little, and stared at her breasts. "I'm going to work my way down until my mouth

194

is between those lovely thighs of yours." His tongue slid over his lips to wet them. "And taste every inch."

She struggled with the silken ties. "Let me go. I'm a vampire. Why can't I break free? Where're my super-vamp powers?"

He grinned, holding her gaze. "You're still thinking as if you're human."

"What does that mean?"

"You *expect* not to get free. You're holding yourself back."

She frowned, looking up at her wrists. She pretended they were being held there by wet spaghetti instead of material—and was surprised when she ripped free.

Lethal chuckled. "Push beyond what you believe to be your limitations."

She grasped his shoulders. "That's awesome! Now weren't you going somewhere?"

He nodded, inching lower. "I was."

"Feeding was so fantastic I thought I might not survive it, so I can't wait to see how great your version of sex is."

"You're going to love it."

She had no doubt.

# Mine to Chase

# Chapter One

The stench of death hit him the moment Chase crept inside the abandoned house on the outskirts of town. A human wouldn't have picked up those slight traces, but he wasn't one. His nose flared as another scent teased his senses—sweet feminine fear. His predatory instincts immediately rose to the surface as his fangs began to ache. He raised a hand, motioning for the two werewolves to circle the property.

"We found him," one of them confirmed before he disappeared, skirting the porch to make sure no one escaped out the back.

*Yes. We did.* Rage gripped Chase instantly. Rogue vampires were the enemy, risking discovery by humans of *all* Others. No one wanted that. It would mean the beginning of a war if the killings didn't stop. Humans far outnumbered Others. It was better to live in peace, their existence nothing but myth and entertainment, than the alternative.

A board above him creaked, betraying where the enemy hid. A smile curved Chase's lips as he stealthily maneuvered through the lower floor to the open stairwell. One whiff assured he was close to the enemy and he withdrew two blades. His knees bent slightly before he leapt, effortlessly sailing over the upper railing to land gracefully on booted feet.

The vamp sitting in the chair appeared surprised as his eyes widened. The book he held fell from his hand in the open lofted area. "Who are you?" He paused, nostrils flaring. "*What* are you?"

"Your worst nightmare. You've been found guilty."

Chase moved before the rogue could react, the speed he'd inherited from both sides of his bloodline assuring the outcome. With the slash of his hands, steel sliced into skin and bone, and then he jumped back to avoid any dust touching his trench coat.

The body exploded into gray ash, slowly falling onto the carpet. In seconds, feet pounded up the stairs. He turned to give his pack orders.

"Find a vacuum and get rid of any trace of what happened."

"Damn, Chase." The wolf smiled. "That was fast. You didn't even let him try to make a run for it."

"Should we burn down the house? I smell rotting bodies." The other wolf breathed through his mouth. "Multiples. He probably hid them in the basement."

"I'm aware." Chase sighed. "It's best to dispose of them without drawing notice. Fire and police would come if we torch his lair. They'd investigate and discover remains in the rubble."

"Gasoline would probably take care of it if we soaked the corpses first."

Irritation rose, and so did a menacing growl deep within his throat. "You heard my orders."

Both wolves dropped their gazes in submission. "Yes, Chase." They rushed to do his bidding.

He wiped the blades clean on his kill's clothing before putting them away to use his cell phone. The call connected as he walked downstairs. It was answered on the third ring.

"We located the rogue who murdered Lacey's sister. She's been avenged, Lethal. Give her a kiss for me." He disconnected with an amused grin when his friend snarled, more than a bit possessive of the woman he loved.

Chase's job was done. He inhaled but then winced. *Almost done.* The bodies of the rogue's victims would have to be disposed of. He located the basement door right off the kitchen and paused, bracing for the worst. Running security for his vampire friends could sometimes get messy, but corpses were rarely involved, unless it was those of the bad guys. This was different.

The stench intensified to a nauseating level when he jerked open the door. He regretted killing the rogue so swiftly. It was clear humans had been slaughtered to feed the bastard. A needless waste. It was easy for vampires to get blood without murdering their food sources—just a quick mind swipe would clear their memories—but the rogue obviously enjoyed taking lives.

Chase could guess why. The sick bastard got off on tormenting them first and watching them suffer.

He breathed through his mouth to suppress some of the offensive odor as his eyes adjusted to the darkness below. The stairs creaked under his weight as he descended.

The unfinished basement had piles of dirt in at least six locations, the corpses under the thin layers of earth too obvious to be anything else. "Fuck." His voice rose. "Get six body bags." He didn't wait for a response, knowing his pack heard him. Their hearing was almost as keen as his.

He scanned the room for something to dig with, not a job he wanted to do with his bare hands. The level of decay he smelled promised to make it a messy task. The rogue had to have used a shovel to bury them.

Jasmine held very still, her gaze locked on the tall, massive man standing at the bottom of the stairs. Light from above revealed enough of his features to scare her into absolute silence. A very masculine face turned just enough to make out full lips and a strong chin. It wasn't the man who'd taken her, but he appeared just as dangerous. Perhaps more so.

It had been days since Jasmine had slept, too terrified to close her eyes. The madman who'd kidnapped her was pure evil. He hadn't given her food and had savagely bitten her a few times. It wouldn't surprise her if she had become delusional from the wounds being infected.

No tears filled her eyes. She'd passed that stage already. First she'd been terrified, pleading for her life. It had pleased her kidnapper. Then she'd hit the acceptance phase that her death was imminent. The bastard had watched her cry as if it fascinated him. The bruises along her arms still hurt from where he'd viciously pinched them, making her kick and hit him in a weak attempt to protect her body. He liked that too. It was the only reason he hadn't killed her outright. He admitted to being bored, said she amused him.

There was something familiar about this man but she figured it was her mind playing tricks. Then he lifted his face, turned toward the door at the top of the stairs—and Jasmine recognized him.

Chase Woods. A very memorable client from almost a year before.

The striking features were his. He was the man she'd dreamed about—muscular and big, with the sexiest brown eyes she'd ever peered into. He'd bought some land on the edge of town as an investment. She'd tried to tell him that the two hundred acres of forest were too dense for building. The cost of clearing and leveling the land would be extreme.

She'd liked him a little too much, despite it not being mutual. He had never flirted, though she'd given him green lights to do so. He'd ignored her subtle hints that she had been interested.

He'd claimed his work didn't allow time off and had wanted her to show him properties after hours. She probably would have been terrified of meeting a man in such remote locations at night, but her attraction to him had made her shove common sense aside.

A memory surfaced in her mind. They'd been surveying a parcel of land after dark and she'd been distracted, a little unnerved by the odd request that she show it to him at night, but there had been something about Chase that she couldn't resist. Something different...

~ ~ ~ ~ ~

She never saw the tree root and nearly fell. His strong arm wrapped around her waist and suddenly she was in the circle of his arms, held against his body.

"Careful." His deep voice was sexy.

"I don't know how you see anything. Wouldn't it be better to return in the morning?"

"The moon is almost full, and I have great eyesight."

202

She grabbed onto his biceps. Her hands didn't come close to encircling the thick muscles. He was strong, much bigger than her, and smelled wonderful.

"I'm almost blind out here." She realized she should release him, but he kept hold of her. It seemed only fair to touch him back. She lifted her chin to stare up into his face. She couldn't make out much but she could tell he wasn't looking at her. He had turned his head to the side. "Are you okay?"

"Yeah." His voice came out even deeper. "I told you to wait in your car."

He had, but she'd wanted to spend as much time as possible with her client. There was something about him that drew her. It wasn't just his handsome face. She'd dated men who were good looking before and had learned the hard way that some of them had less-than-stellar personalities. It could be how fit and muscular he was. Every woman would notice Chase Woods when he walked into a room.

She discarded that as well. It was just *him*. He was sweet, mysterious, and looking into his eyes always did something funny to her entire body. She'd never been more attracted to a man in her entire life.

"I wouldn't be doing my job if I made you view the properties alone. You might have questions."

He chuckled—a deep, rumbling sound. "Can you identify all the tree varieties? There are plenty of them out here."

Jasmine glanced to the side, seeing nothing more than a lot of dark shapes. "Um, no," she admitted. "I can tell you how long it's been on the market and how much we could haggle on the asking price."

He drew her closer when the wind suddenly picked up, shielding her from it. He really did smell wonderful, and she suddenly had an urge to rest her head against his solid chest. Other thoughts came to mind as well. Wild, naughty ones that were shocking. Stripping naked in the woods with a man she barely knew wasn't something she'd ever considered before. It didn't stop the images from filling her head though.

She wanted him to kiss her while lifting her higher into his arms. The skirt she wore would be easy to shove up to her waist after she discarded her panties. Chase was strong enough to hold her up during sex. His jeans would be simple to unsnap to free his cock and then nothing would be between them. They'd be skin to skin. Her knees weakened slightly just imagining the way he'd feel entering her body.

Chase suddenly stepped back and his arms were gone, leaving her feeling cold and sexually frustrated.

"I've seen enough." He cleared his throat. "I'll take it. Let's get back to your office and draw up an offer." He was brusque after that.

The next day, Chase agreed to the seller's first counteroffer. The paperwork was finalized for the sale and he refused to allow her to take him to dinner to celebrate his purchase. It hurt. The warmth and friendliness was gone. He was cold and withdrawn once their business had been concluded.

The attraction was so powerful that it was almost unsettling. She couldn't stop wishing he'd call and ask to see her again.

It hadn't ever happened. That had been the last time she'd seen Mr. Woods, but his memory lingered in her dreams. It explained why her imagination would bring him into her nightmare.

His voice drew her out of her memories and back into the hellish basement...

~ ~ ~ ~ ~

"Hurry up," he demanded. "I don't want to be here all night."

That sexy voice was one she'd never forget. It still made the feminine parts of her respond. It was whiskey and honey, husky but full of strength. A bitter laugh threatened to burst forth. She was dying, and her mind had decided to create more fantasies that included him. It beat fixating on the horrific way her life would end.

The slats in the door were wide enough to watch him cross the room to retrieve a shovel. She reached out to touch the rough wood, wishing she could get closer. The chain jerked her in place when the length, shackled to her wrist, pulled taut. The cuts, caused by her struggles to wiggle free, hurt enough to make her whimper.

Mr. Woods suddenly spun to face her. She couldn't see his face in the shadows but his eyes seemed to glow blue—and he was looking right at her. He dropped the shovel and headed toward the wall.

She froze in place, barely breathing as he crouched on the other side of the door. The change in the color of his irises was stunning, only strengthening her belief that it was just her mind playing tricks.

"Hi," she got out, barely a whisper, not caring if she was talking to a figment of her imagination. Her voice came out rough, dry, and it hurt. She'd kill for a sip of water.

His eyes definitely radiated blue as they widened, and then his fingers dug between the slats. Wood snapped when he yanked hard, tearing it away.

"Son of a bitch." His tone deepened into a snarl, his anger clear.

Jasmine swallowed, trying to stay in the fantasy. It beat the alternative. "Did you ever build those condos?" She wanted to wince at how horrible her voice sounded. It seemed pretty pathetic to screw up a daydream.

"Jasmine?" He leaned closer, a dark shadow.

He gently gripped her upper arms. It still hurt but she didn't pull away. He had big hands, and the warmth of them was worth the pain. His glowing gaze traveled down her body where she sat in the dark, cramped space, before lifting to meet hers.

"I'll get you free." One hand released her and he magically withdrew a knife from his long coat. "Hang on."

He dropped his other hand to grip the shackle on her wrist. It hurt enough to make her cry out but he didn't stop. The tip of the metal stabbed the lock and he flicked his wrist. The shackle parted, releasing her. He tossed it aside and the chain fell to the dirt next to her knee. He repeated the process to free her from the other restraint.

"Come here." He shoved the knife back into his coat and opened his arms. "Crawl to me. I don't want to drag you out."

Every movement hurt but she managed to shift to her knees, careful of the low roof of the storage area she'd been confined inside. He backed up enough to give her room. She straightened the second she was clear and threw her arms around his broad shoulders. Her breasts were smashed against warm cotton and a firm torso.

His soft, silky hair was down now, testament to him being a fantasy. The real man had always kept it secured in a leather tie at the base of his neck. She'd always wanted to see how it would look free from that confinement.

His strong, thick arms wrapped around her waist. She breathed him in instead of the atrocious stench she'd adjusted to. Her nose buried into the long strands of his hair. "You smell so good."

His massive body tensed.

"Don't let me go." She didn't mind dying if she could just hold on to the memory of him. It meant she wouldn't die alone, despite him not being real. "Please. Don't leave me."

He drew her closer by tightening his hug. "I've got you, Jasmine."

She wished that were true. "I'm glad it's you."

He stroked her back. "You're safe."

Exhaustion took hold as his warmth surrounded her. Her eyes closed for the first time in days as she clung to him, and the fantasy that had brought him.

Chase softly cursed as the woman in his arms turned limp. He could hear her steady heartbeat as he lifted her more securely into his arms. He stood and turned to stare at the wolves. One of them spoke.

"What do we do with her? Can you wipe her memory? It would be a shame to kill her after all she's survived, but there may be no choice."

Chase hesitated. "She's none of your concern. Clean this up and remove all evidence of what happened. I'm taking her somewhere safe. There's been enough death here."

He strode out of the basement with Jasmine cradled in his arms. He'd liked the sweet, soft-spoken woman a little too much. She'd bravely met him—a stranger—at night to show him possible sites for the pack to roam. She'd also easily bought into his lies, making it possible to avoid altering her thoughts. He'd found her attractive and had picked up her very subtle hints that she was interested, but he'd ignored every one. She was the type of woman he'd destroy.

He refused to allow that to happen, despite the way his body had reacted to Jasmine. She had wavy hair that reminded him of coffee and cream. Most of it was shades of brown with blonde highlights. He'd fantasized running his fingers through those tresses of hers. Her eyes reminded him of the sky, pale blue, and they held a look of innocence. Her curvy body was the opposite, drawing a man's lust with her full breasts and flared hips he wanted to touch and explore. She was human though, fragile, and bringing one into his world could become hazardous to her health. He'd never allow harm to befall her, even if that meant he was the one she needed to be protected from.

Of course, now everything had changed.

"Chase?"

He clenched his teeth as a shadow near the front door moved. Arry stepped into his path, her green eyes narrowed. She shouldn't be there, yet she was. Irritation flashed as he stared back at her, knowing she'd purposely arrived in hopes of him needing her somehow. It was never going to happen.

"Open it and move."

"Who is she? Dinner?" A pink tongue darted out to swipe ruby-red lips. "Not very appealing."

A growl of anger burst forth before he could halt the instinct. Arry might actually mean her words. He and Arry were as different as night and day. "Do as you're told. She's a survivor."

"Not for long. She's circling the drain."

He trusted Arry's sense of smell better than his own. She was older. "Get the door," he snapped. "You're visiting my territory, and you'll do as you're told."

"Fine." She opened it wide, stepping out of his way. "You should let me drink her and just end it. She's got twelve hours at most."

Not if Chase had anything to say about it. He glanced around, certain no one watched. His senses didn't tingle as he strode to his car and gently adjusted Jasmine in his hold as he situated her in the passenger seat then closed the door. He paused at the driver's door to peer over the top of the car. Arry stood silent, her blonde hair white under the streetlights.

"Help them clean up that mess inside."

"I'm here to see you, not dispose of rogue kill."

"It's an order. Do it or leave my territory."

"So forceful." Arry smiled. "I always liked that about you." She stepped closer, running her fingers over the curves of her breasts on their way to hug lean hips. "I'd rather help *you*."

The meaning was clear, and he was tired of it. "Go help them or leave, Arry. There's no reason for you to be here. Do as I say or I'll have to escort you out of my territory by force."

He climbed inside the car and started the engine. Chase didn't miss the way the blonde stormed back into the house. She was going to be a problem, but she had been since her arrival a week before. Arry had always been determined and selfish about getting her way. And she was set on *him*.

He pulled away from the curb, darting glances at the unconscious woman in the next seat. She was too pale, had lost weight since he'd last seen her, and Chase decided Arry was correct—Jasmine wouldn't survive the next day unless he saved her life.

"Shit."

The vampires in the area might have a problem with him taking in a human. They posed a threat. But the werewolf pack was strong enough to win a challenge if anyone protested. He'd kill any vampires who attacked.

That would definitely piss off his two bosses, Blaron and Lethal, but ultimately they wouldn't be a problem. They were friends.

Taking Jasmine to the club wasn't an option. She would need his full attention while she recovered, and he didn't want to deal with any bullshit. He headed to the place he kept on the sly. No one would find him until he'd decided how to deal with the consequences of what he planned to do.

One more glance to his right confirmed that the woman clung to life. He refused to allow Jasmine to die.

The long driveway was cracked from years of purposeful neglect, to give it an abandoned appearance, but the small light on the entry keypad was on when he stopped the car. He punched in the code and the gate blocking his path slowly wobbled to the side. He drove through and up to the two-story hillside house.

As he lifted Jasmine out of the car, he sensed a presence behind him. One sniff assured him it was Jenny. He didn't look back as he spoke. "We have a guest."

"Is she one of us?"

He disliked being questioned, but he had a soft spot for his half-sister. "No."

"I smell vampire and death all over her. Is she turning?"

"No. She's just a human victim and a special friend."

"She's in bad shape."

"I know." He kicked the car door closed and quickly walked up the porch steps. "Open the door and prepare a bath in my room. I'm also going to need blood."

Jenny darted around him and threw open the front door. "Okay."

He went inside and turned, carrying his light burden down the basement steps and pausing near the wine racks. Jenny gripped two bottles, pushing them deeper into their slots to trigger the panel. The wall soundlessly slid open, revealing a hallway. He strode down it to his bedroom.

He laid Jasmine across the end of his bed and began undressing her. There wasn't much to remove. The sight of the bruising and bites on her pale form once again made him regret killing the rogue too quickly. He'd deserved to suffer.

"The tub is filling." Jenny paused. "Do you want me to wash her?"

It was tempting, but Jasmine was his responsibility. "No. Do what I said. Bring me the blood. And she'll need clothing when she wakes."

"I don't have anything sexy."

He growled, whipped his head in her direction and glared at her. "She's not my lover. Bring her one of those large nightshirts you wear. That will do. Go."

"Sorry." Her gaze dropped in submission. "You said special friend. I assumed wrong."

Jenny rushed off without another word. Chase slid his hands under Jasmine and lifted her into his arms again. It was going to be torture to his libido to bathe her. He avoided looking at her breasts or other tempting sights. It seemed a violation of his duty to notice those things while she was so near death.

"You're going to be fine," he promised.

# Chapter Two

Jasmine was warm and something smelled wonderful. She tried to turn on her side but something held her firm. She opened her eyes to see soft lights and a face hovering just over her own.

"Easy," Chase rasped. "You're safe."

Memory returned. She was delusional, fantasizing that her sexy client had come to her rescue. His eyes were an incredible mocha brown with swirls of blue, as striking as his handsome, tan face. He had the best lips. They were full and lush; the kind she guessed would be wonderful to kiss. Chase Woods was a guy who probably did everything really well.

She lay on something soft and comfortable with her upper body slightly elevated so her head was higher than her legs. Dirt no longer clung to her skin from lying on the basement floor. It took effort to look away from Chase to glance at her surroundings. The room was spacious and a fire burned in a brick-rimmed fireplace. The bed she rested on was large with silky black sheets. She stared at Chase again.

"You need to help me help *you*."

"Okay." She would do anything he wanted as long as it kept her mind from returning to the hellish nightmare of the dank basement.

His eyes fascinated her. She remembered them being dark brown but they were lighter now, and the hints of bright blue were an odd combination. More of the vibrant color flared, spreading as she watched until they glowed as if they were sapphires.

He took a deep breath and parted his lips. The sight of sharp canines made her gasp. They were long, terrifying fangs. The arm around her waist tightened.

"Don't fight. I won't hurt you."

He lifted his other arm and she watched in rapt horror while he bit into his wrist. Chase jerked his mouth away and shoved the wound at her open mouth. Warm skin and blood touched her lips and tongue. It was instinct to twist away but his arm at her waist lifted and his hand fisted into her hair to hold her head in place.

"Stop fighting and drink."

It was as if she lost her will to do anything else. She was aware of swallowing the warm substance. It grossed her out but she didn't gag as she continued to do as he ordered. His voice sounded deeper and her daydream had turned into an entirely new nightmare.

"This will heal you. You've lost a lot of blood and some of your internal organs have begun to shut down. You're safe, Jasmine. You know me." His eyes narrowed. "I'm sorry I have to force you, but this is for the best."

He finally pulled his wrist away and licked it. The second he broke eye contact, she regained control of her body. She tried to twist away again but he held her firmly by the hair. She managed to swipe at the wetness on her mouth with her hand. Red blood smeared across her fingers. A soft gasp drew her attention from the sight of it.

A pretty woman with dark hair stood a few feet from the bed with wide eyes and a gaping mouth. "You're sharing your blood with her? You can't do that!"

Chase stared at the brunette. "Did you bring the blood?"

"Yes. It's on the table. I thought it was for you."

"This is none of your concern. Leave."

"How can you say that? You should have asked me first."

"This is *my* house." His voice deepened into a snarl. "You're welcome to move out if you have a problem."

The woman spun and fled the room. Jasmine stared at Chase when he met her gaze. *Is that his girlfriend? Wife?*

He seemed to guess her thoughts. "That's my sister. I just surprised her, but she'll adjust to you being here."

"What's going on?" Jasmine hated how soft her voice sounded, a near whisper.

"You were attacked by a rogue vampire, but you're safe now. This is my home." He picked up a warm, wet washcloth and dabbed gently at her fingers. He then cleaned away the blood on her face. "It's your home now too."

She wasn't sure what alarmed her the most. *Did he say vampire?* It would explain his fangs, and why he'd made her drink blood. *What does he mean—it's my home too?* Fear edged up her spine, but admittedly, it wasn't as bad as being chained inside a basement with a homicidal madman.

"Your eyes..."

"Easy," Chase rasped, dropping the washcloth on a side table. He leaned in and cupped her cheek, brushing his thumb along her hairline. "I know this is a lot to learn after what you've suffered. I'll answer all your questions."

The first one that came to mind popped out of her mouth. "What are you?"

"I'm a rarity." His hand dropped from her skin but he stayed close. "I'm a mixed breed—werewolf and vampire."

She wondered why all the really handsome men had such major flaws. Chase Woods was nuts. Of course it wasn't real. "Okay." There was no use arguing with a hallucination.

"That doesn't distress you?" He arched one eyebrow.

"It would if this were real."

He drew in a deep breath then sighed. "What would it take to convince you it is?"

"I'd be in a hospital if I'd survived and the police had found me. Your eyes would be totally brown, too."

"Humans aren't allowed to know about us. They usually scream, and then promptly attempt to kill us. We police our own. The vampire who took you was bad, and I was sent to kill him."

"So you're a vampire hunter?" She must have watched too many movies to create this fantasy. "With magical eyes?"

"I'm an enforcer."

"Nicer title."

Chase really was a good-looking man when he grinned. "Yes."

"Okay."

"You're being very agreeable."

"This beats reality. It isn't the kind of dream I usually have about you though."

Interest sparked in his eyes. "You dream about me?"

"All the time. You're hot, Chase. I flirted but you ignored me. I don't blame you," she went on. "I drove by that Goth club you work at a few times and saw some of the women going inside. They all looked like strippers, lingerie models or porn stars...and I don't."

"I don't date anyone I meet at Mooning." His hand returned and he stroked her cheek with his thumb. "You're much more attractive to me than any of those women."

Jasmine laughed. Her body didn't ache anymore and she felt good. "Now I *know* this is a dream. That's such a load of bullshit."

He grew solemn. "Never put yourself down."

"I'm not. My boobs are real, I like to eat, and no one is ever going to want to pay me to be on film without my clothes. I'm more of the girl-next-door type."

"Exactly. There's a sweetness about you that I find very appealing. You fascinate me."

"I would say you must lead a very boring life but I know better. Your club has a reputation for being pretty wild."

"It's not technically my club. I just work there, running security."

"Ah. Do you get tired of patting down all those super-skinny girls? Are they too bony?"

He chuckled, his eye color fading to brown. "Let's just say I prefer someone with curves and a personality. Those women didn't last long the few times I attempted relationships."

"You dumped them?"

He leaned back and stopped touching her. "No. They couldn't handle my lifestyle."

"Jealousy." She could understand that. "It would be tough knowing you were hanging around all those women with your looks. You must get hit on often." She paused, unable to resist. "You admitted to being part dog." She laughed at the joke. He didn't.

"You're almost fully recovered."

He took her hand to study her wrist. Jasmine looked too, and the ugly injuries from the shackles she'd fought were gone. Pink, healthy skin appeared unmarred.

"Very cool dream. I wonder if I can fly."

His gaze held hers. "No. That's one thing you can't do. You'll be a little bit stronger, faster, and you'll heal quickly from most injuries."

"Am I a vampire now?" The concept was intriguing.

"No."

"You're almost his mate!" The cold voice belonged to a rail-thin, tall blonde who stepped closer to the bed. Her eyes—fixed on Chase—resembled two chunks of jagged emeralds. "How *could* you?"

He rose to his feet. "How did you even find this place, Arry?"

"You were so worried about *her* that you didn't notice my car trailing yours." She glanced around. "Tell me you aren't completing the bond. She's *human*."

Jasmine could hear the insult in the other woman's tone and she looked to Chase for answers. "Who is she? What is she talking about?"

"Leave," Chase ordered the blonde coldly, ignoring the questions. "You aren't welcome here, Arry." He took a threatening step forward. "I told you it wouldn't happen when you showed up."

Arry planted her hands on her hips. "Everyone fears us and we're both alone. It's a given that we'll mate!"

"We're not feared. We're *pitied*. Vampires believe we're inferior and werewolves think we're unable to form tight bonds with others." He paused. "I chose *her*. There's nothing for you here."

Arry chewed on her bottom lip. "It's easier if we mate."

"I want to be happy."

"Sex would be good between us."

"It's not enough."

Arry glanced at Jasmine. "What can she give you that I can't?"

"Her thoughts are easy to read. She's sweet and funny." He paused. "Smart. Honest. She's everything I want in a mate."

Jasmine slid out of bed and walked to Chase. One glance down her body revealed a frumpy, faded nightshirt that hit just above her knees. It was comfortable, covered her for the most part, though she'd never seen it before in her life. Her attention returned to Chase and she tapped his shoulder. He turned, peering down at her. His eyes were blue again.

"You read my mind?"

"It's a vampire trait. I can only read surface thoughts, but yes."

"She isn't even sure this is reality," Arry said. "It's too crazy to be real. *That's* what she's thinking. That, and something about infection from the bites…" She smirked. "I see the attraction is mutual. She thinks you're hot but your eyes are confusing her."

Jasmine was stunned as she looked at the blonde. The dream was becoming more than a little disconcerting. "Stay out of my head."

"It's real, honey. He saved you from that basement and healed your wounds. Vampires and werewolves *do* exist. His eyes change color when he's angry, turned on, or using his special traits." Arry opened her mouth, wicked fangs extending. "See? The better to bite with. You're beginning to believe, aren't you? You're afraid now."

It was true. Everything seemed too real and denial was great, but it could only last for so long. Jasmine dropped her hand and backed away from Chase as fear crept up her spine until the hairs at the base of her neck stood on end. He reached for her but she jumped out of the way to avoid his touch.

"Trouble in paradise." The blonde snorted. "Wipe her memories and send her home." She approached Chase. "Mate me. We're the same!"

His head snapped forward. "We aren't. Leave, Arry. Return to wherever you came from. We'll *never* be mates."

"We're in a world that has no place for our kind," she argued. "Your vampire friends don't trust us completely, regardless of your faith in them. While your little wolf pack tempts me to try to find one of my own, you know you only rule them because they fear your strength. They'd chop you into pieces if given half the chance, because you aren't truly one of them. I catch some of their thoughts, the way you must too when their guards are down. It has to be tiring to always worry they might come after you. I'd have your back, and you'd have mine."

"My friends and pack are none of your business. I'd be more worried, if I were you, that they'll come after *you*. They swore allegiance to me. You're just a visitor who refuses to follow orders. Watch your own back— and get out of my house. Never return here or reveal the location. I'll hunt you down and kill you myself if you do."

Jasmine watched them stare at each other as more chills ran down her spine. It was obvious the two weren't friends, not even close, and the dangerous vibes pouring from Chase were strong enough for her to feel. The room seemed to grow colder as the seconds passed.

The blonde raised her hands in defeat. "I'll go. But call me after this blows up in your face. No human is going to accept and love you for what you truly are. She's already frightened, and it hasn't even fully sunk in yet."

Arry spun around but hesitated by the open doorway, turning her head to peer at him. "Your den is safe. I'd never betray you, regardless of the stupid mistakes I believe you make." She glared at Jasmine, and then retreated.

221

Chase watched Arry go before facing Jasmine. She'd backed into the corner by the fireplace. He knew her thoughts centered on using the fire poker as a weapon if he attacked. He wanted to assure that wouldn't happen.

"I'd never hurt you."

"You're really part vampire and werewolf?"

"Yes."

"How?"

She was too cute. Part of her wanted to bolt but she was also very curious. Her strong attraction to him helped. She'd fantasized about him often since they'd met. He could read all that as he concentrated on her thoughts. It would be easy to force her to agree to mating him, but once the bond took, she'd have free will. It would be a bad way to start their future together. It was also forbidden.

"My parents had sex."

She frowned, not appreciating his attempt at humor.

"My father was a vampire, my mother a werewolf and vampire half-breed."

"Vampires don't have kids. They can't."

"You read that in a book?"

"Yes."

"I don't sparkle or burst into flames in the sun. I bet you read that, too." He continued before she could voice her thoughts. "I don't shift into a wolf. My bloodlines aren't pure enough. I don't have a tail, nor do I howl at the moon when it's full. I don't kill people to drink blood, but yes, I need it. Blood banks are willing to make some extra income by selling contaminated blood instead of destroying it."

"Contaminated?"

"We can't catch human diseases. Contaminated blood doesn't affect us. They can't use it on humans, so they believe they're helping medical research by selling it and reinvesting the profit."

Her lips parted.

"We set up a fake medical research company with a small office for deliveries. It avoids suspicion."

"You really drink blood?"

"Yes. You will too after we mate."

"That's gross."

He fought to hide his amusement when she purposely refused to acknowledge the part about mating. "You'd only drink mine. I promise you'll enjoy it." His dick hardened thinking about her at his neck or chest, taking from him while he fucked her.

"Why? I mean, if you want to turn me into a vampire, couldn't I drink anyone's blood?"

She was so enchanting and had inner strength he respected. His words disturbed her, she was afraid, but she was attempting to be brave. "I don't want you to be fully vampire. You couldn't withstand the sun. My blood will protect you from having that weakness."

"Because you're also a werewolf."

It was difficult to follow her thoughts. Many of them were streaming so quickly he could only catch a word or two. Jasmine was smart, something he already knew. She was trying to make sense of it all, using books she'd read and logical guesses to fill in the blanks.

"Exactly."

Mate. That word kept popping into her thoughts, and he concentrated harder, attempting to focus on just the ones on that subject.

*Mate. Sex. God, he's hot. It wouldn't be so bad. Who am I kidding? The guy would probably blow my mind with sex if he didn't suck me dry of blood and kill me first.*

"I barely know you. I need to think about this," came out of her mouth.

*I love his eyes, regardless of what color they are. And his chest. He's so big. I wonder if he's one of those guys who are all muscle because he uses steroids. Did it shrink his package to a tiny size? Don't you dare glance at his crotch. He's watching and he'd notice. That would be so embarrassing. Are you kidding? Who cares about that? He says he's a vampire who's also a werewolf. Of course, I'd have to be attracted to him, right? Of all the men to pick to obsess over. Good going, Jas. Oh my god. How can this be real? Do I run? Scream? Fight? What the hell do I do? I'm so out of my league. Shit! He's staring at me and his eyes are glowing again. Can he really read my mind? That disturbs the hell out of me. Who could date someone like that? There'd be no privacy at all. What relationship could survive that? Shit. I think he is reading my mind. La, la, la, la, la. Does that even work? Maybe I should start singing nursery rhymes. I know I'd want to get the hell out of my head if I had to hear my singing.*

Chase shielded her thoughts to prevent any more from reaching him. He had expected her reservations about becoming his mate, but not how bothered she'd be by his ability to read her mind. He decided to make it clear there really wasn't a choice. She was logical. "Your life was already taken, Jasmine. It belongs to me now."

He regretted the words instantly when she lunged at the weapon, waving the curved point of the poker at him. It was the wrong approach.

"Get back!"

"Sweetheart, you couldn't hurt me with that." To prove his point, he moved fast, removing it from her hold before she could even gasp. One arm wrapped around her waist and hoisted her off her feet to pin her against the wall. "The important part is that we'll be together."

She flattened her hands on his chest as her eyes widened with fear. He hated her reaction but could understand. He dropped the poker and slid his fingers into her hair to protect her head from the bricks if she attempted to pull back.

"Let me go."

"I can't. You're mine, Jasmine. I wanted you when we met, but I didn't want to introduce you to the darker side of life. Someone else did that when you were taken."

"You could make me forget it all, couldn't you?"

"Yes." He lowered his gaze to her mouth, wanting to kiss it. "But you were almost killed. It could happen again. I'm not willing to risk that. I wanted you, and destiny brought us together for a second time for a reason." His gaze held hers.

"Destiny? You believe in that?"

"Yes." He was tempted to read her again but resisted. It made him feel guilty, considering she was probably singing "Old McDonald" or some other childhood song inside her head right now, believing it would protect her from that invasion of privacy.

"I don't."

"Not yet, but I'll convince you."

"I don't think you can."

"Kiss me."

He'd show her there was passion between them. It had always been there, but he'd resisted it when they'd spent those four evenings together viewing properties. Seeing her in that basement, understanding how close she'd come to death, changed that. She was everything he'd always wanted, and she deserved better than living in a dark world. But she could have died—and good intentions be damned.

The second her mouth parted to voice a protest, he was there.

Jasmine's lips were as soft as they looked when he covered them. She gasped but his tongue muffled the sound as he asserted his dominance to his mate. White-hot fervor rolled through him when she kissed him back, her hands fisting his shirt. The animal side of him snarled, wanting to claim her.

# Chapter Three

No one had ever kissed Jasmine the way Chase did. It wasn't just lips coming together. Her entire body seemed affected by each thrust of his tongue against hers. A spark of warmth turned into a burning need that flared to life and slowly spread to her lower belly. His fingers tangled in the hair at the base of her neck and tugged her head back to gain better access. Carnal images were forced into her mind.

She clawed at his shirt, tearing at the fabric in desperate need to feel skin. One of her legs wrapped around his waist to hook over his muscular ass. It was as if pure lust poured out of him and into her. Jasmine couldn't get close enough—rubbing against him, she moaned. She'd gone from frightened to burning alive with sexual need.

Her back flattened against the wall as Chase's body pressed tighter to her front. His pelvis ground between her thighs, rubbing his trapped, stiff cock along the seam of her panties.

The nightshirt she wore rode up, only the barriers of her panties and his jeans separating them. The rigid length of his cock brushed back and forth, heightening her desire to feel him inside her. It was insane yet it all made sense. She didn't want to question—just feel.

This was the guy she'd fantasized about almost nightly. He had been a gentleman, holding her hand while they'd traipsed around woods in the dark, and he'd always opened her car door when she'd met him. He made her laugh with his quick wit. Chase had been mysterious with his short replies about his personal life but he was a good man. She'd known the difference after dealing with a lot of clients who hit on her at the first opportunity. Not once had he made her feel uncomfortable or afraid.

It had been the complete opposite instead. She'd felt safe with Chase—protected and comfortable. He was smart, talking about books he'd read and current events. They had things in common. He loved to watch the same action films she did and enjoyed cooking. He'd listened to her as if what she said mattered, and he was attentive. She'd just really liked him. It had been disappointing when he hadn't asked her out after she'd dropped hints that she'd welcome more time spent together.

And his package was impressive—not small at all.

His hips slowly rocked against her clit, drawing her closer to climax. It felt so good she almost bit him when the pleasure grew too strong. He seemed to know it too, as he tore his mouth away to shift attention to the column of her neck instead. Hot, wet kisses trailed from under her ear to the top of her shoulder, where the nightshirt stopped him from going lower.

His teeth raked her sensitive skin and she moaned louder. She was pretty sure those were fangs, and they felt amazing. He could bite her, but no fear rose over that thought. Instead, she almost wanted to feel them just for the sake of knowing any part of him was inside her.

He untangled his hand from her hair, gripped the nightshirt, and shoved it higher as he adjusted his body to put space between their hips. A slight tug was the only warning before her panties were ripped away. She opened her eyes to watch them sail across the room. It was a speak-now-

or this is-happening moment as he worked his zipper open to free his cock. She wasn't a virgin, and she knew silence implied consent.

She wanted Chase Woods. Right or wrong, crazy or not, she wasn't going to say no.

He didn't do what she expected. Instead of entering her, his fingers explored her sex. She was wet and ready but he pressed his thumb over the bundle of nerves, drawing circles over her clit. She moaned louder as the pleasure grew more intense, digging her fingernails into his shirt where she clutched at his shoulders to help support her weight, which he held with one arm. It seemed easy for him.

"Jasmine," he rasped, slightly out of breath. "Say yes."

"Yes!"

She had wanted him for a long time—too long. It had taken months for her to abandon all hope that he'd call to ask her on a date. It had been depressing. He wanted her now though, and it wasn't just a one-night stand. He was looking for a mate.

"Wait," she panted, suddenly filled with questions before they went any further. The memory of their past gave her pause.

He growled in frustration but stopped kissing her, and his thumb stilled as he pulled his face back until their gazes met. "What?" His eyes narrowed as he peered deeply into hers. "Yes," he said, obviously reading her mind. "I'm serious about the mating. We'll live together here, where you'll be safe. I'll still have my job but you'll never have to worry about me cheating. You'll be it for me, the only one I want, Jasmine." He paused. "How can you be sure? Mates are bonded. You'll be able to read my thoughts and feelings. We'll feel a type of addiction to each other that nothing else can compare to."

"Do you have to keep reading my mind?" She glared at him, irritated. She didn't want to think about that.

"Sorry. I want you too." He adjusted her in his arms, pinning her tightly to the wall again. "I've wanted you since we met, and I really need you to agree to spend your life with me." A smile tugged at his lips. "Yes. You'll live a lot longer. We could have hundreds, if not thousands of years together. No, we won't grow bored of each other. The bond won't allow it. The sex will be incredible, and we'll be emotionally intertwined. Two becoming one, is how it's been explained to me. We'll have our own identities but we will complement each other."

"I'm a little afraid," she admitted. "This is going way too fast."

"I know, but I can't give you the time you want. There's no way you're leaving here without becoming my mate. I almost lost you once—I won't risk it again. You're too vulnerable as a human to return to the outside world. There won't be dinner dates and courtship first to assure you I'm the right choice."

"What if I regret it after it's done? We don't know each other that well. Can't you give me a few days? I haven't seen you in almost a year and there was a lot you wouldn't tell me."

A pained expression crossed his handsome features. "You can't leave here, but I understand your need for time to make the decision with confidence."

"What do you mean I can't leave?" That alarmed her. Was she a prisoner?

"No, you're not a prisoner," he answered, still seemingly aware of what she was thinking. "It's not safe for you to be anywhere else."

"I have a life, a house I'm paying off, and a job." A dozen other objections filled her head. "You can't expect me to give up my entire world to live in yours." It was too much for any sane person to ask of another. "We need to discuss this."

He glanced down between their bodies and growled. "There is plenty of time for that later. Do I have to keep my hands off you?" He looked up, reading her again. "We make love while sharing blood to mate. I'll bite you to take yours while you drink mine to seal the mating bond."

"You already gave me your blood."

"To heal you. We have to exchange blood and sex at the same time to lock the mate bond." He ground his hips against her again, this time nothing separating them. "I can't get you pregnant. We'd have to be mates already for it to take. I don't need a condom. I don't have any diseases."

All her questions and insecurities fled at the feel of Chase's thick cock sliding against her bare clit when his pelvis pressed against her. Pleasure had her shaking in his hold, clutching him frantically just to keep grounded. He rubbed their bodies together in a slow, erotic dance, their hips rocking together.

She'd worry about the future later. The man she wanted most was making thought impossible as he seduced her. Chase was doing a fantastic job too. Need and desire conquered logic.

"Say yes." His husky demand against her ear was too sexy. "Let me in."

She couldn't speak, too overcome with passion, but she managed a sharp nod. She wanted him, and no way would she deny the sexual chemistry and mind-blowing orgasm he silently promised.

He kept moving, torturing her with each stroke of his rigid flesh sliding against her clit. He felt big, extremely hard, and knew how to take a woman to the edge of losing her mind enough to beg. It was on the tip of her tongue to do just that when he shifted her a little higher.

"Wrap your legs around my waist."

She adjusted her thighs higher, wishing to feel skin instead of his shirt. Part of her regretted they weren't naked. It would mean halting what he was doing though, separating to strip, and she was too close to coming to do that. She ached from need and wasn't strong-willed enough to find patience. She had none when it came to Chase Woods.

He growled low, an animalistic sound that just turned her on more. It reminded her that he wasn't all human. It wasn't a deterrent. Instead it just heightened the desire for him to take her. His pelvis shifted away but then he was back. The broad crown of his cock nudged against her wet vaginal opening and paused.

She wiggled, rolling her hips with him poised there, wanting him. "Chase," she urged. "Please?"

"There's no going back," he swore in that same rough tone. "You're mine."

Then he shifted and grabbed her ass with his big hands while his hips slowly thrust upward.

Jasmine moaned at the feel of him entering her. He was as wide as she'd estimated and the feel of being stretched and taken was all-consuming. She was wet, ready, and the nerve endings inside her pussy sent ecstasy straight to her brain as his cock completely filled her. It barely registered that she cried out his name.

"Fuck," he snarled. "I knew it."

She wondered what that meant somewhere in the back of her mind, but then he was moving inside her, withdrawing, slamming home deep, over and over. There was nothing but their heavy breathing, sounds of their bodies slapping together, and the eager need to reach that wonderful place they both sought.

It hit Jasmine first, the climax tearing through her with such force, she wondered if she'd survive. Her body trembled and Chase followed when her vaginal muscles clamped around him, fluttering from her release.

"Son of a bitch," he panted, his body shaking too.

She felt him coming. Strong jets of semen filled her. She could feel every blast as he groaned and buried his face against her throat. It just drew out her own climax, and she was sure he felt a little bigger, as if that were possible. His thrusts tightened into sharp jerks.

Chase barely remained on his feet. It was a miracle his knees hadn't buckled but he'd been too afraid of Jasmine getting hurt if they crashed to the floor. She was his weakness in every sense, both physically and emotionally, the way he felt with her in his arms.

He'd known she was special the moment they'd met, and those indications had grown with every minute they'd spent together while searching prospective properties. It had been tough walking away from her when their business concluded, but she'd been too sweet to horrify by introducing her into his world.

He'd chosen to let her go rather than damage her innocence about all things Other. It would have been impossible to hide his true nature from her if they'd dated. He wouldn't have been able to keep his hands off her, and she would have noticed when his eyes changed color and his fangs grew during the heat of passion. Making her forget by controlling her mind had been an option, but long-term exposure to memory wipes could damage her sanity.

The rogue had changed all that. She could have died, and Chase wouldn't allow it to happen again. Her job put her at risk of meeting unpleasant strangers and giving them opportunity to harm her when they were alone. He should have seen it coming, but he'd been too focused on protecting her from the harsh reality that humans were lower on the food chain than they assumed.

Any residual doubts of her being his mate were gone. His werewolf traits weren't usually dominant but they had flared to life with a vengeance. The animal inside him recognized her for who she was—*his*.

His dick was aching—swollen still, even after coming so hard—and wouldn't be leaving Jasmine's snug pussy anytime soon. *I get it*, he told that part of himself. *She's mine. I'm paying attention.*

It was tough to turn around and walk to the bed. He really did feel shaky and weak. It was another symptom of her being his mate. Nature's way of bitch-slapping the toughest of his kind came with physical symptoms to emphasize it, making them realize they weren't complete without someone to share their lives with.

He stretched out on the mattress with Jasmine on top of him. She didn't protest, just shifted her legs to straddle his. Her rapid breathing slowed as she recovered, and he yanked up the nightshirt to stroke his fingers down her back and ass. She had a nice one, and he'd marked it up a little when he'd gripped her too firmly. His blood inside her would assure there'd be no bruising, but the red imprints of his hold were there when he lifted his head to peer down.

*Bastard*. He should have taken her on the bed, made love to her instead of nailing her against the wall. She deserved better, but he'd denied himself far too long. He'd tried being noble by resisting his attraction to her. *No more*.

He'd never forget seeing her in that basement with torn flesh where she'd been bitten, her wrists raw and bleeding, and how she'd trembled in his arms when he'd held her. One more day and she wouldn't have survived. He hadn't even known she'd been in trouble.

*I should have kept tabs on her. I should have watched out for her. I should have— Fuck!* He'd left her exposed to danger, is what it boiled down to. She was his mate and he'd been too stubborn to admit the reality of it. He'd shrugged it off as strong attraction and nothing more. Seeing her so near death had been an instant wake-up call.

"How are you?" He nuzzled her cheek.

"Good."

He loved her voice, so feminine and pleasant to his ears. Her skin was soft and she had the sexiest curves. He trailed one hand to her hip, giving it a gentle squeeze. His mate wasn't bony the way most werewolves and vampires tended to be. She'd been right about the women who frequented the club. They were too perfect, thanks to their bloodlines. Or because of plastic surgery, if they were groupies there for the thrill of living dangerously. The humans thought it was just a place to meet rich, handsome men in the Goth scene, and were interested in having sex with them in hopes of a fun time or a benefactor. They weren't aware they were volunteering to be late-night snacks for any vamp whose eye they caught.

Jasmine was all his, perfect just the way she was, and he'd make sure that didn't change. He could protect her by keeping her hidden inside his den. No way did he plan to expose her to the people he knew. His vamp bosses were trustworthy but other vampires were pricks. They viewed humans as the weaker species, only good for drinking and fucking. There were rules in place to stop them from killing for either purpose, but she'd view vamps as monsters. He could relate. Sometimes he hated their cold indifference to anyone they believed inferior.

He cringed when thinking about his pack. He'd never intended to become their leader, but they'd smelled the wolf inside him. Their alpha had challenged him the moment he'd taken the job as head of security at the club, refusing to take orders or back down. He'd had to kill the idiot when he'd refused to submit.

Some of the females in the pack aggressively pursued Chase. He wasn't interested, but Jasmine wouldn't easily be accepted as his mate. He could think of two bitches who would challenge her for the right to be at his side. *Not going to happen.*

He'd walk away from the pack, his job, everything just to keep Jasmine safe.

He and his sister would protect her if Arry ever gave away the location of his secret den. It was doubtful it would happen. They had too much in common, came from the same vampire nest where they'd been raised, and while she was a pain in the ass, he didn't count her as a threat. She just annoyed him by believing they should settle for each other as mates. He'd set her straight.

Jasmine stirred on his chest and raised her chin. Uncertainty shone in her direct stare. He easily read all her concerns. It was good that she was taking all this better than he had guessed she would. Screaming and crying had been options he'd considered.

"You're safe here with me. I'd never allow anyone or anything to hurt you."

"What do you really want from me?"

It was a tough question. The answer would scare her. *Everything.* "Your life as you knew it is gone. The rogue might have friends. I didn't find any indications of anyone else living with him, but it's a real possibility that someone is keeping tabs on him. They would seek revenge. You could become a target."

Dismayed thoughts hit him in waves. She'd worked hard to buy a house she loved. Her family wasn't close but she worried about never speaking to them again. Real estate was all she knew. Financial concerns came next.

"Enough," he ordered. "I have more money than we could spend. You don't need to return to your office. I know you enjoyed it but it's too dangerous to go back to the life you had. I am the alpha of a werewolf pack, and we're always accepting new members who need homes. You could help find housing for them to avoid becoming bored. You'll be able to call your family and friends sometimes. It would be best if you tell them you fell in love and married someone from another country. I can handle the cell phones to block our location. I'm good at that. Your house, well...I'm sorry. You'll have to sell it, but I think you'll love this one after you take a tour."

"Married?"

She was stunned and it amused him more. "Mated is married. We could have an official ceremony if you want. I'm not opposed. Though, what's a piece of paper and some guy saying words compared to the kind of bond we'll have?"

"I don't know what that means."

"It's deeper than anything you could imagine. You'll learn soon enough though." *Just as soon as you agree*. He didn't want to rush her but he wanted to seal the bond. He closed down his ability to read her, swamped by how rapidly she could come up with new things to worry about. "It will be fine."

"Says you." She tried to wiggle away but his arms hooked around her waist to hold her secure.

"Kiss me."

"I know how that ends. Are you going to keep seducing me until I agree to stay here?"

It was a great plan. "Maybe." He chuckled. "I could do worse things." He hated the fear that ghosted in her eyes. "It was a joke. You have to believe I'd never hurt you."

"I kind of do, but we've spent so little time together and I haven't seen you for all these months. You didn't even call...but you want to get married? That's kind of nuts."

"Welcome to my world." He rolled, pinning her under him. She gasped but didn't fight when he lowered his mouth to her throat. "Wrap your thighs around me. You won't regret it."

The swelling had gone down but they were still joined at the hips. He loved being inside her welcoming body. She fit him perfectly, blew his mind, and he wanted her again. Jasmine lifted her thighs to press against his waist and her calves settled across his ass. He began to move slowly, kissing her lips and neck. Her moans of pleasure spurred him on.

*No, seducing her isn't a bad plan at all.* He'd do anything to assure she'd stay and be his. He lifted up slightly, adjusted the angle of his cock sliding in and out of her to make sure the shaft rubbed against the still-swollen bundle of nerves at the top of her pussy. Louder moans came, and her vaginal walls clamped tightly around him. He had to fight the pleasure to avoid embarrassment. He was ready to come as if he were an untried teenager again.

Jasmine was so hot, so wet, and so his. She was heaven and hell, temptation and salvation. He'd spent a solitary life, knowing he'd never completely fit in with a pack or a nest after his mixed bloodlines became more pronounced. He couldn't shift at all, and didn't stand a chance of taking a dominantly werewolf mate. They feared he wasn't warm enough to love or feel deep emotions, and instead was too fixed on his need for blood.

They were wrong. The woman under him was the most important thing in his life, and would remain that way until death claimed him.

Her muscles tightened more until he clenched his teeth, fighting to move inside her without losing his control. He leaned in, so his mouth could reach her breast. Suckling on her taut nipple, he used his teeth to nip her. It was enough to send her over the edge as she cried out, clawing at him with her fingernails. Her pussy milked his shaft until he threw back his head, let go, and filled her with his seed.

# Chapter Four

Jasmine woke alone in the big bed. The fire had been tended recently, the flames high and bright in the room. Chase must have covered her with the sheet, since the last thing she remembered was him making love to her until she'd passed out. She sat up and glanced around.

The room was big, with brick walls and portions of old oak-wood paneling. It was tastefully furnished with dark antiques. The dresser was massive and there was a matching wardrobe. A door to a bathroom was open. The two closed doors next to it were probably closets.

Her wrists were unmarred as she closely studied them. Not even a faded scar from her injures remained. The infected area on her shoulder where she'd been bitten by the rogue had healed as well. Pink, healthy skin denied any proof of the attack. The other wounds had disappeared too. Chase had healed her.

The handsome man she'd obsessed over was part werewolf, part vampire. It screamed insanity but she believed.

She shoved the covers back and put on the nightshirt Chase had relieved her of during one of their bouts of sex. The stone floor was cold under her bare feet as she padded to the bathroom. It was a nice room with a Jacuzzi tub. She longed for a bath but showered instead.

A new toothbrush had been left on the counter for her use. It touched her that Chase had obviously thought about her needs. He'd also left folded clean clothes next to it. She eyed the oversized T-shirt and boxers, assuming they were for her. They hung on her a little due to his size, but were comfy, and after brushing her wet hair, she reentered the bedroom. He hadn't returned.

Hunger and curiosity drew her to the bedroom door. She gaped a little at the thick metal door and the locks on it. She gripped the knob, half expecting it to be locked, but it turned without difficulty. The door was heavy when she pushed, and revealed that instead of just a typical frame, there were deep-set ridges, as though it could be sealed air-tight when closed.

The fact that she hadn't been locked in implied she wasn't a prisoner, surprising her. It stunned Jasmine further when she realized she was underground, and she followed a hall toward an open doorway. Now that she thought about it, she couldn't remember seeing any windows in Chase's bedroom or bathroom.

A surprise waited as she realized it wasn't another door at the end of the hall, but instead a wall. She pushed against it, stepped into a basement, and turned to study the wine racks attached to the front of the wall. All but two of the bottles were dusty, as if they hadn't been touched in years. When the wall was closed, the hallway and bedroom would be concealed to the casual eye.

Jasmine glanced around. The rest of the basement was large, appeared old, and a musty scent hung in the air.

The stairs were solid stone, reminding her of a castle. Part of her feared she wasn't in the town where she'd been raised anymore. There was a black hole in her memory between Chase finding her and reaching his home. Had he taken her out of the country?

Again, the door at the top was metal and thick. It creaked slightly when she eased it open to peer at a big, modern kitchen. Sunlight streamed through a window. She padded over to look out into dense woods.

"You shouldn't be up."

The feminine voice startled her. She spun, gaping at the brunette from the night before, whom Chase had claimed to be his sister.

"I'm Jenny. You're Jasmine." She smirked. "I guess 'J' names are popular."

"Where is Chase?"

"He had some business to attend to. He'll be back in a few hours." The woman's gaze dropped to her waist. "Hungry? I can hear your stomach rumbling."

"That's weird." Jasmine regretted saying it the moment the words were out, not wanting to offend.

"You'll adjust to keen hearing once you're fully mated. It will enhance your senses all around." Jenny pointed to a table. "Have a seat. I hope you don't mind cereal. I don't cook unless my brother demands it."

A hundred questions popped into Jasmine's head, but she settled for a few while she watched the woman prepare a quick breakfast. "I could do that myself."

"It's easier if I just do it. You don't know your way around the kitchen yet." Jenny glanced at her. "But you'll need to learn at some point."

"You live here then? Why would Chase tell you to cook? Do you work for him?"

"He's my protector, so I do whatever I'm told. It beats living on the streets and he's good to me. He isn't around much, but I suppose that will change now that he has you." The woman stared at her.

"Protector?" A few hundred more questions resulted.

"Our mother really loved to seek out older vampires, the stronger the better, so we got the vamp genes from them. It made some of the werewolves we lived with nervous, knowing we needed so much blood to survive. Mates don't mind you sinking fangs into them, they kind of get off on it, but they get testy if you drink otherwise. Blood banks weren't around where we come from."

"Where is that?"

"It doesn't matter. When we were older our mother became a companion to a vampire so we lived with a nest." Jenny put a bowl of cereal in front of her. "Eat. Ask Chase your questions."

"He's not here," Jasmine pointed out.

"Too bad for your curiosity then. I have things to do outside." Jenny left through the back door.

*So much for us becoming friends.*

Jasmine ate, rinsed the bowl, and then washed it. She wasn't sure if she was allowed to explore the house, but no one had said she couldn't. Chase had mentioned it was her home too.

The first floor of the house was big, obviously a mansion built in the forties, from the architectural details. Some were confusing, as if parts of

244

the house had been remodeled sometime in the seventies. The formal dining room was dusty and it seemed no one had used it in a really long time. One door was locked. The living room had more modern furniture and a big-screen television. A small sitting room held tons of older leather-bound volumes of books in the built-in shelves. Two bathrooms were located on the first floor as well, and she paused at the steps, peering up the curved staircase to the second floor.

"Please don't go up there."

Jenny startled her again, and Jasmine spun around. She rested her hand over her racing heart. "You scared me. I didn't hear you come in."

"I'm quiet. It's the predator in me."

"Um, I'm not sure how to respond to that."

A smile curved the brunette's lips. She was pretty, with blue eyes very similar to Chase's when they glowed, but slightly paler in color. "It's what we are. We may appear human, but never forget things aren't what they seem." She jerked her head toward the stairs. "That's my space up there, and I like my privacy. I can't outright order you to never go to the second floor, but I'd appreciate it if you didn't. Chase doesn't like to sleep above ground. It's probably because of what happened twenty years ago."

"What happened?"

"Vampires attacked us. They knew what we were and tried to kill us. It was a deadly mistake." She chuckled. "They sent only five of them after us."

"Five vampires?" Jasmine was taken aback.

"They should have sent twice that many if they were serious about killing my brother and me."

"So what does that have to do with sleeping upstairs?"

"They came in through the windows of the home we used to live in. It was a full breach in the dead of night." Jenny waved her hand to a chair. "Sit."

Jasmine took a seat on one of the sofa benches in the entryway. They weren't the most comfortable things but they were attractive. Jenny sat on the opposite one ten feet away.

"I refuse to give up having a real bedroom with windows, fresh air and sunshine. My brother feels more secure underground. Fewer points of entry in case of another attack. That's where he lives most of the time. Under that club he works at, they supposedly have a lot of underground chambers, but that could just be rumors. It's not as though he's ever taken me there, so I'm not certain if it's true."

"You don't like the club where he works?"

"It's owned by two vampires." Jenny watched her as if she were something fascinating. "Did you meet my brother there?"

"No. I was his realtor. He bought some land."

Jenny nodded. "I'm glad. I'd hate to think he'd accept leftover goods."

"What does that mean?" Jasmine wasn't sure if she really wanted an answer or not.

"The women who frequent that club are playthings for the vamps. They fuck them, bleed them, and mess with their minds so they forget everything but the sex." She paused. "It doesn't even have to be good sex, but they can make them believe it was the best they ever had so they return again and again. I've heard that's how they keep a steady food supply."

It was a little disturbing. "And Chase?"

"What about him?"

"Does he do that? Have sex and feed from women at the club?"

"Not anymore, if he ever did." Jenny smirked. "You have no clue about mates, do you?"

"I didn't even know vampires or werewolves were real until last night."

"He wouldn't bond with you if he wasn't sure you were the one he wanted. It's extremely rare for a mate to cheat. They'd have to be mentally unstable and heartless. Your pain would become his, and vice versa. It's kind of like shooting yourself in the foot. Isn't that the saying? The bond amplifies emotions, passion, and nothing else can compare to that. It would be unsatisfactory if he nailed another woman."

"I'll take that for a no. Why is Chase's bedroom hidden? Because of the attack? I saw the fake wall."

"Yes, it's to protect him, and now you, in the event of another attack. There are four inches of steel and concrete surrounding his sleeping area. No one would be able to breach it without a lot of work and time. We have dangerous enemies. Chase and I argue often about my preference to sleep upstairs, but he's not here enough to make me comply with his wishes. I spent too many years living underground as a child. I won't continue to do it as an adult just in case a few assholes attack us."

"Like the rogue vampire who grabbed me?"

"Try Chase's own pack and the bloodsuckers in this area. He can never let his guard down around the club members. Lethal and Blaron have extended Chase their protection as their head of security, but not all vamps are sane."

"I'm confused," Jasmine admitted. "What does protection from this Lethal and Blaron mean?"

"They are his vampire friends, and their protection means they've warned other vampires to never target Chase because he's a mixed breed. That doesn't mean all of them will listen."

"Do vampires hate mixed races?"

The other woman licked her lips and clasped her hands on her lap. "We're stronger in a lot of ways than vampires or werewolves. It means we could kill them. None of them are comfortable with that. Vampires can't day walk without burning to a crisp, while the sunlight only gives us a tan. They resent that we have that ability, and they know we could attack them when they're at their weakest. We can do everything they can do but we're *more*."

Jasmine understood. "And the werewolves?"

"We can't shift, but we have all their other abilities, plus the vampire traits. Most packs living within the cities work for the vamps, and the pack members naturally attempt to follow the strongest wolf. Chase's scent is wolf, despite not being a full-blooded one. And he's very strong. Any alpha would have to challenge Chase. Werewolves respect strength and dominance the most."

"But you said they posed a danger."

"Chase scares the shit out of them. Any of them would take him out if they were able. They're never going to completely trust him to put them first because he's not fully wolf, yet they can't help but follow him."

"Have any of them attempted to kill him?"

"A few."

"What happened?"

"Chase killed them first."

The words were said so simply, without any emotion. A chill ran down Jasmine's spine. "That's horrible."

"It's survival of the fittest." Jenny stood. "He's home." Her gaze turned. "Hello."

Chase leaned against the wall just inside the room, and appeared to have been there for a while, judging by his relaxed stance. His eyes were another matter, the blue nearly glowing as he regarded his sister with a cold stare.

"What are you doing?"

"Answering her questions."

A deep growl rumbled from him. "You know better."

His sister lowered her chin and gaze. "I apologize. I didn't think you'd mind."

"Bullshit. You didn't expect me back so fast and didn't hear me enter the house. Go upstairs and stay there until dinner. We'd like steaks, and you're cooking."

"We don't have any. I bought chicken."

"Then go back to the store."

She nodded quickly. "Of course." Jenny fled up the stairs.

Jasmine got to her unsteady feet, a little afraid and nervous. Chase watched her, unmoving.

"I asked her those questions. Get angry at me if you're upset."

He scowled.

"She's your sister, not your servant. *You* go to the store if you want steaks, and I'll cook them."

It was slightly scary when he pushed away from the wall and stalked closer. He had exchanged his jeans for black leather pants that molded across muscular thighs and lean hips. The black cotton shirt outlined his broad shoulders, chest and muscular arms where it stretched tight around his upper body. He stopped a foot away. They almost touched.

Jasmine had to tilt her head to keep eye contact with him, a reminder of how tall he was. Her fear increased as the silence grew uncomfortable. "She didn't do anything wrong." Her voice came out soft—a whisper—but she refused to back down the way his sister had. "I had questions and you weren't here to answer them."

"Don't interfere again with Jenny. She knows the rules."

"Is this how mating works? I'm supposed to do everything you say? Are you going to punish me if I disobey?"

He shook his head. "I already told you I'd never hurt you, and you can always speak your mind."

"Good. I planned to, regardless of how you'd react. I'm not the submissive type. You were just a jerk to your sister."

His lips twitched. "I see."

"She said she doesn't work for you, but you just treated her as though she does. Worse, actually. I have a housekeeper that comes in a few days a week, and I'd never speak to her that way. I'd politely ask her to do something instead of just snap out orders."

"Any other suggestions?"

"There shouldn't be any rules concerning your sister and me talking. This mate thing is like marriage. That's what you said. That would mean she's going to be my sister-in-law if I agree, right?"

"Yes."

"Then there shouldn't be any rules about us talking."

"Fine."

It surprised her that he'd caved so easily. "You mean that?"

"I'm not accustomed to being corrected." Amusement sparked in his eyes. "I apologize."

"I think you should tell that to your sister."

"I will." He lifted his hand and used his fingertips to caress her cheek. "How did you sleep?"

"Great."

"You've eaten."

"How did you know that?"

"By smell. You had cereal with milk."

Jasmine covered her mouth. "Do I have bad breath? I'm sorry."

"I love that brand of cereal, and I drink milk."

*And blood.* She wasn't about to forget that. "You really do eat food then?"

He peered into her eyes and she felt something inside her head. It was a faint tingle at the back of her mind.

"Vampires don't need to eat food but some of them do. They enjoy the taste of it and some believe it keeps them more human to partake in the experience. Werewolves eat a lot of food because they need it to survive. I love my meals, and yes, I drink blood as well. I need both." He paused. "It wouldn't be good if I didn't drink blood. My body needs it or there are side effects that would eventually kill me."

"You're reading my mind again." She wasn't comfortable with it and placed her hand on his chest. It was warm and firm. "Stop."

"Sorry." He shrugged. "It's another adjustment I need to make. It comes naturally to me. I don't mean to invade your privacy or make you uncomfortable."

"It's not fair. I can't read *your* thoughts so just stay out of my head."

"I'll try."

"Do you mean that?" The tingling stopped as if something withdrew from her mind. "I felt that!"

"What?" He frowned.

"You leaving my head."

The tingling returned sharply and she pushed at him. "You're doing it again, aren't you? Get out."

He stepped back. "Amazing."

"Get out!"

The tingling stopped.

"You can feel it. It must be my blood inside you."

"That would do it?" She wondered what else had changed about her.

"Yes. I gave you a lot. You were severely injured. Your organs were shutting down." His hand wrapped around the back of her neck as he drew closer. "May I attempt something?"

"Stay out of my head."

"Not that. I want to see if you can read my thoughts."

"I can't do that."

"You might." He paused. "Close your eyes and clear all thoughts away."

Jasmine hesitated but then did as he asked. It took her time to push back all the questions she still had. She hadn't thought it was possible to actually read minds but that belief wasn't set in stone anymore since Chase had proven otherwise.

"Can you hear me?"

"Of course."

"Damn!"

The deepness of his voice surprised her and she opened her eyes to look at him. "What's wrong? My hearing is fine."

253

"Honey," he whispered, "I didn't say that aloud."

"Say what?"

He stared at her.

"Say what aloud?"

His eyes narrowed. *Can you hear me?*

Jasmine gasped, almost tripping on her own feet when she stumbled back. No sound came from Chase but his voice was inside her head all the same.

"I'm shouting in my mind but you heard that, didn't you?" he asked aloud.

"Yes."

"It's my blood. I knew I probably gave you too much."

"What does that mean?" It was a frightening moment. "Am I turning into what you are?"

Anger tensed his features. "It's the damn vampire traits." He suddenly closed the distance and gripped her chin, forcing her head up. His other hand touched her face, pulling down her bottom eyelid for a second. "Shit."

"What?" Alarm was a mild description for what she felt.

"I gave you too much. You're slowly turning."

"Turning into what? What you are?"

"Vampire."

That wasn't good. She didn't need to be told that, since he paled and his voice deepened into a snarl. Panic rose but she tried to tight it down, to remain calm. Freaking out wouldn't do anything but make the situation worse.

"I told you that I'd give you time, but this changes things. We have to mate or you're going to actually die."

"You gave me blood to save me. Now it's killing me?"

"It would be a vampire death. You won't remain dead."

Jasmine didn't know what to say. Her mouth opened but no words came.

"It means you'll be totally vampire if we don't mate."

"And that's bad?" *Of course it is*. The shock of what he said made her heart race, and her mind wanted to shut down to avoid the unpleasant truth.

"Do you like the sun, honey?"

She nodded, sealing her lips.

"Then yes, it would be bad. Even my blood wouldn't protect you from burning in the sunlight if we allow you to fully turn. You need more of my blood on a regular basis to keep you alive. You were too drained from that damn rogue. Shit." He released her, combing his fingers through his hair. "You were too close to death but I didn't realize this would happen. I thought my blood would just heal you."

"I don't want to have to drink blood to survive." More disturbing consequences filled her thoughts of what it would mean if she became the undead. That one just topped her list of what she'd hate most.

"It would only be mine. We've been through this."

"How long do I have? I feel fine."

"We need to mate within twenty-four hours. No longer than that or it's going to be too late. You'll go into an unnatural death and once your body dies, you will be completely vampire when you wake. I'd prefer we do it right now."

That wasn't good at all. Jasmine stared up at him and tried to remain calm. It wasn't easy. The new world she'd been exposed to was too foreign, and she had tough choices to make. Chase made it sound simple—just accept being his mate—but she wanted more time.

*Twenty-four hours.* She could almost hear the ticking of a clock inside her head. "I need to be alone. I have to think this through."

He didn't appear happy with her request, but he nodded.

# Chapter Five

Chase paced the kitchen until his sister entered, just back from the grocery store. "Thank you."

"For what?"

"Jasmine pointed out that I don't appreciate you enough for all you do."

Jenny had started putting away the steaks but paused to gape at him.

"What?" Irritation flashed inside him. "Quit staring at me that way."

She recovered and closed the fridge. "You protect me and give me a home. I don't know what I'd do if you hadn't taken me in."

"It doesn't mean I should be an ass. I have been."

"Yes." She suddenly smiled. "I wasn't sure about you taking a mate but I like it so far."

"Why wouldn't you be happy about it?"

"She's human, but I suppose it's better that you ended up with one of them instead of a werewolf."

He scowled. "What would it matter?"

"Most werewolf bitches are power hungry. I wanted more for you than to end up locked to someone who would never truly love you." She stepped closer. "Jasmine really didn't know what you were?"

"No."

"You met her before but waited until she nearly died to claim her? Why?"

"I was deeply attracted to her but she was too sweet and good to enter this life. I felt very protective."

Jenny nodded. "I understand. I met a human but avoid him now because he can't ever find out what I am."

That statement drew a frown from Chase, and a new sense of worry. "What human?"

"He's a neighbor. I've run into him more than a few times where our land meets at the river. He enjoys fishing."

"Single?"

"No scent of a woman is on him."

"Is he interested in you?"

"He's male, Chase." She grinned. "What do you think?" She sobered. "I'm really attracted to him, he smells so good and he's funny."

"Why don't you date him and see where it leads?"

"We both know what would happen. He'd either freak out if he learned what I am or, if I mated him, he'd go on a power trip. Sharing my blood would make him stronger, more aggressive, and change him for the worse. He wasn't raised with that kind of strength."

"He could be different than most."

"He might not be." She walked to the counter to unpack a bag. "You'd have to kill him, and I couldn't stand it."

"I wouldn't do that."

She peered up at him. "You'd have to if he started showing off to his human friends. Can you imagine? 'Hey, look at me. I can lift a car!'" She rolled her eyes. "Rule number one is keeping the secret of our existence."

"You could take him to live with the nest."

Jenny's expression hardened. "No."

"Mother?"

She gave a sharp nod. "She attempted to make me a vampire's companion."

Anger burned through Chase. "Why didn't you tell me?"

"I knew you'd be furious. She thinks that's what's best, Chase. I came to stay with you before she could send me to London. That's where most of the old masters live."

"I'm glad you came to me." He silently swore to have a talk with their mother. "Is that where she is? I don't keep in contact."

"Probably." Jenny shrugged. "I ditched her at the airport and haven't spoken to her since. I refuse to return to the nest, though, on the off chance that she's returned."

"You could mate with a werewolf that you like to get our mother off your back."

"No thanks!" The sadness in her eyes belied her laugh.

"Do they believe you'd be too cold to mate?"

"No. That was just you because you were always such a hard ass. I just don't find all that growling and aggressiveness charming."

"Understood. I get enough of that shit from my pack."

Her eyes sparked with real amusement. "If only our mother could only see you now. She'd be horrified that you're so sweet."

"Shut up." He playfully swatted her arm. "Don't ever tell her."

"Why do you work for vampires?"

"Blaron and Lethal aren't like the others. They are good souls."

"Some say vampires don't have those."

"Those two do. They aren't anything like our fathers."

"You mean they wouldn't abandon their companion and their young just because they're an embarrassment with their mixed bloodlines?"

His humor died. "No."

"Have you heard from your father?"

"Not since he wanted me to take out one of his vampire enemies."

"You didn't!"

He shook his head, sighing loudly. "I'm not a weapon to be used when he needs an assassin during daylight hours."

"Mine was the one who suggested to our mother that I become a companion to one of his friends. I think she still loves him."

"We don't need them. We never did. Mother needs to realize she was used by them to have offspring. The concept fascinated them, but the reality didn't fulfill their expectations."

Jenny suddenly stepped forward and pressed her hand to the center of his chest. "Do you love Jasmine?"

"I believe I do. I think I have since we first met."

"Be sure. Mating is forever."

"I've never felt anything this strong before. She makes me happy, and I look forward to a future with her. She's all I think about."

"You're such a dork." She laughed, grinning. "That's love."

"Now I just have to get her to immediately agree to mate with me."

"I thought you were going to give her time."

"She's turning."

"Shit." Jenny backed away. "Why are you standing here talking to me? Get it done. You don't want to doom her to an existence without sunshine and cause her to be weaker than she needs to be. Your mate shouldn't have to endure vampire flaws."

"I don't want her to regret it."

"I'm pretty sure she'd hate bursting into flames if she ventured outside during the day and having to drink blood on a daily basis. Jasmine doesn't know enough to make that kind of decision, Chase, but you do. Do what's best for her."

He knew his sister was right. "I'll go find her." He sniffed. "She's not upstairs."

"She headed downstairs, last I saw."

"She'll be suffering exhaustion while her body goes through the first stages of transformation."

"Go mate her."

Chase spun on his heel and stalked to the basement. "Do you mind cooking dinner in an hour? She'll be hungry."

"I've got this. You deal with her."

261

He paused by the door and turned, holding his sister's stare. "About the human you mentioned..."

"What about him?"

"I wouldn't kill him. I'd just guide him until he understood how important it was to protect you and what we are. I don't want you to be alone."

"You mean you'd scare him into submission and beat him if needed."

"Better me than someone else attempt to kill him for revealing too much."

"That's true. I'll think about it."

"Good."

He closed the door after him, following Jasmine's faint scent still lingering in the air, tracking her to his bedroom.

Jasmine stared at the ceiling, trying to make sense of everything. A slight noise drew her attention and she sat up as Chase entered his room. It was still a bit awkward between them since they didn't know each other that well. No words came to mind as he slowly stalked closer.

She noticed the way he moved, graceful but with an aura of danger. He wasn't a typical guy, had never been one, but now she knew what was so different about him. Being part werewolf and vampire was a lethal combination. His dark stare didn't frighten her though, but instead made her aware of various parts of her body. Her belly tightened and her nipples tingled. Another part of her reacted too, but she tried to ignore that.

"How are you feeling?"

She wasn't sure why he didn't just read her mind. That ability still unnerved her. "Okay. A little tired but restless. I couldn't fall asleep."

He sat on the edge of the bed, his weight dipping that side slightly as he shifted to face her. "Are your eyes sensitive to the light in here? Any numbness in your body?"

She *wished* the second part was a current symptom. Every time Chase was near, it was impossible not to notice the way her body reacted to him. It had been that way since the first time they'd met at her office. One look, and her heart rate had increased and her palms had been sweaty when they'd shaken hands.

"No. I'm good."

"It's a slow process, fortunately." He reached out but he didn't touch her. Instead his fingers traced a crease in the bedding. "We still have a bit of time."

"Before I turn into a full-on vampire?"

"Yes."

"Will it hurt?" That was a real fear.

"No. Your body will start going numb while it shuts down until you fall asleep. Your heart will stop beating at that point, and you'll die." He glanced anywhere but at her. "The next evening, after the process is finished, you'll wake."

"Will I still have a beating heart?"

"It does to a degree."

"What does that mean? It either does or it doesn't."

"It will slow to a standstill if you haven't eaten or if you're sleeping during the day. When you wake and feed, it accelerates. The fresher the blood in your system, the more it will pump at a normal rate."

"What about air? Will I need to breathe?"

"You could go without for quite a while. You technically don't need it but it isn't pretty when your body is starved of oxygen for extended periods of time."

"Can you elaborate? I don't know any real facts about vampires, just the fiction I've read in books."

"Think white or a greenish tint, depending on whether you're in a dry or wet climate." He grimaced. "We need to take care of this situation, Jasmine."

She knew what that meant. "You want to make me your mate."

"You know I do." He leaned closer, holding her gaze. "I promise you'll never regret it."

"How can you possibly do that?"

He hesitated. "I'm over a hundred years old, Jasmine."

She studied his features closely. He didn't appear older than early thirties, if even that. She bit her lip, trying to guess his point, besides shocking her.

*You can hear me when I concentrate on projecting my thoughts to you.*

The sound of his voice inside her head was as clear as if he'd spoken the words aloud.

*Believe in what you think is impossible. I'm proof of that, my love. I'll always keep my promises to you.*

Hot tears filled her eyes while she gazed into his. The brown irises turned cobalt as she watched, more proof that everything she'd once known to be factual wasn't quite true. Chase changed everything. Her life was turned upside down by his very existence.

"Take a chance," he murmured, inching closer, staring deeply into her gaze. "You have everything to gain." His voice deepened. "My love. Me. Happiness." He paused before giving her a sexy, devastating grin. "Great sex."

He wasn't playing fair. He was too close, smelled really good, and who was she kidding? She adored Chase Woods. It ran deeper than that though, had almost been an obsession since they'd first met. He was the man who'd captured her fantasies on a nightly basis, made other men insignificant in comparison, and he'd saved her life.

"I'll lose my house, my job, my friends and family if I agree, right?" *How can I do that to be with this man?* It went against everything she'd ever believed in. She was a strong, capable woman. The concept of walking away from her life to be with Chase left her feeling lost and confused.

"I know it's difficult, but if the rogue had friends, you're still in danger. They will seek revenge and come after you. They would destroy the people you care about to get to you. I'm strong enough to defeat anyone who dares come after you. You're my mate, Jasmine. I won't let anyone harm you. And there are other things to consider. How will you explain the changes you've undergone to the people you know, especially over time?

They will notice. That will put you at risk because you'd have to lie to the people you care about, causing you pain. That would hurt you more. And that would hurt me."

"I didn't ask for this." Bitterness rose over the impossible situation she'd been placed in.

"The rogue did this, not me. I walked away from you once when it was the last thing I wanted to do. I did it because your happiness came first." His tone softened, and so did the look in his eyes. "I'd do anything for you."

"Can't you fix me so I don't turn into a vampire? Can't we just date and my normal life can resume? I need more time."

Chase hesitated, a pained look crossing his handsome face. "I'd give you anything if it were possible. The rogue harmed you too much for a hospital to save your life. My blood was the only option to keep you alive. I didn't mean for this to happen, for you to start to turn into a vampire, but he'd taken you too close to death. You have only two options now—become one of them, or agree to be my mate. Either way, I can't turn back the clock and undo what has been done."

Jasmine didn't like it but she knew he spoke the truth. He had supernatural powers but time travel wasn't one of them. Putting anyone else in danger wasn't something she'd ever willingly do.

"I'd die for you, Jasmine." Sincerity deepened his voice. "I know it's asking a lot, perhaps too much, but please agree to be my mate. I swear you won't regret it. I'll do whatever it takes to make you happy. We'll work out all the issues."

Her heart squeezed tightly while she stared deeply into his beautiful eyes. He meant every word. She believed that, and the love she felt for him grew stronger until it was tough to breathe. It was a once-in-a-lifetime opportunity to be with him forever. Her concerns and fears faded as they watched each other.

Only one word came from her lips. "Yes."

She wasn't sure who was more surprised by her agreement. Becoming his mate was a lifelong commitment. He'd made sure she understood there would be no turning back, and they'd live for a very long time. Chase's smile faded as a low growl emanated from deep within his chest.

"You won't regret this."

Jasmine really hoped she wouldn't. "What do we do?"

He leaned closer. "What comes natural."

"That didn't answer my question."

"I'm going to make love to you." His warm hand gently cupped her cheek. "And when the time is right, I'm going to bleed for you. You'll drink more of my blood while I bite into you."

"Will it hurt?" It sounded oddly sexy but she didn't want to feel pain.

"Never."

The husky promise was one she wanted to believe as he closed the distance between them and his full lips brushed hers. Just the whisper-soft feel of their mouths touching was enough to make her heart race with excitement. His masculine scent and taste was arousing.

"Undress."

She leaned into him, kissing him when he would have pulled away to give her room to maneuver out of her T-shirt and boxers. She grabbed the curve of his shoulder and hung on. The shyness of their new relationship had her longing to get lost in the moment before she was naked. It would be easy to do with Chase. The man almost screamed raw sex appeal.

Another growl rumbled from him and her nipples tightened in anticipation. The sex between them had been amazing, wonderful and intense. She wanted to be that mindless again and pushed up, going chest to chest with Chase. His free hand wrapped around her back, pulling her more snugly against him.

Tongue met tongue as they explored each other with an eagerness born of pure fervor. The memories of the last time they'd touched excited her as much as his kiss. No one had ever made her as hot as he did. It might have been the forbidden delight of being with the ultimate bad boy but her ability to think faded. Whatever the reason, she squirmed, wishing she'd stripped when he'd asked so no barriers were between them.

Chase pushed her onto her back and she didn't struggle when his weight pinned her down. He tore the T-shirt at the sides, the material easily giving way to his strength. The sound of it shredding only heightened her desire to be skin to skin with him. His knuckles caressed the skin he bared, teasing her where they skimmed.

He pulled his mouth away, trailing kisses from her lips to her throat as he lifted up just enough to yank her destroyed shirt away. With one tug, he ripped away the boxers. Jasmine's fingers tangled in his hair, seeking something to hold on to. The urgency and purely primal way Chase touched her was an exhilarating experience. No one had ever wanted her as much as he did.

"Mine," he growled in a deep, sensual voice before his teeth gently nipped just under her ear.

"Yes," she agreed, out of breath, despite his tone leaving it clear that it wasn't a question. He was staking his claim and she was willing to let him.

He released her and she wanted to protest when he sat up, until she realized the cause. It was with regret that she stopped touching him too, unable to hold on as he shifted away. She instantly missed exploring his heated, muscular body. His shirt was quickly shed but he just unfastened his pants and shoved them down before he was on top of her again. Her thighs spread to give him access to settle over her once more. It made the ache to have him inside almost unbearable while she waited to see what he'd do.

His brilliant blue eyes blazed when their gazes met as his rigid cock nudged against her pussy. She was wet and ready to accept him as he entered her in one slow drive of his hips. The sensation of being filled and stretched—taken—was all-consuming to Jasmine.

Chase froze, buried deep inside her.

"Mine," he repeated. "Forever." He leaned in closer until their noses pressed together. "Agree to be my mate."

"I do." She meant it. She wanted to join with him in every way. "Take me."

A snarl came from his parted lips. That animalistic sound might have frightened her at any other time, but then he began to move in and out of her. She wrapped her legs around his waist, her heels finding purchase on the waistband of his leather pants, which were snagged on the back of his thighs. Every slide of his cock against sensitive nerve endings brought her closer to coming. Her nipples grew taut, her vaginal muscles clamping around his thick girth. The pleasure intensified until it threatened to drown her. Moans tore from her throat.

"Suck on me," he demanded. "Don't stop."

Her first thought was that he wanted oral sex, but then his wrist was suddenly against her mouth. Hot liquid with a metallic taste coated her tongue, and she knew it was his blood. At some point, without her realizing, he'd cut himself. His fingers curved around her jaw, turning her head away slightly but keeping his wrist bleeding over her parted lips.

He fucked her harder, the intense pleasure making her almost oblivious to the tingling inside her head. She swallowed his blood, too focused on the coming climax to care or think about what it meant.

His teeth clamped onto her neck where it met her shoulder and Chase bit down. His fangs punctured her skin.

Pain and pleasure blurred together, making it impossible to distinguish one from the other as sheer ecstasy struck. She exploded from within, orgasms jolting through her in an endless loop. Chase bit deeper, sucking her blood, and groaned. Their bodies were locked together, trembling, when his hips finally stilled.

*Sweetheart? Can you hear me?*

She attempted to turn her face away from his wrist but the hand holding her jaw tightened.

270

*Don't. Keep drinking. Send your thoughts to me. I'll hear you.*

It was difficult to put words together while her body still twitched and reeled from making love. Chase's voice was inside her head, his mouth still locked on her neck, so it was impossible that he'd spoken aloud. She breathed through her nose and tried to calm her erratic breathing.

*Chase?*

*We're mates. No speaking is needed. You can let go of me now. I'm going to gently withdraw my teeth. Hold still. This won't hurt. Just relax. I'm blocking your pain.*

It stunned her that he could do that. He pulled his wrist away and she sucked air into her mouth. The taste of his blood wasn't gross, but instead something she wanted more of. It worried her, but her mate was suddenly speaking inside her mind again.

*It's normal, sweetheart. You're different now but you were already changing before we formed our life bond. You'll crave my blood and it will taste sweet to you.* He pulled his fangs away and the area he'd bitten had gone numb.

Jasmine turned her head, staring up at him when he looked down at her. The way his eyes glowed was spectacular. His mouth was closed and none of her blood showed until he licked his bottom lip. His tongue was bright red.

"You're not comfortable with silent conversations." His voice came out husky. "You'll quickly adjust to our mate bond and learn to appreciate that we can communicate without others hearing us." He chuckled. "Read me. You can. Just try. It's all there for you if you open up."

271

She closed her eyes to concentrate, a tiny bit afraid of what she'd find if she were able to do the impossible.

His thoughts didn't transfer to her, but intense emotion suddenly filled her. Love. Tenderness. A deep sense of protectiveness. Passion. He wanted her again.

*Yes, I do. I'll always want you. I do feel all those things. Did you believe I'd want to mate you if I wasn't willing to die for you? You're mine, and I'm yours until the end of our time.*

Jasmine's eyes opened to stare at him in wonder. Tears blinded her as her own emotions surfaced. She loved him and he loved her back. All doubt left.

*I'm still not comfortable talking this way. I love the sound of your voice. It's sexy.*

He laughed. "Okay, sweetheart. Anything you want."

"Anything?"

His eyes narrowed as he read her mind and lowered his mouth to hers for a kiss.

*Always. We can definitely do this more. My sister and our dinner can wait. I'm going to make love to you again.*

*Good. Stop thinking at me and do it.*

# Chapter Six

Chase was tense when he reached the club. He hadn't wanted to leave Jasmine but he needed to confront the fallout of taking a mate.

The two guards stationed outside the doors whipped their heads in his direction. The sound of them sniffing seemed amplified as he approached. They'd smell the change in his scent now that Jasmine was his mate. Her scent was mingled with his.

The one on the left took a step back, his gaze instantly dropping. The one on the right growled, shock clear in his dark eyes.

The threat was clear. Chase didn't hesitate to grab Jacob by his jacket and slam him hard against the wall.

"Do you have a problem, wolf?" he snarled.

"No." Jacob's eyes flared before he dropped his gaze, darting it everywhere but at Chase's face.

Chase dropped the werewolf to his feet and stepped back, releasing him. "Good. You're my enforcer. I expect you to respect my decision *and* my mate. I'll leave it to you to notify the pack." He growled low in his throat. "Can I count on you to dissuade anyone from causing trouble? I want the truth."

"Of course." Jacob gave a sharp nod. "You're my alpha."

"Don't forget it," Chase warned. He glanced at Paul. "Do you have a problem?"

"No." He shook his head wildly, his chin tucked. "Congratulations. When do we get to meet her?"

"When I believe no one is stupid enough to challenge me or her."

Both werewolves were silent. Chase paused for a good minute but they refused to speak. It was going better than he hoped. Otherwise he'd have already had to fight and kill at least one of them.

"I'm going inside now. Hold your posts. Has there been any trouble tonight in the club?"

"No, alpha." Jacob lifted his head and met his gaze, before glancing away. "It's been quiet."

"Full house but no disturbances," Paul added. "Just the way you like it."

Chase passed them and yanked open the door. The sound of music spilled out as he entered. All that soundproofing his friends had paid for worked. Flashing lights from the ceiling jumped around the dance floor to spotlight the swaying bodies. He breathed through his nose, taking in all the humans and vamps. He sniffed again, identifying the bartender and other members from his pack.

A few of the vamps turned their heads as he slowly strolled through the club toward the offices. Their senses of smell would note the change in him as well.

Marcus, one of the club regulars, stood, blocking his path.

"Who is she?"

"None of your concern. Do you want to move or shall I put you back in your seat?"

The bloodsucker grinned, revealing his fangs. Blood coated his tongue, proof that the human at his table had already been tasted. "You know what they say about mates, freak. They are a weakness—and now you have one." His pupils dilated. "I won't forget to share the good news with your fans."

Chase swiftly gripped him by his throat. "And I never forget a threat," he growled. "You're dead if you or any of your friends attempt to go after my mate."

"Is the lad being a problem?"

The deep voice with the Scottish brogue came from behind him. "No, Blaron." It annoyed Chase that his friend could move so silently that he hadn't heard his approach, but the noise in the club had helped mask it. "Just making friendly conversation with one of the customers."

"Ah." The big kilt-wearing vamp stepped closer, pausing next to him. "Marcus, a bonny lass is at your table and you're bothering my friend? Shame on you. That's the thing I find most annoying with the younger generations. Stupidity and rudeness run rampant."

Chase squeezed enough to prevent the vamp within his grasp from responding. It would have crushed a human's throat but the bloodsucker just winced in pain.

"I resent that. *I'm* younger, but I have manners. His head is still on his shoulders. I know the staff hates to clean blood off the floors, and it would spook the guests who aren't aware of what he is," Chase returned.

"True." Blaron grinned, fingering the long blond braid that fell over his shoulder. "I assume this is about the lass you took as a mate?" He glanced at him. "I never forget a scent. I've smelled her before on you."

"Let's discuss this in a more private setting." He didn't want his friend to give anyone hints on the identity of Jasmine. She had family and friends that his enemies could target.

"Sure." The older vamp's humor disappeared as he circled around Marcus to stand at his back. He leaned in to put his lips near his ear. "You're in my house, and this is my friend. Am I clear, young'un?" He clamped his hand on the vampire's shoulder. "Should I allow him to rip off your head to save me the trouble?"

Marcus whimpered, panic widening his eyes.

"That's what I thought." Blaron stepped back. "The staff hates cleaning up piss, too. Drop him before he wets his pants."

Chase grudgingly released Marcus. The frightened vamp would have returned to his table, but Blaron halted him with a chilling glare. "Anyone who threatens or goes after someone under my protection won't see the following night. Am I clear?"

"Yes." His voice came out raspy, but at least Marcus could talk.

"That includes mates. His, specifically, and any of her kin. Are you hearing me?"

Marcus gave a sharp nod.

"And don't be thinking you can have someone else do your bidding. Anyone so much as breathes on them, and I'm blaming you."

Marcus nodded again.

276

"Now go sit your arse down and be nice to that bonny redhead waiting for you. She's a looker, and I want her to return here often. It's good for business." Blaron stepped to the side. He glanced at Chase and jerked his head in the direction of the offices.

Part of Chase was relieved. His friend had just announced to the entire club that his protection extended to Jasmine. Every vamp in the place would have noted the exchange.

He followed Blaron to the side doors, down a set of stairs, and beyond the noise of the club once he sealed them inside the office.

Lethal sat behind a desk, and he peered up at him with lively blue eyes. "Interesting." His nostrils flared. "The real estate agent?"

Alarm shot though Chase and a snarl burst from his mouth. "Were you having me followed? We are supposed to have trust."

The tall vampire rose to his feet, his leather pants rubbing against his chair. "Easy."

"How do you know about my Jasmine?"

"I can smell her."

"How do you know what she does for a living?" Suspicion grew.

A smirk twisted the male's lips. "I recommended her to you, remember? I've used her a few times."

Chase reacted on instinct, leaping over the desk and shoving the big bastard into a wall to pin him there with the claws that shot out from his fingertips. "You touched my mate?!" The urge to kill his friend was so strong, he barely resisted. "*Fed* from her?"

277

Lethal's blue eyes widened. "Hell no! The lass helped me buy a few homes. I never tossed her skirts up and bedded her. Nor did I bleed her."

"She didn't mention you to me."

"She wouldn't." Lethal cleared his throat and frowned. "I blurred her memory of my name and what she helped me acquire. I still paid the lass. You know I don't like anyone knowing where I buy property. They were my safe houses."

Blaron cleared his throat. "Gentlemen? Are we going to fight? Allow me to move the computers at least. It's payroll day, and nothing is worse than snarling employees bent out of shape."

Chase withdrew his claws and stepped back. "We're good."

Lethal grinned. "She's a bonny lass who will make you a wonderful mate. You hid her scent well. I had no idea you were even dating anyone."

He hesitated, glancing at them both. "It was spur of the moment. You know that rogue you asked me to hunt? She was one of his victims."

A growl sprang from Lethal. "Is she well?"

"I healed her. She will be fine." Chase rounded the desk. "She was the only one who survived. We need to keep a closer eye on missing persons' reports."

"Agreed." Blaron fingered the sword attached to his belt. "We'll dispatch those damn rogues from our city. We don't need any more problems."

"You're going to hate to hear this then." Chase sat in a chair. "My pack isn't going to take it well that I mated."

278

His friends took seats too. "What makes you believe that?"

He held Lethal's curious gaze. "My lead enforcer backed down when I gave him the opportunity to challenge me outside, but he didn't want to. He's not happy my mate isn't a member of the pack, and that means I can't trust him as far as I can throw him. It will lead to strife in the ranks and they'll eventually come after me once some of their anger overtakes their fear."

"Aye," Blaron mused. "They will. It would have bonded you to them if your mate happened to be a werewolf from the pack. They've been looking for a reason to spill your blood since you arrived. So have most of our regular customers. Your bloodlines are an issue. You're of both worlds, but they only see you as different."

"I'm giving my notice."

Lethal reached up to shove his long black hair over his shoulder. "No. We refuse to accept it. You're our head of security and you'll stay in that position."

"We're friends." Blaron smiled. "You can't leave us in the lurch. We trust you."

"It's going to make your club a target if they can't find my den."

"Is that where you're hiding the bonny lass?" The dark-haired vamp grinned. "With your sister—the one you refuse to allow us to meet?"

"They are both safer far from here." Chase sighed. "I don't want my trouble coming to your door."

"We love trouble." Blaron winked. "It gets too boring around here otherwise. We're friends 'til the end, but I'm not preparing to die." He glanced at the other vampire. "Tell him we have his back."

"You just did." Lethal chuckled. "It goes double with me."

Chase studied them. "You don't owe me for saving your asses when you decided to visit the pack I lived with. You didn't know about the war between wolves and vampires. It started before you came to America. You're used to the city packs that depend on you for steady work. That pack has a long memory, and they hated you both on sight. They shouldn't have blamed you for a history you had no part in."

"They decided to behead us but you got us out of there." Blaron leaned back in his chair. "You were the first mixed breed we'd ever met. We're friends, and we stand together when trouble comes." He patted his trusted sword again. "I say we set a trap and wait to see who comes."

Chase didn't like the idea. "It would be easier if I just didn't work for you anymore."

"We trust you, Chase." Lethal grinned. "Friends don't abandon friends in bad times. They stick together. You're the best one for the job, so forget quitting."

"Shit." Chase eyed both men with dread. He knew them well and they'd already made up their minds. They wanted to help him whether he wanted it or not. "And if it means losing an entire pack? Who is going to guard you when you sleep? I can't do it every single day. I have a mate who might not enjoy being alone all the time."

"We have our safe houses. I don't plan on sleeping below the club anytime soon." Blaron stood. "Let's plot our enemies' demise. I'm sure they are doing the same."

Chase stared at Lethal, hoping he'd be the voice of reason.

He rose to his feet with a deadly look on his features and gripped his sword, strapped it on before grabbing a leather trench coat. "To battle, men." He chuckled. "May the blood of our adversaries flow so we may be victorious."

"You both are nuts...but I'm glad you're on my side." Chase pushed out of his seat and glanced at them. "I think I have an idea how we can lure them out tomorrow night. Let's go upstairs and handle the customers. Afterward, we'll talk strategies."

\* \* \* \* \*

Jasmine set aside the book and slid off the bed to peer at Chase when he suddenly stormed into the bedroom. It was apparent he was upset, but she didn't know why. His gaze fixed on her as a deep, scary growl burst from his parted lips.

"What did I do wrong?" She hated the fear that quickened her pulse.

"Nothing." He took a deep breath. "It was a rough night and the drive home didn't calm me any. I'd hoped it would."

"What happened?" Strong emotions of anger hit her suddenly but she had a feeling they were coming from him.

The sight of him shrugging off the leather jacket to reveal muscled arms in a black tank top was one she admired, distracting her from the feelings she picked up from him. Chase's body always had an effect on her. He tossed the jacket across the back of the chair by the door, sat down hard and tore off his biker boots. They were dumped on the floor.

"Chase?"

His intense gaze lifted to meet her curious stare. "Don't freak out." Then it was as if a mental door closed between them, and suddenly she couldn't pick up anything he felt.

*That's not good.* She wondered why he thought she'd be alarmed, but then realized he was snarling his words. "I know you're not going to hurt me. I believe that. I'm not going to run screaming from you just because you're in a bad mood."

"That's not what I meant." He stood, reached down to fist his shirt, jerked it up his body, and tossed it away.

The bruising on his ribs was horrible enough, but the smeared blood on his side had her stumbling closer. "What happened?"

"It's not mine. The damn jerk bled all over me though. The black clothes hide it well enough, but it's all over me where I couldn't wash it off without undressing."

To prove his point, he removed his belt and unfastened his leather pants. The red stain continued down one hip and thigh. Jasmine's mouth fell open.

"One of my pack decided to jump me in the parking lot. He thought it would be a good time to challenge me, after I'd already fought some vamp ass when a few of them got out of line with customers at the club." He bent, pushing the pants completely off. "I'm guessing he figured I'd be too tired to win."

Jasmine inched closer to get a better look. The blood trailed all the way down to his knee, and it was worse when he turned to stalk into the bathroom. More blood covered his back, but it was brighter red and wet. Four slash marks scored his shoulder blade.

"Chase? You're hurt."

He halted by the door with his back to her. "I could have undressed in the bathroom so you didn't have to see this, but it's part of my life, and now yours. There's no sense in hiding it from you. The enforcer got in a lucky strike with his claws before I got hold of his throat. I'll heal by morning. Everything is going to be okay." He glanced at her then. "I'm fine."

Jasmine stood statue-still while Chase continued into the bathroom. The sad expression on his face didn't convince her. He'd left the door open so she didn't hesitate to follow him inside. The clear glass door allowed no privacy as she watched him stand under the showerhead.

"One of your pack tried to kill you?" She wanted clarification.

"Yes. It happens from time to time."

"He. Tried. To. Kill. You." She was horrified. "That's not okay. I thought packs were supposed to be like family."

He avoided looking at her as he dumped soap on a washcloth to scrub at the blood. "They are. Human family members kill each other too. Our worlds aren't so different in that regard."

"Your world sucks."

That drew a quick grin from him as he shot her an amused look. "Only the vampires."

"I'm not joking around. Someone tried to kill you." The rest of it sank into her perplexed mind. "Is he going to come after you again?"

"No." His gaze narrowed. "It was a fight to the death."

*You killed him.*

"I walked away. He wouldn't give up. I had to carry him to my car and go dump the body."

Her knees weakened, causing her to sway a little on her feet and grab hold of the counter for support. Fear hit hard, more so than horror. She figured that would come later. "Are the police going to be looking for you?" She thought quickly. "We need to leave the country." She'd flee with him. She might not be sure everything being a mate entailed, but it was for life. Losing Chase wasn't an option she wanted to consider.

"We?" Eyebrows lifted. "You'd come with me?"

"Of course."

She pushed away the reason they needed to leave. It made it easier to handle. He'd saved her life and she'd made a serious commitment by agreeing to be his mate. He also wasn't human so, in her mind, normal rules didn't apply to him. It had been a case of self-defense.

His features softened. "Humans don't get involved in our business. There won't be any missing person's report filed. His family or friends will make it appear as if he left the country if anyone questions what happened to him. It's what we do to stay under the radar." He paused. "It's his family and friends I have to worry about, along with any other wolves in the pack who have a problem with what I've done."

"Because you had to kill him? Won't they understand he attacked you and you had no choice?"

"No, challenges and the resulting deaths are expected. It's because I mated you." He turned in the shower, facing away to duck his head under the spray.

Guilt nagged at Jasmine. She'd mourned the loss of her life as she'd known it while Chase had been at work. It didn't seem fair that she had to give up her house, her career and the people she cared about to be with him. *It's no picnic for him either*, she suddenly realized. People were trying to kill him because they were together.

"What can I do?" She wanted to help him.

Chase glanced at her over his shoulder. "You could come in here and wash my back. I'll heal faster if the wounds are clean. My body won't have to fight off infection as it mends the damage."

One glance down his body had her more than willing to strip and join him. Tan, muscled skin tempted her to do more than touch his back. There had been changes since the mating, ones that she couldn't deny. Her libido seemed to have gone into overdrive. Just staring at him naked made her ache.

Her hands shook as she removed her clothes while he watched through the glass. Passion was an easy emotion to read as his eyes began to glow. They fascinated her. She slowly approached. He pushed open the door and stepped back to make room. Steamy hot water ran over her as she waited for him to reach around to secure the door.

He was so tall compared to her that she had to lift her chin to see his face. A soft growl rumbled from him and the muscles in her belly clenched. Her nipples also responded by growing taut. Desire rolled through her with a jolt. Chase inhaled and his hands gently cupped her hips.

"You're so sexy and smell so good. So mine."

All she wanted to do was reach up to cup his face and pull his mouth down for a kiss. It was difficult to remember that he was injured. "Your back."

"It doesn't hurt. Don't worry about it."

"I need to wash it."

He snarled something under his breath, but dropped his hands and turned. "Do it fast. I'm impatient."

He wanted her as much as she did him. She hadn't missed the state of his dick before he'd spun around. Chase was sporting an impressive erection that matched the rest of him—all hard, masculine perfection. The sight of the ugly slashes across his shoulder blade cooled her passion a bit as she stared at them.

"I don't want to hurt you. Should I just use water but not soap?" She reached up to unhook the showerhead from the holder, making it easier to maneuver.

He grabbed the soapy sponge and handed it to her over his shoulder. "I'll get a fever if infection sets in. It won't kill me but it's not pleasant. I need to be at one hundred percent by morning."

"Why?" She accepted it and hesitantly began to wash the wounds. His muscles tensed but he held still, making no sound.

"I have to work early in the morning. It's going to be a long day."

Part of her was hurt by that. The least he could do was take some time off to spend with her. She had a lot of adjustments to make, ones that would be easier if he were with her. "Do your bosses know you took a mate?"

"Yes."

She wondered how that had gone, but kept silent. It was a handy distraction, pondering their responses while she finished washing the gashes in his skin and rinsing away the soap. They appeared to be healing at an accelerated rate that would have been alarming if she hadn't known he was a supernatural being.

"All done. They aren't bleeding."

He spun back, grabbed the showerhead, and replaced it in the holder. "I want you."

His hands returned to her hips and she gasped when he lifted her off her feet, pinning her to the tile wall. Overpowering emotions slammed into her. The mental door had been thrown wide open with an explosive charge.

"Do you feel how much I want you?" He brushed kisses across the top of her shoulder.

Jasmine moaned, spreading her legs and wrapping them around his waist as fiery need burned bright. His passion and hers seemed to combine until all she could think about was having him inside her. She clung to him, her nails digging into his wet skin as she used her hold on him to rub against his body.

"So mine," Chase softly growled. "You need to feed."

"I ate while you were gone." It annoyed her that he'd think about food while they were touching.

"Blood."

His lips returned to her throat, the points of his fangs drawing erotic twin lines down to her shoulder. One shift of his hips, and his cock nudged against her pussy. She was wet and ready for him as he slowly entered her.

"Chase!" Raw pleasure blinded her as she closed her eyes, and he drove into her deep.

He froze there and pulled his mouth away. "Drink."

Her hips twisted as she tried to ride his cock, but he pressed against her tighter, making it impossible.

"Mine? Look at me."

Her eyes snapped open. His were glowing, staring directly at her. One hand lifted and she saw his fingernails had lengthened into claws. They would have frightened her before, but not anymore. His index finger dug into his muscular chest above his right nipple.

"Drink now if you want me."

Her mate mentally sent her waves of lust. Her mind wasn't able to block them and she cried out, hurting for him to fuck her.

"Drink," he demanded.

She sealed her mouth over the bleeding wound and the taste of blood wasn't gross. Instead, the flavor burst on her tongue, a mixture of something erotic and delicious. She moaned, hungrily sucking. A snarl tore from Chase as he adjusted to grip her hips and began to slowly thrust in and out of her pussy. Pleasure rocked through her system as his thick, rigid cock rubbed against her sensitive tissues.

All thought left Jasmine as ecstasy gripped her. She kept drinking, overloaded from his addictive taste and how wonderful he felt, until the climax struck and she had to pull her mouth away from his chest to scream out his name.

His release followed and she cried out with their thoughts linked, coming a second time when ecstasy tore through her again. She could feel his pleasure, making it her own, every jet of his semen filling her with another burst of rapture until blackness threatened to take her.

"Easy." Chase tightened his arms more firmly around her, one shelving her ass while the other curled around her waist.

Her head fell forward to rest against his shoulder as he kicked open the shower door and carried her to the counter to gently place her there. Jasmine didn't want to let him go, but she knew he wanted to dry her off and take her to bed. The link between them was wide open and while she couldn't hear his thoughts as words, she knew his intentions. Her hold loosened.

Jasmine hated the loss as he stepped back to grab towels, but he returned immediately. Big hands were gentle as they patted her dry with the thick cotton. She peered into his eyes as he looked into hers. A strong sense of love filtered through—but also fear.

"Why?"

He studied her closely with a frown. "You're confused and alarmed."

"You're afraid of something."

The link between them snapped closed. It hurt, as if he'd rejected her.

"Chase?" She cupped his face. "Don't just turn it off like that."

He bit his bottom lip and opened up to her again as he stepped between her parted legs to stand there. "I'm sorry. You're adjusting to being my mate and this bond is new to both of us. I felt your pain. I didn't mean to hurt you."

"What are you afraid of?"

His arms wrapped around her, lifted and carried her into the bedroom. "I didn't want you to see that."

"You can't possibly be afraid of *me*. I'm not going to leave you or ever betray you by telling anyone what you are."

He sat on the bed with her on his lap. "I know that. You're a new mate, and that makes you vulnerable. That worry is what you caught through our bond."

"Why?"

"You're fragile right now. In time you'll grow stronger and gain some of my abilities." He pulled her closer to his chest until they were nose to nose. "Your bone density will be tougher than a human's, you'll heal faster

290

and you'll be harder to kill. You'll be able to defend yourself better once I teach you how to fight." He smiled. "I plan to do that."

"Fight what?"

"My enemies. I have many, but I'm working on dealing with them to make you safer. They will never get near you if I have my way, but I want you to learn how to protect yourself just in case you ever need to. We'll start your training in a few weeks, when your physical changes are over."

She allowed that information to sink in. "Am I going to look any different?"

"No. Denser bones won't make you physically larger. They'll just be more difficult to break. You won't grow fangs either. I'll always have to cut my skin to feed you."

Jasmine glanced down at his chest. The scratch had already begun to heal.

"I won't have scars from feeding you. A wound has to be pretty deep to do that." He suddenly turned, coming down on top of her, where he caged her body on the bed. "Do you know what I want, Mine?"

"Why are you calling me that?"

He brushed his lips over hers before smiling. "It's what you are. Mine." His mind opened up to her and strong emotions struck.

"You want me again." She wrapped her legs around his waist. "I want you too."

# Chapter Seven

Every muscle tensed as Chase tilted his head, listening for the slightest sound. The club was unusually quiet.

"Easy," Blaron rasped from across the room. "They will come."

A human wouldn't have heard his words but they were clear to Chase. He glanced up into the rafters, where lights were strung, immediately wishing he hadn't spotted his friend standing on a narrow beam. The Scottish man wore a kilt.

"Underwear," he muttered, quickly looking away. "Wear it."

His friend chuckled.

"Aye," Lethal whispered from behind the bar. "I tell him but he won't listen. I wear pants to avoid a breeze."

"Leave me alone. I enjoy the freedom." Blaron laughed.

"I'm not enjoying the view. I never want to see that much of you again." Chase refused to look up a second time as he scanned the shadows in the club. "Did you hear that?"

"Aye." Lethal crouched out of sight. "We have company."

The scent of blood was strong as three recently fed vampires strolled into the main part of the club, their scent helping to mask the presence of his friends. Chase walked out to greet them, arms folded over his chest. "Gentlemen, the club is closed tonight. Private party."

"We heard." The brunet vamp grinned to reveal his fangs. "We came to introduce ourselves to your lovely bride. I hope we haven't missed the wedding?" He glanced around. "Where are she and the minister?"

"In the back," Chase lied, his fist tightening on the stake he hid between his forearm and ribs. "You need to leave."

The second vampire positioned himself to Chase's left. "Not without meeting your human." He inhaled. "A–positive? That's my favorite."

Slight guilt struck Chase that he'd purposely cut Jasmine with his fingernail to stain his shirt with a little of her blood while she'd slept. He'd needed to fool anyone within range that his mate was nearby. She'd never know, since he'd licked the tiny wound to heal it, but he should have asked her permission. He just hadn't wanted her to worry if he shared his plans.

"I'm surprised you can smell anything over the stench of you three. I hope you weren't feeding in the parking lot? You know it's against the rules."

The third vampire moved to his right so they nearly surrounded him. "Of course not. We fed inside the club."

A new scent reached Chase—and his shoulders tensed as he glanced at the hallway that led from the front door into the main area. Four of his pack males sauntered in. His jaw clenched and it took willpower to mute the snarl that wanted to rise.

"Feeding from my pack?" He glanced at the wolves. "Since when do you offer up a vein to vampires?"

Damon, one of his enforcers, growled. "Since you chose a human over us. Vamps are stronger when they're hyped up on our blood."

293

"You're no longer our alpha," Ronny snarled. "We've come to kill you *and* your new mate."

Fury burned inside Chase. "You mean you whored yourselves out to vamps, hoping *they* could kill me since you know you're too weak to do it." He glared at his pack members. "Which one of you thinks he's going to take my place?"

Damon stepped closer. "I will."

"Then you'll die first." Chase kept his gaze moving, watching, trying to judge which of them would strike first. "I won't be the one to do it though. That's unfortunate," he jerked his head toward one of the vampires, "but I have to deal with them first, since you made this an unfair fight by giving them an advantage with your blood."

The brunet vampire hissed. "What does that mean? You're the one who'll die. We'll let you watch us play with your mate first though, while she begs you to save her. Her screams will be the last thing you hear. Where is the little bitch?"

Chase didn't wait to be attacked. The idea of them planning to torture Jasmine was enough to send him into a rage. He moved fast, threw out his arm, and embedded the stake deeply into the vamp's chest.

The idiot appeared stunned as his eyes widened a second before lines appeared on his face and it turned an ashen gray. The skin split as he turned to dust, his solid form disintegrating.

The other two vampires weren't going to be so easy to kill, now that he didn't have the element of surprise.

Chase saw Blaron drop from the rafters to land in a crouch next to Damon. His friend's sword flashed in the dim light as he rose to his full height and ended the life of the werewolf in seconds.

Satisfaction was short-lived as both of the dead vampire's friends recovered from the shock of realizing they'd walked into an ambush.

Lethal lived up to his name as he sprinted across the room to join the fray and took out a second werewolf. The sound of bones popping as the remaining two pack members shifted wasn't a concern to Chase. His attention fixed on the two bloodsuckers intent on killing him.

One of them came at him with fangs and claws. Chase barely dodged away in time to avoid a painful slash at his throat. The adrenaline from the wolf blood they'd sucked down was going to be a problem, but nothing he couldn't handle. He'd make certain his enemies died, to ensure his mate's safety. He almost felt sorry for the stupid bastards for not understanding how deadly an opponent he'd become.

The second one leapt into the fray, and Chase shoved the stake into his chest but missed his heart. The bloodsucker screamed in pain, but managed to stagger away when Chase had to release his hold to avoid the first one grabbing him from behind. He unleashed his claws and drove them into the jerk's neck, bleeding him out a bit to weaken him.

Swords clashed with claws across the room. Chase didn't have time to check on Blaron or Lethal. His friends could handle themselves. They were old vampires with impressive battle skills. He had his own ass to worry about as the blood-drugged vampires unsuccessfully tried to corner him.

They were bleeding and hurt, but they'd be harder to kill with the wolf blood in their systems.

Jasmine's image flashed in his mind, and he howled in rage as he dodged and lashed out with his claws once more as one of the vamps came too close. He couldn't lose the fight. His enemies would track Jasmine down eventually and kill her just for the hell of it if they were able to take his life. The bad thing about living for so long was the boredom that could take hold. She would become an obsession to the bastards.

Lethal was suddenly at his back, and he beheaded one of the vampires with his sword. Chase launched himself at the remaining vampire, taking him to the floor. His claws tore through the bastard's chest as his opponent screamed. In seconds, he'd removed his heart, and watched in satisfaction as the solid body turned to ash.

He staggered to his feet and glanced around at the carnage of what had been his enemies. Four dead wolves and three ash piles were all that remained. His friends had both survived.

Lethal grinned, holding his bloodied sword. "That was fun."

Blaron's white shirt was torn and wet with blood where claws had marked his chest. "Aye. It's not over yet though." His gaze fixed on the door. "We have more company."

Six of Chase's pack mates entered the club. Four males and two females. He growled low in warning, waiting to see if they'd submit or challenge him. He wasn't surprised at seeing them. Tina led them. She was a pushy bitch who'd tried to tempt him into mating her since he'd first taken the alpha role.

"Surrender your mate to death and allow me to take her place," the she-wolf growled, her fangs showing. "Don't force us to kill you, Chase. I want you."

"The feeling isn't mutual." He snarled and glanced at the other female. Her presence surprised him. Mora was one of the most docile females in the pack, and he'd trusted her enough to make her his secretary. He'd just seen her an hour before.

Her gaze dropped when he looked into her eyes. "You too?"

Fear showed when she glanced up. "They made me," she blurted.

He could believe that. Mora was half human, couldn't shift, and had mated to another half-breed who couldn't protect her against the full-bloods.

Tina's arm flew out and knocked the smaller female to the floor. Mora stayed down and the smell of her blood filled the air. Chase shook his head, giving Tina his attention.

"You'd make a cruel alpha bitch. You're supposed to protect the weakest members, not bully and abuse them." He moved slowly, placing his body closer to Mora and getting between her and the other werewolves. "It's over."

Mora stood and moved behind him but he didn't glance back. It might be a mistake to turn his back on her but he liked the little she-wolf and her mate. They'd been the only pack members to actually welcome him when he'd arrived. The previous alpha had looked down on them for their weakened bloodlines while he hadn't, being a mixed breed himself.

"They made me steal your phone," Mora whispered. "Tina has it."

Rage gripped him as he glared at the bitch in question. "Why?"

Tina smiled. "We told her we'd kill her mate if she didn't bring it to me. She was quite helpful."

"I meant, why did you want my phone?" He had a sinking feeling that he knew.

The club doors opened and his worst fear came true as a scent reached his nose. "Son of a bitch!"

* * * * *

Jasmine was irritated as she glanced at Jenny. "I thought Chase didn't want me to leave the house? He said it was too dangerous because he has enemies who could target me. I had to promise him I wouldn't leave the house before he left this morning."

The woman behind the wheel shrugged. "Don't ask me why my brother does anything. I got the text message for both of us to come to the club, so that's where we're going. I'm not thrilled either. I hate blood bags and howlers, but my brother wants us at Mooning."

"Vampires and werewolves? Aren't you one of them?"

"I'm talking about the full-bloods. They snub our kind but they also fear us. Some will attack without provocation just because of what we are."

"Is Chase the only family you have left?"

"No. We have cousins, aunts and uncles."

"Are they living close to here?"

"No. We left the pack that most of them live with."

298

"Why did you leave?"

Jenny glanced away from the road to frown at her. "You're full of questions."

"I'm curious, and your brother isn't around to answer them. You won't get into trouble for telling me what I want to know."

A chuckle broke from her new sister-in-law. "He told me. You laid down the law. Okay, I'll share. Our people don't think we're werewolf enough to make good mates. They believe our vampire blood runs too strong, since our fathers were ancients and really powerful. They fear we're dead inside."

"Fathers?"

"We're half siblings. Chase left home before I did, but I followed him here after spending ten years with our mother. She wanted me to follow in her footsteps."

"What does she do for a living?"

"I am not talking professions. She wanted me to hook up with an ancient blood bag to give him a few children. They find it an ego boost to have the ability to create offspring if the circumstances are right, but I didn't want to become some jerk's science project."

"It sounds so cold."

"It is." Jenny sighed. "That's why I went to my brother for his protection. I met my father a few times and he's the cruelest, most vicious creature imaginable. It amazes me that my mother ever warmed to him enough to allow him to touch her. Then again, our mother isn't quite right. She's got too much of her father's blood in her."

"Who is her father?"

"An ancient blood bag. Let's just say that Gramps isn't the warm, cuddly type, either. He once grabbed Chase and took a bite out of him just to see how he'd taste. He enjoyed it enough to keep doing it until my brother grew strong enough to make him stop. No one likes to be an unwilling snack."

Horror washed through Jasmine. "Your mother allowed it?" She couldn't imagine that any woman wouldn't protect her own child.

"That's Mom." Jenny snorted. "Very maternal, wouldn't you say? Let me assure you that she's one mother-in-law you don't want to spend holidays with. Never pressure Chase into taking you to meet her."

"I won't." It was an easy promise to make. The concept of meeting someone so cold gave her chills, and made her doubt what she'd signed up for as Chase's mate.

Jenny seemed to read her mind. "Chase hates our mother, and I can't blame him. He's nothing like her, I promise. That's why I came to him for protection."

More questions filled Jasmine. "Why do you need protection? Are the men stronger?"

"They are." She nodded. "Mother Nature, or whoever you want to blame, gave them bigger bodies, more muscle, and a shitload of aggression. It's safer if we stick together." She paused. "I'm safer. He did fine on his own."

"He's pretty tough, isn't he?"

300

A smile curved her sister-in-law's mouth. "You did very well, picking him for a mate. No one will be able to care for you better."

"I want him to really love me," she admitted softly.

"He does." Jenny laughed. "You doubt it? Many females tried to lure him into marking them, but none succeeded."

"We barely know each other."

"It isn't always about how long you know someone. For us, it's more important how strongly you feel when you meet the right person. We're instinctual creatures."

"And you can read minds."

"That too. It helps us get to know someone really fast and well. He didn't make a mistake picking you for his mate."

Jasmine voiced her inner fear. "He did it to save my life."

"No. He did it because he wanted you. We're...older than we look, and we chose to leave our people. Humans die faster than we do, so death is something we've adjusted to. He would have allowed you to die if you weren't the one he wanted to mate. Don't think for a second that it was pity that prompted him to bring you home for keeps."

"Says you."

"I'm the only expert on our kind you know." Jenny glanced her way. "You'll just have to take my word for it."

"I guess I will."

"Haven't you felt it through the mate bond?"

Jasmine remembered all the sensations that had invaded her mind when Chase opened up to her. "Yes."

"He loves you. Stop rationalizing with your human side and trust your instincts. Mating bond links don't lie. It's impossible to fake emotions. You'd feel the deceit."

"Okay. Thank you."

Jenny chuckled. "Is it so hard for you to believe you mean everything to my brother after all you've seen since becoming a part of his life? Vampires and werewolves are real. True love exists, and you have that with my brother. It will last as long as you two are alive."

Jasmine silently wondered how long a life she'd lead with Chase. It was a question she wasn't sure she wanted answered. Would they have fifty years together? A few hundred? Maybe more? In the end, it wouldn't matter. Every day they had together would be one she spent with the man she loved.

The last of the sunlight faded as they drove into town. "I really hate these places," Jenny muttered, parking in the lot beside the nightclub.

"It looks pretty dead. Does it open later since it's geared toward vampires?"

"They're out and about. The nonsense about them being totally helpless while they sleep during the day only applies to the newly turned. And even *they* wake about an hour before sunset. They can't wait to leave their lairs once they can." Jenny shook her head. "I don't like this."

Jasmine glanced around at the few cars in the parking lot. "Maybe they don't open until later, since I'm sure they probably don't close until just before dawn."

"Maybe." Jenny didn't sound so sure. "It's not as if I frequent blood-bag hangouts. Let's go. Chase doesn't like to be kept waiting."

"Are you sure we should go in there?" A bad feeling hit Jasmine.

"He wouldn't order me to drive you here if it was dangerous. Maybe they're closed tonight so he can introduce you to his friends. He swears the two blood bags who own this joint aren't soulless pricks."

"That makes me feel better." Jasmine hoped the sarcasm wasn't missed as she climbed out of the car and took in the parking lot once more.

Jenny stared at her from across the roof as she jerked her head toward the front doors. "We should get inside." She glanced around. "I don't like being in the open in unfamiliar territory."

"Okay." Jasmine said. "But I don't see anyone."

"I feel as if we're being watched. The hair on the back of my neck is tingling."

"Maybe we should leave." A chill ran down her back as she watched the other woman tense up and circle the car to reach her side.

"No. Chase is waiting. I'm sure we're safe. Let's just get inside the building." Jenny grabbed her hand and led her forward. "Hurry up."

The front doors to the club were unlocked. They entered—and Jenny jerked to a halt and snarled. The sound was aggressive, and Jasmine gasped.

"What's wrong?"

"Blood. Lots of it."

"It's a vampire club. Didn't you say they drink it here?"

Jenny stepped in front of her and pulled something from beneath her shirt. It had been tucked inside the waistband of her pants—a wooden stake with a leather handle.

"Why do you have that?"

Jenny released her, reached back and withdrew a small gun. "I have this too. Just in case." She paused. "One for vamps, one with silver bullets for wolves. Stay behind me and stick close."

"Shit."

The urge to flee was strong, but Jasmine followed orders.

She trailed her into a large room that wasn't well lit—but the bodies on the floor were visible due to a few overhead lights. She peeked around Jenny and her dinner nearly came up as she realized two of them had missing heads.

"Oh my God."

"Defend my mate!" a deep voice roared.

Jasmine tore her attention from the horrific scene of death to locate Chase. He stood beside two tall men, one in a kilt, one in leather pants, and they faced off against a group of five people. The tension in the room was obvious, even if her mate's face hadn't been contorted in rage. His fangs were showing.

"Right on time," a woman snickered.

Jasmine watched as the woman turned around. She was pretty, but that only lasted a few seconds before her features began to change. Her nose pushed outward as hair grew rapidly along her cheeks. It was obvious she was a werewolf.

"Crap," Jenny groaned, pushing Jasmine back when she bumped into her.

The four men dropped to their hands and knees to change into their werewolf forms too. The sickening sound of bones popping reached Jasmine.

"That is so wrong!"

Jenny glanced back. "Get against the wall, *now*. They're here to kill you. Take this." She lifted her arm, offering the gun, handle first. "Aim for the head or heart. Don't hesitate to pull the trigger. They'll tear you to shreds if any of them get past me. Shoot anything that does."

Shock held Jasmine still for a few heartbeats before she swallowed hard and grabbed the weapon. "I've never fired one," she whispered.

"It's a good time to learn," Jenny muttered. "Just don't hit me."

*Good advice.* Her hands trembled as she wrapped them around the cold metal and found the trigger. Her mind wanted to shut down but she didn't allow it to happen. They were all in danger. "Is the safety off?"

"It's never on." Jenny suddenly crouched, stake fisted in one palm, her weight braced with the other. She growled in warning, taking a protective stance.

Chase and his two friends didn't wait for the werewolves to finish their transformation before they withdrew swords and attacked. The second her

305

mate moved, Jasmine noticed a short woman who'd been hiding behind him spin around to dash to a far door.

*Who is she? Why is she behind Chase?*

Jealousy was short-lived as two of the werewolves rolled out of the way of the sharp blades. They righted themselves on four legs and their thick, furry bodies barreled in the direction of the front door.

*Right at us*, Jasmine realized. She couldn't look away from their vicious teeth.

A big body suddenly landed just feet in front of Jenny, and Jasmine wondered how Chase had suddenly appeared. Light reflected off a long blade as he swung it and something slammed into the wall that almost hit her. She whimpered when she realized what it was. The decapitated head thumped to the floor and almost hit her foot. An arm was the next thing to come sailing up into the air as her mate took out the attackers.

"I'm going to be sick," she warned.

"They're the enemy." Jenny sounded calm. "Better them than us."

*What the hell did I get myself into?* Jasmine thought, just before everything went black.

# Chapter Eight

"Mine? Come on. Talk to me."

Jasmine realized she was cradled in strong arms and knew that husky voice. She'd had a hellish nightmare. She opened her eyes to stare at Chase. His hair was damp and so was his chest, which she was pressed against, as if he'd just showered.

"How are you?" The concern in his eyes was clear.

"I..." She cleared her throat.

"It's over. They're all dead. We're in one of the apartments under the club. You're safe."

"That was real?"

His arms tightened. "Yeah. The stench of all that blood overwhelmed you. It's to be expected, you being a new mate."

"I think it was the flying body parts."

His mouth curved into a smile. "Life with me is never boring."

She would have used another description to explain how things had changed since her kidnapping and rescue.

Chase sobered. "You weren't supposed to be here or see any of that."

"Jenny said you wanted us to come to the club."

"No. My phone was stolen and someone from my pack sent that message. I told you to stay at home where you'd be safe."

Memory fully returned. "Who was that woman?"

"A bitch who got what was coming to her."

"I saw her escape out a back door. Will she come after us again?"

"Oh. You must mean Mora. She's one of the pack. I thought you were referring to Tina."

"Who are they?"

"Mora and her mate are half-breeds. Tina is a full-blooded wolf who thought she could impress me by showing her cunning nature, but instead it got her killed." He shifted his hold and stroked her cheek with his thumb. "She made the unforgivable mistake of going after someone I love."

The bond between them opened and his feelings warmed her, showing how strong his emotions were. Lust also hit, leaving her no doubt he wanted to lay her on the bed they sat on to make love to her.

"Chase." She cupped his face to pull him down for a kiss.

His full lips brushed hers before he withdrew and smiled. "I have good and bad news before I allow you to seduce me."

"Me?" She laughed. "You're the one projecting images of bending me over in front of you, making me all hot."

A sense of seriousness cooled some of the heat between them. She took a deep breath. "Give me the good news first, since you're determined that we talk before following through with what I just saw."

"The deadliest of my enemies won't be a problem anymore. It will send a strong message to anyone who considers coming after me or mine."

"Okay. What's the bad news?"

"You left the house after I told you not to. You're in deep trouble."

"Jenny thought the text was from you."

He arched one eyebrow, giving her a stern look. "She's not your mate."

Disbelief filled her. "She figured that you wanted me to meet your friends. It wasn't her fault someone swiped your phone."

"True. I'll make sure it always stays in my possession at work from now on instead of leaving it in my jacket pocket at my desk. But...I gave you an order, and you didn't follow it. I'm going to have to punish you for disobeying."

Her temper flared. "Disobeying? Did you really just say that?"

Humor sparked in his eyes. "Don't you want to know what your punishment is?"

She tried to wiggle out of his arms but he was too strong. "No. I'm a person, not a pet. Don't even think about spanking me because I'm not into that crap."

"I'd never hit you." He chuckled. "I took the next month off so we could spend time together. My vacation is effective as soon as I finish getting dressed and we leave the club."

"You did?"

He nodded.

"I'm not the blind-obedience type."

"I'm glad to hear it. I like it when you stand up to me." He leaned in, smiling again. "Besides, you project your thoughts forcefully at times. You weren't happy when I left this morning. You want a honeymoon, and I agree."

"This all sounds like good news to me."

He kissed her with a quick brush of his lips. "We're going to get to know each other really well." A memory of them together in the shower flashed through her mind as he shared it with her, so she knew exactly what he meant.

"I'm still waiting for the bad stuff."

"I heard what you said to my sister. You are going to learn how to use a gun, and you should know how to fight. I want you to always be safe."

"Honeymoons are supposed to be fun."

"It will be."

"Uh-huh." She wasn't convinced.

"Me. You. Mostly undressed." He pressed a kiss to her forehead. "Wrestling around. Getting up close and personal. Sweating will be involved." His lips moved lower as he tucked his head, homing in on her throat. "I'll pin you down. You can try to pin me."

She gave him freer access as his voice lowered into that sexy, soft growl that turned her on. "I'm still not hearing anything bad."

He nipped her skin and a jolt of desire shot from her neck to her lap, drawing a moan from her.

"I have to deal with one last issue before the honeymoon starts."

"What is it?" Worry struck. *Will he have to fight again?*

"I doubt it." He read her mind. "At least I don't believe I'll meet any more resistance. The strongest wolves were already taken out, and I need to assert my position as alpha with the pack. A little time will be good for them to mull over what happened and how futile it would be to challenge me in the future. I just need to speak to them first."

"Okay." She'd worry, but she understood that he'd have to deal with the werewolves. "If you're not expecting more fights, what's the bad part?"

"You're looking at thirty days of me not leaving your side," he rasped. "No respite. No reprieve. I really want you." He softly growled again. "And I'm going to have you, over and over. I'm going to love you so much and so often, you'll be sorry."

"Never. I'm really happy to be your mate, Chase."

He held her tighter. "Me too."

33832203R00183

Printed in Great Britain
by Amazon